AN EVANS NOVEL OF THE WEST

Don Worcester

GONE TO TEXAS

M. EVANS & COMPANY, INC.

MAY (1) '93

M. Evans & Company, Inc.
216 East 49th Street
New York, New York 10017

Library of Congress Cataloging-in-Publication Data

Worcester, Donald Emmet, 1915–
    Gone to Texas / Don Worcester.
        p.   cm. — (An Evans novel of the West)
    ISBN 0-87131-697-8 : $16.95
    I. Title. II. Series.
    PS3573.0688G6 1993
    813' .54—dc20   92-43126
                                                        CIP

Typesetting by AeroType, Inc.

Manufactured in the United States of America

9 8 7 6 5 4 3 2 1

A Note on Sources

For accuracy concerning individuals and events, this book is based primarily on Bennett Lay, *The Lives of Ellis P. Bean* (University of Texas Press, 1960) and on Bean's memoir in Volume I of Henderson Yoakum, *History of Texas* (1854). Also useful were Ohland Morton, *Terán in Texas: A Chapter in Texas–Mexican Relations* (Texas State Historical Association, 1948), and Wilbert H. Timmons, *Morelos of Mexico: Priest, Soldier, Statesman* (Texas Western College Press, 1963).

Chapter One

The double column of horsemen wound through the woods in Spanish territory beyond the Mississippi following powerful, black-haired Philip Nolan, who sat his blooded bay Kentucky stallion with grace, looking every bit the gallant leader. At the young Irishman's side was a taciturn, eagle-eyed old Spaniard, the veteran scout Luciano García. Close behind them rode swarthy, straight-backed, unsmiling David Fero, who appeared to be in his late twenties. He wore an old army jacket and slouch hat that had seen better days. Nolan had introduced him as his *segundo*, his second in command. "An order from him is an order from me," he told Ellis Bean.

Ellis was a long-nosed, muscular Scotch-Irish youth with bold brown eyes and brown hair. He turned to his companion, Duncan McPherson, who rode at his side. Blond-haired, blue-eyed Duncan was, at sixteen, a year younger than Ellis and already an inch or two taller. He flashed Ellis a quick smile. "I can't wait till we get to Texas and see the wild horses."

Ellis nodded and turned in his saddle to look back at the riders behind him. Most of them also seemed excited at the opportunity to accompany Nolan on one of his famous mustang hunts. Texas was a name that had some magic about it. Ellis gazed at Emphraim Blackburn, a tall man whose pleasant face was lined with wrinkles, and whose hair and beard were already gray. He was considerably older than most of the others, who were in their twenties. At his side was Joel Pierce, a slender, frail-looking, sandy haired, freckled youth whose wide blue eyes always seemed to have a startled expression. The pair looked like a father and son out for the first time to see the world. Ellis shook his head. Neither of them belonged on a mustang hunt in a wild land like Texas.

Behind them was Natchez farmer Mordecai Richards, who was also older than most and whose son Stephen rode at his side. Mordecai's jaw was set, and he wore the expression of a man whose conscience warned him he was on the road to sin. The others, among them Nolan's black slaves, Caesar and Robert, were only dimly visible in the dust that hung over them all. Bringing up the rear, seven Spaniards from Texas or Louisiana led pack mules loaded with guns, axes, spades, provisions, and blankets, and knives to trade with the Indians.

Nolan and Luciano suddenly checked their horses. The rest of the riders also stopped and stared. Across a grassy space a few hundred yards away a Spanish cavalry column emerged from the woods. The soldiers spread out in a battle line and advanced at a walk with leveled lances. Ellis stared at the long, polished lance blades and held his breath, his spine cold at the thought of catching a lance blade between the ribs. He glanced at the priming in the Kentucky long rifle he held across his saddle.

The cavalry kept coming until it was fifty yards away, when the officer signalled it to halt. He seemed to be sizing up Nolan's party, deciding whether to attack. Ellis licked his dry lips and rubbed a sweaty palm on his pants leg.

What do we do if they charge? he asked himself. We'll have time for only one shot apiece, and if we miss. . . . He hastily counted the lancers and saw there were only twenty. *At least we outnumber them.*

2

Gesturing to his troops to remain in place, the officer rode forward to meet Nolan halfway between the two parties. Ellis stared at the soldiers, wondering why they had come. Nolan had said he had a Spanish passport and permission to hunt mustangs in Texas. Everyone knew he'd gone there several times since his first trip nine years earlier. The previous year, 1799, he'd brought back a big herd and had taken a few head to Virginia before visiting Vice-President Jefferson in Philadelphia. Now it almost appeared that Spanish troops were looking for the Americans, just a few days after they'd been ferried across the Mississippi at Walnut Hills, or Vicksburg, as some called it.

After a few minutes the Spanish officer saluted Nolan, wheeled his horse, and led his troops on to the east at a trot. Nolan smiled as he rode back to his own men. "That's the commander at Fort Washita," he explained easily. "He's after Choctaw horse thieves and wanted to know if we had seen them." Ellis exhaled. He didn't know how tightly he'd been holding his muscles until he relaxed. Nolan spoke quietly to Luciano, who nodded and led the way west.

"I thought at first they were after us," Ellis said quietly to Duncan.

Duncan nodded. "It looked that way for sure."

Ellis thought back to the flatboat trip he and Duncan had made down the Holston and Tennessee rivers six months ago, in the late spring of 1800. Their fathers had staked the two youths to a load of whiskey and flour, both in demand at Natchez. They had safely navigated the Narrows, but their flatboat had been wrecked at Muscle Shoals. Unwilling to return so soon, they caught a ride on another flatboat and continued on to Natchez, where Ellis' uncle, Robert Bean, farmed and raised cattle.

Outside General Wilkinson's headquarters in Natchez they'd met the impressive young Irishman, Philip Nolan, who had just returned from visiting Vice-President Jefferson in Philadelphia. His business, he told them, was catching wild mustangs in Texas; he'd be going again in October, and he could use good men. "Catching mustangs is more fun than work, but I'll give you both a share of what we catch and a peso for every day we're away after three months," he told them. When both eagerly agreed to go with him, he added, "In the meantime, each of you get a horse and saddle. I'll count on you, and send word a few days before I leave."

They had worked for Robert Bean clearing land and building cowpens in exchange for a mustang and saddle apiece for the long ride back to Tennessee. In October a young man brought them word that Nolan would leave Natchez in three days and was expecting them.

"Mr. Nolan is going to Texas again to catch wild horses," Ellis told his uncle, "and he wants us to go with him." Robert Bean looked shocked. He took his pipe from his mouth and stared at Ellis as if he'd said he wanted to go to China in a canoe.

"Don't either of you consider it for a moment," he warned, shaking his pipe stem at them. "Governor Sargent got a letter from Captain Vidal over at Concordia. He says they're convinced Nolan is up to some mischief, and catching wild horses isn't his real purpose. It would be folly to go with him. Go back to Tennessee where you belong." They had ignored his warning and slipped away to join Nolan's party, twenty-eight men in all.

Ellis also recalled overhearing Nolan talking that same morning to Mordecai Richards. "We'll go through the Caddos to the mustang prairies and build a small fort." Richards looked surprised, almost shocked.

"A fort? Who might attack us? The Spaniards?" Ephraim Blackburn listened intently, a worried look on his lined face.

Nolan smiled, as if reassuring a child there were no bears under its bed. "Oh, no. Armed as we are, we've nothing to fear from them. Indians, only they won't attack a fort. But we have nothing to fear from the Comanches. I lived with them two years.'' He glanced around at the others, then continued. ''After we round up a big herd, we'll take it to Kentucky. I know many men who are ready to conquer Texas. The horses are for them.'' Richards appeared far from reassured.

Ellis' thoughts were interrupted, for the cavalry troop trotted past them on its return to the fort at Washita. The officer and soldiers grimly stared straight ahead, ignoring Nolan's party. As he watched them disappear, Ellis' thoughts returned to Nolan's words. If he knew many men who wanted to conquer Texas, they'd obviously talked about it. The Spaniards probably had spies who reported such talk, and that must be why Captain Vidal was suspicious. Nolan seemed supremely confident the Spaniards wouldn't interfere; the cavalry troop hadn't, but it might be returning to the fort for more men. They weren't after Choctaws—that much was clear.

''They were really looking us us,'' Ellis said softly, ''but they figured we're too strong.''

''They'll probably cut us off when we go by their fort,'' Duncan said, with a grimace. ''But we came to catch horses, not to fight Spaniards. I don't understand it.''

Instead of continuing past the fort, however, Luciano led them north of Fort Washita, and they rode steadily through the woods all night. Feeling like a fugitive, Ellis listened for sounds of pursuit. They didn't stop until they crossed the Washita River, where they made camp on a hill. Hunters killed two deer, and they hungrily sniffed the roasting venison until it was ready to be devoured. No one had much to say, for all were now sure the troops had been sent to stop them.

''I wrote that honest woman I married back in Carolina that I'd earn me some horses and come fetch her,'' young Joel Pierce said. ''Now it looks like maybe that wasn't a good idea.''

5

"I bet he ain't even got a passport," square-jawed Thomas House said, rubbing his bushy eyebrows. "Leastwise one that's valid." Ellis glanced at House, envying his bulging biceps, the mark of his blacksmith's trade. Out of the corner of his eye he saw someone walk away and turned his head. It was Jonah Waters, a hawk-nosed tailor from Virginia, whose shifty eyes were never still. Waters sidled up to Nolan and spoke softly to him without looking him in the face.

Nolan's face turned red, and, looking larger than usual, he strode to where House and the others sat on the ground. His black eyes flashed with anger; he was no longer the jovial Irishman. "You're trying to discourage my men, talking like that," he snarled. "Don't meddle in my affairs; you'll find I'm the only law here." He glared around to be sure the others were listening, then raised his voice. "If anyone tries to leave, Luciano will track him down and give him what all deserters deserve." He nodded toward the old scout, who stood like a grim statue, with his rifle in hand. No one could doubt that he'd willingly carry out any order from Nolan. Ellis felt like he'd just stepped out of a swimming hole into an icy north wind.

"My uncle was right," he said under his breath to Duncan. "I wish now we'd listened to him, but it's too late. We're stuck." Duncan gloomily nodded in agreement.

While they rested their horses for a few days, Mordecai Richards, John Adams, and John King went hunting early one morning. When they failed to return that night, Stephen Richards feared that Indians had attacked his father and the others, or that they were lost. They hunted for the missing men for several days, when Nolan grimly called off the search and they rode on. Everyone knew that Mordecai Richards was an experienced woodsman and hadn't gotten lost. The three men had deserted and made their escape.

"God help us if they tell the Spaniards where we are,"

Duncan remarked, looking around as if expecting to see another cavalry troop.

"Surely they wouldn't do that to us, Ellis said. "After all, they didn't take Stephen, so he's in the same fix as we are."

"I wish they'd taken me with them," Ephraim Blackburn added. "I'm a Quaker and I couldn't kill another human being even to save my own life."

"Why *did* you come? Duncan asked.

"I'd heard of Mr. Nolan even before I came to Natchez, and I knew General Wilkinson regards him almost as his own son. He assured me there was not the slightest danger of our having to fight. He'd been to Texas several times, and he told me about the herds of wild horses. I was dying to see a wild horse hunt, and knew this might be my only opportunity." He paused and his expression grew rueful. "They say curiosity killed the cat. I hope that won't be true in my case, for I left my family in Natchez, and they need me." He brushed his gray hair back and stared at the ground. Joel Pierce listened, looking sad enough to cry.

As they rode past Lake Bisteneau, Ellis stared at the flocks of ducks and geese, but he didn't feel like hunting. Gone were the high spirits he'd had after crossing the Mississippi. As they rode through the tall pines they startled grazing deer and a brown bear with two cubs. Ellis noticed that Nolan, Fero, or Luciano always seemed to be watching for signs that indicated any of them might be thinking of turning back. When they camped, William Danlin, a young frontiersman in greasy buckskins who limped from an arrow wound in one foot, and broad-shouldered carpenter Charles King, who always seemed to be measuring things with his eyes, announced they were going hunting and asked Fero for ammunition. He gave them only three rounds apiece. "If you can't kill a deer with that," he said, "let someone else try." The two men shrugged and accepted the rounds. No one would risk traveling through Indian country without plenty of powder and lead.

At the site of Old Caddo Town on the Red River the carpenters built a raft to ferry their supplies across while the horses and mules swam. Continuing on through the cool shade of towering pines, they forded the Trinity, then rode through grass that reached their stirrups to the Cross Timbers, a belt of trees that stretched to the north and south as far as they could see. Beyond the woods they came to the Brazos.

"Look! Buffalo!" Ellis shouted as a herd emerged from beyond a hill on its way to water. His father had killed buffalo in Tennessee in the early days, but he'd seen only a few buffalo robes. Everyone wanted to stop and kill buffalo, but Nolan insisted that they keep traveling. "Plenty of time for that later," he said.

The herds of elk excited Ellis almost as much as the buffalo. As Nolan topped a hill he stopped his horse and waved the rest up. When they formed a line alongside him and Luciano, he pointed and said, "There they are, boys. There's what we came for." In the valley below them were half a dozen bands of mustang mares and colts, each guarded by a powerful stallion that kept them from mingling with others. Ellis stared at the mustangs of many colors as they cavorted about, their long manes and tails flying. "Wow!" he exclaimed. "Just look at that!"

Blackburn, too, gazed at the wild mustangs in admiration. "What a sight!" he exclaimed. "But they're so happy free, it'll be a shame to make them slaves." At his side Joel Pierce also watched, his lips quivering.

As they rode across the valley one mustang band playfully circled them, coming closer and closer, as if challenging them to a race, while Ellis gazed at them in admiration.

"Hang onto the mules!" Nolan shouted to the Tejanos. "If they run off, we'll never see them again!" The Tejanos already had firm grips on the lead ropes, for the mules were trembling with excitement and snorting, eager to join the mustangs.

"When tame horses or mules get in with the wild ones," Nolan explained, "they're harder to catch than the wildest mustang. I guess that's because they know what it is to work for a living."

Reveling in their freedom, the mustangs were as beautiful as any wild creatures. Ellis watched them in awe, almost regretting that they'd soon deprive some of the handsome little animals of their freedom. He was, nevertheless, eager for the chase to begin, and he forgot about the Spaniards.

Between hills near a small creek beyond the Brazos, Nolan set the carpenters to work building a crude, square, roofless fort of five-foot-tall log walls. The rest of the men built pens of stout posts set close together for corralling the mustangs.

One day when the pens were nearly ready for use, Danlin shouted, "Injuns!" Ellis ran to the fort for his rifle, Duncan by his side. He'd fought Cherokees in the forest, but he knew Comanches only by their awesome reputation. He leveled his rifle over the log wall and held his breath.

The Comanches approached in a long line, with grim-faced warriors in the lead, followed by the women and children with the travois and pack ponies. Nolan walked toward them, making signs with both hands. One Comanche, who looked like he might be the chief, replied with similar signals, then rode forward and shook hands with Nolan, who turned to his men. "Put down your guns," he called. "They're friendly." The chief dismounted, and the two talked in Spanish, which many Comanches seemed to understand.

Ellis stared at the short, stocky warriors, who weren't like any Indians he'd ever seen. They wore fringed elkskin leggings, breechclouts, and buffalo robes. Most carried mean-looking lances as well as bows and arrows, and a few had old guns. They controlled their well-trained ponies with thin rawhide ropes looped around the animals' lower jaws. They looked fierce, but all seemed pleased to see Nolan. Ellis watched in amazement as the women and children quickly unpacked the travois formed by lodge poles tied over the ponies' shoulders, and put up more than twenty tipis of mellow buffalo hides, blackened at the tops by smoke.

Nolan returned to his men. "They're headin' south to hunt buffalo. We can trade with them tonight. The Comanches are the most powerful tribe in Texas, so we've got to keep them friendly. Don't do anything to anger them. Above all, leave the women alone."

Broad-shouldered, thin-legged Charles King spat. "Even horny as I am that oughta be easy," he said. "I ain't ever seen a squaw worth diddlin' nohow."

Nolan smiled, a knowing smile, Ellis thought. "Don't be so sure," he said. "Some of the young ones are real beauties. But if you fool around with them and survive, you'll be singing soprano. Leave them be."

In the morning, Ellis watched as the Comanche women quickly took down the tipis while the boys drove the pony herd into camp. In fifteen minutes the travois were packed with large bundles tied to the dragging tipi poles behind the ponies' heels. The warriors rode ahead and the others followed.

The next morning eleven of the best horses were missing. Nolan was outraged. "It's not like Comanches to steal from their friends," he said, "and I know the chief doesn't approve. It's just that every man does what he wants to, and the chiefs have no power to stop them. We can't run mustangs without those horses, but we should be able to catch up with them in a day or two when they stop to hunt."

With Fero, Robert Ashley, Joseph Reed, Ellis, Duncan, and Caesar, Nolan set out on foot, grimly following the tracks made by the dragging travois poles. But the Comanches didn't stop soon to hunt; it was nine days before they came upon their camp. All but the women and children and a few old warriors were away hunting buffalo. Nolan spoke to one of the old men.

"He says the one-eyed man stole our horses," he told the others. "He'll be easy to recognize." The Comanche women fed them roast buffalo meat, then they wearily lay down to rest from their long journey.

Late in the afternoon they heard children squealing and dogs barking, and knew the hunters had returned. The pack ponies were loaded with huge pieces of dripping red meat. Dogs followed the pack ponies of their masters, snatching hungrily at their loads. The women drove the dogs away, immediately unloaded the ponies, and began slicing the meat into thin strips to put on racks for drying in the sun. The hunters came to see Nolan and his men, but Ellis didn't see the chief. I bet he doesn't want to see Nolan now, he thought.

The powerful Caesar walked up behind One Eye and pinioned his arms, while Fero bound him hand and foot. The other Comanches ignored them, and they left the thief tied up all night.

In the morning One Eye's wife led the stolen horses to Nolan two at a time and handed him the lead ropes without looking him in the face. She was obviously fearful for her husband's life.

After mounting his horse, Nolan warned One Eye and all who were listening that although his men were few they were well armed, and they could defeat many times their number. Then pushing hard, they reached the fort in four days. The horses were worn down and had to recover their strength before they could run mustangs.

At dawn a few days later Ellis heard the hoofbeats of many horses. "Injuns!" he shouted, leaping to his feet, and grabbing his rifle. Wondering why the five guards at the corrals had given no warning, he peered over the log walls of the fort and gasped. In front of him were Spanish cavalrymen, militia, and Indians; he looked over the other walls. They were completely surrounded and the five guards were prisoners, their hands tied behind their backs. All of Nolan's men hurried to the walls, rubbing their eyes and cursing when they saw they were badly outnumbered.

Seeing the fear in their eyes, Nolan shouted, "We must fight to the death or they'll make us prisoners for life!" Ellis stared at the Spaniards training their weapons on the fort, and his clammy hands trembled as he put fresh priming in his rifle. It looked like everyone in Texas must be after them. He glanced at Nolan but saw no fear in his eyes. It's him they're really after, Ellis thought, not us.

The Spanish officer, accompanied by a bearded, middle-aged, heavy-set civilian who didn't look Spanish, rode toward the fort with forty cavalrymen following. "That's the son-of-a-bitch William Barr," Nolan growled. "He's a trader at Nacogdoches. He's wanted to get me ever since I refused to do some smuggling for him." He and Fero and a few others walked out to meet them, while Ellis held his breath and stared open-mouthed.

Nolan held up his hand. "That's far enough," he called. "Come no closer or some of us may be killed." The soldiers stopped. Ellis looked around for some place to hide. The Spanish officer, Captain Miguel de Músquiz, rode forward, with William Barr at his side.

"Our only hope is for Nolan to get them to let us go," Ellis whispered. "Against so many we haven't a chance. There must be three hundred of them." Duncan nodded and licked his lips, glancing anxiously from Nolan to the officers. Joel Pierce and Blackburn stared at the soldiers, their faces white with fear.

Ellis listened as Músquiz spoke and Barr translated. "You must lay down your arms and surrender," Barr said in an Irish accent. Ellis listened for Nolan's reply, almost afraid to hear what he might say. He must know now they're onto him, Ellis thought, but the rest of us didn't know about that. He should explain why we're here so they'll let us go.

"No!" was Nolan's curt reply as he spun about and stalked back to the fort, Fero and the others at his heels. Ellis saw one of the militiamen raise his carbine and aim it at Nolan's back. Instinctively Ellis aimed and dropped the man. With a sense of unreality, he bent down to reload and saw two of Nolan's Tejano mustangers bolt out the back of the fort, one of them carrying Nolan's carbine. Fero ran to the door and yelled for them to come back, which made them run faster.

Ellis looked frantically around, feeling like a raccoon treed by a pack of hounds. There was no way to escape. Músquiz raised his sword and shouted an order. Ellis ducked behind the wall as the soldiers and militia raised their guns. Bullets whistled overhead or thudded into the thick logs on every side. Most of Nolan's men were hastily firing over the walls, then crouching to reload. Trembling, Ellis raised his rifle and fired, ducking so quickly he didn't know if he'd hit his target. His hands shook so, he spilled powder while reloading.

Nolan was everywhere, encouraging his men, daringly exposing his head to fire his pistol. "Make every shot count," he shouted over the boom of muskets and bark of long rifles. "Don't miss!"

He opened his mouth to speak again when a bullet stuck his head and his feet flew out from under him. Ellis looked around for him, expecting him to say more, then saw him stretched out on the floor motionless.

"Nolan's hit!" he shouted, and the others turned. Fero leaned over Nolan.

"He's dead!" he called. "Bullet in the head!" The others stopped firing for the moment. Ellis leaned on his rifle to steady himself, for his legs suddenly felt weak. Then, seeing the others firing again at the soldiers, he got off another hasty shot and hunched down. Ephraim Blackburn, his arms around Joel's shoulders, huddled in a corner. Blackburn's lips were moving and Ellis knew he was praying. So far, no one but Nolan had been hit.

The cavalrymen unloaded a small artillery piece from a pack mule and began showering the fort with grapeshot. After only a few rounds, two men were painfully wounded.

"We've got to capture the cannon or make a run for it," Ellis gasped. "If we don't, we'll be killed for sure.

"We'll make a run for it," Fero shouted. "Don't all fire at once or the lancers will get us. If we can only make it to some trees. . . ."

Ellis and the others hastily filled their powder horns and bullet pouches, then Fero gave the rest of their supply to Caesar to carry. Hands trembling and mouth dry, Ellis wondered if his legs would hold up. Running out the back of the fort toward the small stream, they stopped to fire and load in turns to keep the deadly lancers at a distance. Bullets whistled about them and plucked at their clothing; miraculously, no one was hit.

They splashed through the creek, not daring to stop for a drink of water. They fired and reloaded in turns as the lancers closed in behind them. Ellis glanced back toward the creek and saw one of the men wounded by grapeshot sink to the ground, too weak to continue.

"Oh God, look!" Ellis cried. Caesar had dropped the powder bag and was holding up his hands. Now all the Spaniards had to do was wait until their quarry ran out of powder, then pick them off one at a time.

Ellis and his comrades retreated slowly through waist-high grass toward the Brazos, their long rifles keeping the Spaniards out of accurate range of their muskets and carbines. The sun rose high over their heads. Ellis' throat was parched. Finally they came to a ravine and clambered into it. Ellis' mouth was so dry he couldn't swallow, and his heart was pounding. I don't want to die, he thought, but we've gone as far as we can.

They had no water and their powder was getting low. By early afternoon the Spaniards had brought up their little cannon and showered the ravine with grapeshot. Joel Pierce cried out and held his hand to his cheek. When he took it away, blood ran down his chin from a jagged gash. "Hold your handkerchief over it till it stops bleeding," Blackburn urged.

"I got to have water!" the other wounded man panted. He laid down his gun and crawled out of the ravine to surrender and beg for water.

Ellis looked around at the others. Most were fearless men, but their situation was hopeless. There was a look of resignation on their faces.

The wounded man soon returned, wiping water from his chin. "The captain says that since Nolan is dead, he'll send us home if we surrender," he told them. Duncan and Ellis looked at each other and shrugged. The stocky William Barr, carrying a white flag, approached the ravine.

"Surrender now and you'll be sent to Nachitoches," he assured them in his Irish accent. Ellis stared at him to see if he appeared to be telling the truth, if he really believed what he told them.

Ellis doubted it, but that made little difference. They could surrender and take their chances, or they could stay there and be killed. David Fero crawled out of the ravine, walked up to where Músquiz sat on his horse, and handed him his pistol and hunting knife. Since he was Nolan's second-in-command, there was nothing for the others to do but follow him.

The troops herded them back to the fort. When Ellis stepped in a hole and nearly fell, a soldier jabbed him in the back with his own rifle. Robert and Caesar dug a grave for their former master, while the soldiers buried their dead. Just before they lowered Nolan's body, Músquiz spoke to a soldier and handed him Fero's knife. The soldier knelt by Nolan's side while Ellis held his breath, horrified at the thought of having to watch him cut off the dead man's head. But the soldier cut off

Nolan's ears and handed them to Barr. Seeing Ellis' expression, Barr explained, "That's just proof to the governor that he's dead. I'm taking them to San Antonio." He pocketed the grisly trophies. Ellis shuddered.

In the morning the Indians rode away, while the troops, militia, prisoners, and wounded men began the long ride eastward across the flower-covered prairies. Mustang bands galloped out of their way, then stopped to watch them from a safe distance. Ellis gazed at them without really seeing them.

On April 3, they reached the village of Nacogdoches, set on a knoll among tall pines. The cavalry stopped by a large, two-story stone building that looked out of place among the log houses. A middle-aged, portly American with neatly trimmed hair and beard emerged from a nearby building. He was well-dressed and appeared to be prosperous.

"I'm Samuel Davenport," he told them. "That's my trading post yonder." He nodded toward it. "This is the Old Stone Fort; it's where you'll be stayin' for awhile."

Joel Pierce touched his swollen cheek, his eyes glittering feverishly. "I hope they let us go soon," he said in a choking voice. "I wrote my wife we'd be gone only three months and I'd have some horses of my own. Now all I want is to see her again."

"I hope all of us will soon be with our loved ones," Ephraim Blackburn said. Davenport shook his head, a bit sadly, Ellis thought.

"How come you're here?" Ellis asked him. "You're an American, aren't you?"

Davenport took a cigar from his pocket, smelled it, and put it in his mouth. "I was," he replied. "Came here from Pennsylvania a while back and liked it. They let me stay, and now I'm a Spanish citizen and Indian agent for East Texas."

Blackburn put his hand on Joel Pierce's forehead. "He's burning up" he told Davenport. "Have you anything for a fever?"

Davenport looked at the ugly wound and winced. "I'll send the *curandera*," he replied. "She can bring it down pretty quick and dress the wound."

A few days later, Músquiz and Davenport came to the fort. Through Davenport, Fero asked Músquiz when they'd be sent home.

"I'm waiting for orders to release you from the commandant in Chihuahua," Músquiz replied. "In the meantime, you are free to do what you want in the daytime as long as you return to the fort at night."

"Chihuahua is a long ride, more than six hundred miles," Davenport added. "It'll be awhile before the reply comes. I advise you to be patient."

"We surrendered on his promise to send us back to the States," Fero growled. "He doesn't need an order to keep his promise."

Davenport grimaced. "You don't know the Spanish army," he said. "They don't do anything like that without written orders. I know he'd like to release you, but he might be cashiered if he did. I think they'll set you free in time if no one does anything to rile them. My advice is to sit tight and wait it out, even if it takes a year or two." Fero groaned.

"How'd he know where to find us?" he asked.

"Some of your men told the commander at Concordia, and he sent word to Captain Músquiz. He also warned him that you were all well armed and would fight. That's why he took every available man." Fero scowled at news of their betrayal.

Although the taciturn scout Luciano had always appeared unapproachable, as if he preferred silence to conversation, Ellis and Duncan hesitantly spoke to him one day, figuring he understood Spaniards. "Why did they attack us?" Ellis asked, wondering if Luciano would deign to reply. "Mr. Nolan had a passport, didn't he?"

Suprised, Luciano looked them over, as if seeing them for

the first time. "Yes," he replied, "but maybe they learned something about his plans, or someone said bad things about him. *Señor* Nolan was a fine man and my good *amigo*. He saved my life once. I wish I could have saved his."

"Were you with him when he came here before?" Ellis asked. Luciano nodded again.

"Twice. You should have seen the herd we brought out last time—thirteen hundred head. That's a lot of mustangs." He looked at them for a moment in consideration. "Since we have nothing to do and may be here for a long time, I could teach you to speak Spanish. That is, if you want me to. Who knows? It might come in handy one day."

Both eagerly accepted, and met with him every day after that, glad to have something to occupy their time. Before long, both were able to ask simple questions and to understand the answers.

"That Luciano is a wise old owl," Ellis told Duncan. "I like him. I guess he was just waitin' for someone to talk to him."

"Reckon we should steal a couple of horses and make a run for it?" Duncan asked one day as they wandered around waiting for Luciano.

"Make it three horses we can slip away with early some morning and take Luciano with us," Ellis replied. "If we can get even half a day's head start, we can make it for sure with Luciano along. He knows the country."

Later that day, they were at Davenport's trading post looking at the goods on the shelves when Fero walked in. Ignoring Ellis and Duncan, he approached Davenport. "How long are they going to keep us here?" he growled. "Some of the men have families."

"All I can tell you is what I said before," Davenport replied. "I think eventually they'll release you, if no one does anything to anger them."

"Like what?"

"Like trying to escape," Davenport replied. "That would be a disaster. This affair has caused a lot of excitement, and it'll take a while for it to die down. But if anyone leaves, or even tries to, it'll be much worse than before. The others might not be freed for years. Maybe never." Fero cursed.

Duncan and Ellis left the post. "It was sure tempting, and I know we could have made it, "Ellis said. "But after what Davenport told Fero, it wouldn't be fair to the others. They might never be released, and that would be a high price for them to pay for our freedom. We'd better be patient, like Davenport said, but it won't be easy."

Six weeks passed, and still no order came from Chihuahua. "Damn them," Robert Ashley said. "I wish we could lay our hands on our rifles and fight our way out of here. I'd as soon be killed trying as rot here." Others agreed.

"We must do as they say" Blackburn warned. "As long as there's life there's hope. Let's pray we won't have to wait much longer." Ashley scowled.

The next evening when they returned to the fort, Fero counted heads as usual, then cursed. "Someone's missing," he exclaimed. "In fact, four are."

Ellis quickly scanned the faces of those in the fort. Ashley, Nolan's slave Robert, and two others were absent. He thought of what Davenport had said and felt a knot in his stomach.

"Has anyone seen them?" Fero asked sharply. "If any of you know where they're hiding, we must bring them back whether they want to come or not. Otherwise, the rest of us may be in for it." No one had seen the men since morning. They had fled without telling anyone of their plans. Ellis felt like throwing up.

Músquiz angrily confined them again in the stone fort and increased the number of guards, ordering them to shoot anyone who tried to flee. "Damn them," Fero growled. "No telling what will happen to us now."

Chapter Two

For the next few weeks, the prisoners huddled under guard in the old fort, gloomily waiting for the orders from Chihuahua. "I wish we had something to do," Ellis said. "Anything. Choppin' firewood would be better than this. We've got too much time to think." The others gazed at him and nodded their heads.

"I hope they're not goin' to let us rot here for another six months," Tom House said. He stood up, stretched, and began to pace up and down. "It was bad enough before those men escaped. Damn them to hell."

"That honest woman I married must be worried sick," freckled Joel Pierce said to Ephraim Blackburn. "She probably imagines that all sorts of awful things have happened to me. She knows I'd never desert her. I wonder if I'll ever see her again." His voice quavered and he buried his scarred face in his hands, stifling his sobs. Embarrassed, the others turned their backs. Blackburn patted his shoulder.

"Have faith," he said. "Surely we'll see our loved ones again."

One morning, they heard the hoofbeats of many horses. It sounded like a cavalry troop, and the prisoners expectantly rose to their feet. The big wooden door swung open and Captain Músquiz entered, with a letter in his hand and

Samuel Davenport by his side. The prisoners glanced at one another, wondering what this meant. Músquiz frowned and Davenport appeared worried. It was clear they wouldn't be sent home. Ellis suddenly felt chilled.

"This is from the *comandante* at Béxar," Músquiz said, holding up the letter while Davenport translated. "He is furious at me for trusting you and letting some of you escape. He doesn't intend for that to happen again. He orders me to send the rest of you to Béxar in chains. You leave immediately."

"I'm sorry, men," Davenport told them. "It's not fair to punish you for what others did. But. . . ." He shrugged and left.

"Those men who escaped sure played hell with the rest of us," Ellis said. "Maybe we should have made a run for it while we had the chance. The farther we get from Natchez, the harder it'll be."

A blacksmith riveted rough, iron shackles connected by short, heavy chains around their wrists. The edges of the iron bands hadn't been smoothed, and when Ellis raised his hands, he winced as the rough iron sawed into his skin. He mounted a horse with difficulty, cutting his wrists until they bled.

When all were mounted, twenty cavalrymen herded them onto the Camino Real for the long ride to San Antonio. For a day they rode through pine woods before coming to the open prairies. The Royal Road was nothing but a trail traveled by pack trains, couriers, and occasionally by two-wheeled Mexican carts drawn by oxen.

A week later, they forded the San Antonio River and stopped at the Presidio of Béxar, a large stone building in San Antonio's Military Plaza. Towering over the village of stone and adobe houses was San Fernando church. The prisoners were ordered into the guardhouse for the night. Ellis heard the heavy bolt slam shut, barring the door.

They were allowed to lounge around the plaza during the day, but were locked up at night. Ellis and Duncan walked slowly around the plaza, kicking at dried horse droppings and trying to keep the flies out of the wounds on their wrists. They passed Ephraim Blackburn and Joel Pierce sitting disconsolately on a bench. "I'd be willing to stay here five years if they'd let those two go," Ellis said. He looked at his raw wrists. "That is, if they'd take these shackles off."

Three months passed, when orders arrived to take them to Mexico City. "I wonder what they can do to us there they can't do here," Ellis said.

Day after day they rode south across deserts and through mountain passes. Ellis gingerly held up his wrists and blew away the flies. Most of the cuts had formed thick ugly scars, but a few places had little chance to heal. His muscles ached from the hours in the saddle; it seemed as if they were traveling to the end of the world and would never reach it. "I wonder if they'll ever let us go," he said somberly. "And if they do, if we can make it all the way back."

"Nolan told us to fight to the death or they'd make us prisoners for life," Duncan replied. "It sure looks like surrendering was a mistake." He brushed the shoulder-length blond hair out of his tanned face with his manacled hands. His wrists were also scarred and raw.

Finally they saw San Luis Potosí below them in the distance, surrounded by lush green fields and orchards. Shining white churches towered over the largest city Ellis had ever seen. He gazed in awe at the splendid buildings, forgetting for a few moments the oozing wounds on his wrists. He had little time to admire the city, for the cavalry stopped by a massive stone building and the sergeant ordered them to dismount.

They were herded into the dark interior and turned over to

sullen guards. The foul stench of urine, offal, and rotting food that struck his nostrils like a slap in the face told Ellis this was a dungeon. The guards led them down to the dimly lit lower floor, then divided them. Ellis, Duncan, Blackburn, Pierce, Luciano, and Danlin were shoved into a room that received a little light and air from a small grated window high in the stone wall. Fero, Cooley, Stephen Richards, Reed, House, and Waters were ushered into a similar room. Both rooms had heavy iron doors with small openings through which the guards handed them bowls of food and jugs of water. In one corner was a pile of dung left by previous prisoners. The stench was almost unbearable. "Thank God we'll be here just one night," Danlin said to Ellis.

In the morning, Ellis watched impatiently for the door to open, but the guards merely handed them bowls of tepid water with a small piece of boiled chicken floating in each one. No soldiers came to take them on to Mexico City. Surely we'll go on tomorrow, Ellis thought. They can't just leave us here and forget us.

On the third day, when the guard brought the food, Ellis asked in Spanish, "When do they take us to Mexico City?"

"Mexico City?" The guard snorted and laughed. "When you're dead, maybe. No one ever leaves this place alive."

Ellis felt suddenly weak and his hands trembled. For foolishly accompanying Nolan, they had been condemned to die a slow death—it might take years. In a voice as unsteady as his legs, he told the others what the guard had said. In the dim light he saw their faces register shock, then despair. Without feeling hunger or being aware of what he was doing, he ate the little piece of boiled chicken, then lifted the bowl to his mouth and drank the water in which it had been cooked.

Although the others looked ready to lie down and stop breathing, Blackburn's wrinkled face seemed to glow in the dim light. "We are not going to give up hope of deliverance," he said in a firm voice. "We are going to keep our senses, because one day we will leave this place alive.'' He recited from memory a verse from the Bible. Ellis didn't recognize it or any of the others Blackburn recited each morning thereafter. When he had gone through all of the verses he remembered, he started over. He's keeping us all from going mad, Ellis thought, but he resigned himself to dying in the stinking dungeon.

One morning, more than a year later, they were ordered out of the dungeon and herded onto the street. Shielding his eyes from the unaccustomed sunlight, Ellis saw saddled horses and a cavalry troop awaiting them. Still in chains, they were ordered to mount and weakly climbed on. They were escorted out of the city on the same road they'd followed when they arrived.

"They're taking us north," Ellis said quietly to Duncan. "I wonder what that means." Duncan didn't reply, for the officer, a short man with a waxed mustache, was glaring at them.

"Where are we going?" Ellis later asked a soldier who rode near him. The man glanced around to see if the officer was watching before replying.

"We're taking you to Saltillo," he said. "I think from there you go to Chihuahua."

The officer in charge of the escort apparently regarded the prisoners as criminals who deserved no consideration at all, for he showed them none. One morning, Joel Pierce was too sick to rise. "Put him on his horse," the officer ordered. "If he wants to die he can do it in the saddle as well as in bed." Two soldiers roughly shoved the gaunt youth onto his horse's back. Duncan and Ellis rode on opposite sides of him ready to catch him if he started to fall. Somehow he survived, and he was able to ride by himself by the time they reached Saltillo.

When they stopped in the plaza at Saltillo, the people

crowded around as usual to stare at the bearded, ragged, dirty prisoners. What was left of Ellis' homespun shirt and pants was barely enough to cover him. The old women, in black dresses, brought them bread and fruit, although they obviously had little to spare. One gave Ellis a white cotton shirt, then wrung her hands when she realized he couldn't put it on because of his shackles.

The cavalry troop that brought them to Saltillo turned them over to another. Ellis looked at the new officer, a clean-shaven young Spaniard with sparkling black eyes. When he inspected the prisoners, he frowned at the sight of their scarred wrists and called to his sergeant. "Send a man for the blacksmith and remove those chains," he ordered. "I don't care what they did—they don't deserve to be treated like that."

When the shackles were removed, Ellis tore off what was left of his ragged shirt and put on the one the woman had given him. His arms had been shackled so long he could hardly move them.

"That's better, isn't it?" the officer asked in Spanish, and smiled.

"*Muchas gracias*," Ellis replied.

"I thought all Spaniards were mean as hell," Ellis remarked. "Can't say that about the lieutenant."

"Or the townspeople," Duncan added, "although they look more Indian than Spanish."

At every village on the long ride to Chihuahua, the people took pity on the prisoners and brought them food and clothing. One wrinkled old woman with gray braids that reached nearly to her waist stopped by Duncan to admire his long blond hair. She called to her daughter, and both exclaimed over the color, and fingered Duncan's matted locks. Before the cavalry rode on, the daughter brought Duncan a white cotton shirt.

After thanking her, he said to Ellis, "We've both got

shirts. Now maybe someone will give us each a pair of pants."

They reached Chihuahua in the spring of 1803, two years after their capture. Stern-faced General Nemesio de Salcedo, who had recently arrived, was commandant general of all the Interior Provinces. "When General Salcedo learned that you were in a dungeon at San Luis Potosí," the commander of the escort told them, "he ordered you brought here."

Because escaping from Chihuahua and crossing the desert on foot was almost impossible, Salcedo gave them the freedom of the city during the days, but they had to return to the barracks at night. Each was given a little money every day to buy food, but nothing to replace the rags they wore.

One night when they returned to the barracks to be counted, an officer beckoned to Stephen Richards to follow him. Stephen didn't return that night; in the morning when Ellis saw him in a Spanish uniform, he seemed embarrassed. "They let me out to join the army," he mumbled. "I'm leaving for Nacogdoches in a few days."

"How come?" Ellis asked.

"I don't know. I didn't expect it," he replied, not looking Ellis in the face.

"I know why they did it, and he knows," Ellis said to Duncan later. "It's the reward for his father telling them where to find us. It's not Stephen's doing, but I don't blame him for not wanting to see us."

Duncan and Ellis wandered about Chihuahua, grateful for at least this much freedom. The city, mostly adobe houses with flat roofs, had a population of about seven thousand. In the public plaza stood the principal church, which dwarfed the royal treasury building and the shops. The prisoners found the people friendly.

The upper classes ate well, lived in comfortable houses of adobe bricks, and amused themselves by playing cards and betting on cock fights. The poor lived in one-room *jacalos* of sticks and mud and ate scrawny chickens, cheap beef, *frijoles*, and *tortillas*.

Every evening the upper class families gathered at the public walks on the south side of the city under three rows of trees. At each end of the walks were circular seats where people played guitars and sang songs in Spanish and French. Ellis and Duncan greatly admired the sparkling-eyed young ladies, who wore short jackets, petticoats, and shoes with high heels. Over their dresses, unmarried girls always wore a silk shawl, and when men were near, modestly drew it across their faces, leaving only one eye exposed. "With that thing over their faces, you can't tell if they're smilin' or frownin' at you," Ellis remarked. "Don't seem fair." At nine each night the *paseo* ended and everyone went home, for after that hour soldiers stopped anyone found on the streets.

Several of the prisoners, including David Fero, Joel Pierce, and Zalmon Cooley, received permission to move to San Carlos or other towns. Brawny Thomas House, who worked as a blacksmith in Chihuahua, exchanged letters with Fero and Cooley on plans for escaping. House warned the others not to trust Jonah Waters, for he remembered Waters repeating his remarks to Nolan. Waters worked as a hatter in Chihuahua.

"We've got to find a way to earn some money or we'll soon be naked," Ellis said one morning as they accompanied Luciano to the plaza. "They give us barely enough to keep from starving. If Luciano didn't bargain for us, we'd likely starve anyway." Men in sandals, white cotton shirts, and trousers, and women in black dresses were already bringing chickens, fruit, and bread to sell.

"I wonder if there's any work for a gunsmith here," Duncan said. "My father taught me to repair guns, and all you Beans are gunsmiths. Of course, we'd have to have tools." Luciano listened but said nothing.

"I've repaired plenty of guns," Ellis observed. "I'd rather make hats, or something like that, but I don't know how." They bought some bread and fruit, then sat on a low stone wall and watched the girls. Luciano left them.

He returned at noon. "I've been talking to some merchants," he said. "Rafael Núñez will sell you the tools you need on credit," he told Duncan. "Manuel Moreno will supply you with material for making hats," he said to Ellis, who shrugged. "He also knows two good hatters who'd like to work for an Americano." Ellis smiled.

Both got to work right away. With a vise, hammer, files, and other tools, Duncan soon had all the business he could handle. Ellis' hats were soon in demand—none but the Americano's sombreros would do. They bought clothing, ate well, and soon repaid their debts. When Ellis made the last payment, Moreno invited him to his home for dinner.

The Morenos lived in a spacious, well-furnished house of adobe, with a patio and large yard filled with fruit trees and grape vines. Moreno served wine, then his wife and two young daughters joined them for dinner. Ellis admired the attractive *Señora* Moreno but didn't know how to behave in the presence of ladies of her class. He tried to remain silent, but she wouldn't allow it. "Tell me how you came to be in Texas," she said, and little by little drew from him the story of their misadventures. "You are all innocent!" she exclaimed indignantly. "They have no right to hold you!"

When they had finished dinner, she and the girls—Ellis guessed them to be ten and twelve—withdrew, while Ellis and Moreno smoked cigars and talked.

"Spanish officials are slow to act on matters of this sort," Moreno told him. "You could be here the rest of your life. You already speak Spanish well. I advise you to join the church, marry, and settle down. You won't become rich, but you can live comfortably."

"I hadn't thought of that," Ellis replied. "I figured one day they'll get tired of holding us and let us go."

"That's possible but unlikely. Everyone believed Nolan was invading Texas, and some still think he was. I'm afraid you'll be here for a long time. Better think about what I said."

"I will," Ellis assured him. He and Duncan, along with House and Danlin, soon began the process of preparing themselves for entering the church. None of them was ready to abandon hope of being freed one day, so they declined to consider marriage.

"We need to save as much money as we can," Ellis told Duncan. "One day we'll surely have a chance to leave here, but we won't get far without *dinero*." That's not what we did in Tennessee, he thought. No one ever tried to save money. We spent it as fast as we made it and didn't worry about tomorrow. But now it's different.

Late one day in January 1804, Fero, Cooley, Pierce, and the others who'd moved to San Carlos or elsewhere appeared at the barracks in Chihuahua, escorted by soldiers. "Does anyone know what this is all about?" Cooley asked. No one did.

At mid-morning the next day, an officer and a few soldiers marched the whole group into the city. "Can you tell us where we're going?" Ellis asked him in Spanish.

"Certainly. You're on the way to the *juzgado* to stand trial for entering Spanish territory illegally. It's high time they took some action."

In the courthouse they saw dignified, stern-looking Judge Pedro Galindo de Navarro, a handsome, gray-haired Spaniard leafing through a stack of papers on his desk. "That's the evidence against you," the officer told them. "It's taken Judge Galindo a month to read it all. But now he's ready to announce his decision."

The prisoners stood with hats in hands. It reminded Ellis of waiting for a teacher to decide whether or not to whip him. Don José Díaz de Bustamante, the prosecutor, solemnly entered the room and stood to the right of the judge, who had risen to his feet. Don Pedro Ramón de Verea, the prisoners' counsel, entered and stood at the judge's left, his face relaxed, almost smiling. I guess he figures he did all he could for us and is glad it's over, Ellis thought. He wasn't prepared for what followed.

"I order all charges against the accused dismissed," the judge said, "and I recommend their immediate release."

The prisoners appeared at first unable to comprehend the verdict. Then it seemed as if heavy chains had been miraculously removed and they were floating on air. Ellis' legs felt suddenly weak, but he smiled broadly. Freedom! He recommends that we be released! He glanced at Ephraim Blackburn and Joel Pierce, and saw tears streaming down their faces.

"I never had much confidence in Spanish justice," Cooley exclaimed. "It's slow, but I can't complain now."

"Thank God, thank God," Blackburn said hoarsely. "I feared I'd never see my loved ones again."

"I doubt if my wife will even recognize me," Joel Pierce said sadly. "They waited too long." Ellis looked at him and had to agree. He'd never fully recovered his health and was gaunt-faced and pallid, obviously in bad shape. The scar on his pale cheek was an ugly purple line.

"I hope they'll furnish us horses for the ride home," Duncan said. "I'll walk if I have to, but they took our horses in Nacogdoches, so they owe us some."

All of the prisoners remained at the barracks nights, for there was no reason that Fero and the others should return to San Carlos. All of them went from store to store during the days, buying a few extra garments for the journey home. Ellis felt like running around shouting, "We're free! We're free!" but managed to restrain himself. He saw Ephraim Blackburn, his thick hair white, looking more solemn than usual. Ellis smiled. "I thought you'd be celebrating like the rest of us," he said.

"I'd like to," Blackburn replied, "and I would if I could stop thinking about Joel. He's not well enough to travel, but he's determined to go. I'm afraid the trip will kill him, but we can't go off and leave him here alone." Ellis' smile faded. He'd forgotten about Joel.

The next morning, a captain who had always been sympathetic to the prisoners called them together, and Ellis knew from his expression that he wasn't bringing good news. He cleared his throat.

"I regret to tell you that General Salcedo did not agree with Judge Galindo's ruling and suspended it. He is sending the records to Spain and requesting the king to make a ruling." Ellis listened but couldn't believe what he heard.

"Good God!" Zalmon Cooley exclaimed.

"The Lord is my Shepherd," Ephraim Blackburn intoned.

"Son-of-a-bitch!" Fero shouted. Ellis' lips moved numbly, but no words came. If they want to torture us to death as painfully as possible, they're doing a good job of it, he thought. Despondently, he and Duncan went back to making hats and repairing guns. It'll take years to hear from Spain, Ellis brooded. By then I'll be an old man. Why don't they just shoot us?

Months passed and rumors floated about, but nothing happened. Some said that Salcedo hadn't sent the papers to Spain, and they'd never be freed; that was easy to believe. Duncan was called to the village of Aldama to repair the weapons of a detachment of troops stationed there, a task that would take several months. Fero and House again exchanged letters about a plan for escaping. "William Danlin and I are thinking of trying to get away," House told Ellis.

"Me too," Ellis replied. He got permission to go to San Carlos, where he made escape plans for Duncan, House, and himself. Between them, Ellis and Duncan had purchased, through Mexican friends, four horses and three guns.

Before attempting to escape, House and the other prisoners in Chihuahua decided to petition Salcedo to release them. An obliging priest wrote in Spanish a lengthy explanation of how they'd come to accompany Nolan to Texas, explaining that he had assured them he had permission and a passport, and that he had been allowed to enter Texas a number of times before. They had no reason to doubt his word until they met a Spanish patrol searching for them, and then it was too late to back out. While waiting to learn Salcedo's response, Fero and Cooley again wrote House concerning escape plans. From San Carlos, Ellis wrote to Duncan in Aldama and to House in Chihuahua that he had the preparations nearly complete, and that two soldiers had agreed to desert and accompany them. They were to meet at an old church when the day came, and from there set out on their journey. He entrusted the letters to a villager, who delivered Duncan's at Aldama before continuing on to Chihuahua with the letter to House. Duncan hurried his work along so he could return to Chihuahua in time to join the escape party.

Tom House was sick and stretched out on a mat in the adobe house that served as his blacksmith shop, when a sergeant and squad of soldiers entered. "Stay where you are," the sergeant ordered in Spanish, and gathered up the letters on a little table that served as a desk.

"What's goin' on?" House asked in broken Spanish.

"I shouldn't tell you, perhaps," the sergeant replied, "but one of your countrymen—the one with a nose like a hawk— took General Salcedo a letter from *Señor* Bean to you. The General ordered us to see what we could find here and arrest you. That's all I know."

"Nose like a hawk," House muttered. "That can only be that son-of-a-bitch Waters. I'll cut off his balls for this, if he has any." The soldiers escorted him to the guardhouse.

At Aldama, Duncan learned that Ellis, Cooley, and Fero had been arrested in San Carlos, and hastily burned the letter from Ellis. If they force him to talk about our escape plans, they'll come for me next, Duncan thought. Every time he saw soldiers he expected to be arrested, but he was allowed to finish his work and return to Chihuahua, where he found House in the hospital, in bad shape.

One day, Ellis' cell door opened and a guard helped Joel Pierce through it and lowered him to the floor, for he was too weak to stand alone. Ellis recoiled in horror at the sight.

"I'm dying, Ellis," Joel gasped as he lay on the floor. "I'll never see my wife again. I didn't expect to find you a prisoner, but at least I'll die in the company of a friend and a countryman."

Ellis had a little money in his pocket, and he persuaded the guard to buy some wine and bread. After Joel drank a little wine and ate some bread, he was able to sit up. Ellis gazed at him sadly—he was little more than a skeleton; there was no doubt that he hadn't long to live.

"You should go to the house of my friends the Romeros," Ellis told him. "They'll care for you like you were their own son and nurse you back to health. I can do little for you here."

"No. I can't possibly recover. I prefer to die here with you."

At that moment the cell door opened again and the guards pushed a big man with Indian features and shackled arms into the room. "Why is he here?" Ellis asked the guard.

"He killed a man."

The prisoner took a jew's-harp from his pocket, held it to his mouth, and twanged on it continuously until Joel was writhing in agony, holding his head with both hands.

"He's sick. See what you're doing to him," Ellis said. "Why don't you stop?"

The man stopped twanging while he answered. "I'll play whenever I want to," he said.

Enraged, Ellis snatched the little instrument from his hand and tore out the tongue. The man arose and attempted to grasp Ellis by the throat. Ellis raised his shackled arms and brought both fists down hard on the man's head so that the irons around his wrists struck his skull. He went down hard and lay on the floor moaning. Joel tried to rise, but fell limply back on his mat. Two days later he died, and Ellis mournfully watched the guards carry his wasted body away for burial. He thought of Joel's wife. She must have given up hope of ever seeing him again long ago, he thought. It's better if she lost hope and forgot him.

Three months passed, when Ellis was released without explanation and allowed to return to Chihuahua. "I knew you were in prison," Duncan told him, "and I'd have come to see what I could do for you, but Tom House is in bad shape. I was sure he'd die if I left him."

"The first thing I aim to do is see if Jonah isn't too yellow to fight me with pistols," Ellis growled. "He doesn't deserve to live." They found him the next morning.

"You sorry son-of-a-bitch," Ellis greeted him, "get a pistol and meet me outside of town. Then you kill me, or I'll sure as hell kill you." The shifty-eyed Waters turned pale and ran.

Knowing a house that Waters frequently visited, Ellis got a stout club and waited for him. When Waters came out, Ellis stepped from around the corner and blocked the way back to the house. "If you won't fight me with guns, I'll get my satisfaction another way," he growled.

"Please don't hit me," Waters begged in a quavering voice. "I didn't mean you any harm."

"Liar!" Ellis laid on with the club until Waters lay badly bruised and whimpering on the ground.

Ellis and Duncan went to the *paseo* most nights to admire the young ladies. "That one's makin' eyes at you," Duncan said, as a fancily dressed girl walked by with her chaperone, probably an aunt. Ellis watched them walk on—the girl turned her head and looked hard at him with the one eye that was exposed.

One night Ellis went alone to the *paseo* while Duncan took food to House. The young lady was there, as usual, and somehow she slipped away from her chaperone and hurried to where Ellis stood under a tree. She shamelessly pulled the shawl from her face.

"What's your name, *señor*?" she asked. "Mine's Elena," she said before he could reply. Just then the chaperone charged up like a buffalo bull after a wolf, crossing herself when she saw the breach of moral conduct. She dragged the girl away and informed her father, who was a colonel under Salcedo. The next day he sent a soldier to Ellis with a note.

"You have compromised my daughter's honor," it said. "You must marry her at once."

"Be damned if I will," Ellis told Duncan. "After I saw her face she didn't look all that great to me. And all we did was talk. I didn't get in her pants. I didn't even kiss her." Two soldiers arrived.

"You must come with us," they told him.

"Where?" Ellis asked.

"To the *cuartel* at San Jerónimo." The barracks were a dozen miles from Chihuahua.

Early in 1807, twenty-two ragged American soldiers were marched into the *cuartel* in Chihuahua, but the guard refused to allow Nolan's men to talk with them. "Who are they?" Duncan asked a Spanish officer who had been friendly ever since Duncan had repaired his weapons.

"They were with a Lieutenant Pike on the Rio Bravo above Sante Fe, in Spanish territory," he answered. "They were arrested and brought here so General Salcedo could question them."

"Where is Lieutenant Pike?"

"He and a Dr. Robinson are at the house of Juan Pedro Walker, but don't try to see them. The General forbade it." Walker, an American, was commandant of the military academy, and Nolan's slave, Caesar, lived with him as a servant.

Lieutenant Pike came to the plaza one morning to buy a straw hat, and stopped by Ellis, who had a stack of hats of all sizes. "You must be Lieutenant Pike," Ellis said. "I'm Ellis Bean, one of the Nolan men. They wouldn't allow us to talk to you." Pike looked around to see if any soldiers were watching.

"I know," he replied. "But one of your men managed to slip away and see me. David Fero. He was a lieutenant in my father's battalion. He begged me with tears in his eyes to get him out of here. I promised to do all I could for the lot of you. I'm going to send the Natchez *Herald* the information he gave me on all of the prisoners, so their families will know they're alive." He paused and looked around again. "I told General Salcedo the circumstances of your being with Nolan, that you were all innocent of wrong-doing and should be set free. He said he rescued you from a dungeon and has given you all the freedom it is in his power to give. Now it's up to the king."

Late in April, Pike and a few of his men, along with Dr. Robinson, were escorted to San Antonio on the way to Natchitoches. A month later, Ellis' friend Moreno stopped in the plaza, as he often did. He shook hands without smiling. "I just learned that the viceroy has reprimanded General Salcedo for releasing Pike," he said. "It doesn't sound good for the rest of you." He went on his way, shaking his head.

Ellis pondered his words. The only news we ever get is bad, he thought, feeling sick. They'll never let us go. We'll all die here without ever seeing our families again.

One day early the following November, a soldier summoned Duncan to the *cuartel*, where he saw Joseph Reed,

William Danlin, and Jonah Waters. Without explanation, they were locked in a room in the barracks. A few days later, Ellis, Ephraim Blackburn, David Fero, Zalmon Cooley, and Luciano García were brought from San Carlos and San Jerónimo and placed in the same room.

"Does anyone know why we're here?" Fero asked.

"Maybe at last they're going to set us free," Blackburn answered hopefully. "It's high time they let us go."

Wondering if that could be true, the prisoners waited, trying to recall their nearly forgotten homes and families. The next morning, Ellis turned pale when three black-robed priests solemnly entered the room to hear their confessions, for he knew that was what the Spaniards always did when men were about to be executed. Most were afraid to inquire about their fate, but Fero asked, "Does this mean we'll be put to death?"

"We don't know, *señor*," a priest answered. "They haven't told us. Perhaps some of you may be."

"I guess I'm the one they're after," Ellis said gloomily, and some of the others nodded in agreement. "But if they've decided to shoot me, I hope they'll let the rest of you go."

"If they were only after you, they wouldn't have rounded up the rest of us. It looks to me like we're all under the gun," Duncan said.

Blackburn cleared his throat and ran his bony fingers through his shaggy white hair, his wrinkled face solemn. "Most of you are young and have your lives ahead of you," he said hoarsely. "If justice is done. . . ." Ellis interrupted him.

"If justice is done and they shoot the worst scoundrel among us, it's got to be Waters," he growled. "He should have been shot years ago." There were grunts of approval from the others. Waters wiped the sweat from his sharp nose and sighed deeply, but said nothing.

The next morning, the door swung open again, and Ellis

shivered when dignified Antonio García Tejado, adjutant inspector of the Interior Provinces, solemnly entered the room holding a paper in his hand. With him were prosecutor Díaz de Bustamante and the prisoners's counsel, Verea. All three wore black cloaks, and their faces were expressionless. Verea motioned to the prisoners to kneel. They've come to pronounce sentence, Ellis thought; at least they've got bad news. He dreaded to hear it.

"This is His Majesty's decree," García de Tejado intoned. "One man in every five who entered Texas with Nolan and who fired on royal troops must die." Ellis heard gasps around him, followed by heavy breathing, while his own thoughts were racing. How will they decide who to execute? he wondered.

García de Tejado cleared his throat and continued. "Because your man Pierce is dead and only nine of you are left, only one must die." He looked as if it pained him to deliver the order, but since it came from the king, he had no choice.

The Spanish troops had attacked them; they had merely defended themselves, Ellis thought bitterly, but there was little time to contemplate the cruel sentence. A soldier immediately entered the hushed room and placed a big drum on the floor, while another set a crystal cup containing a pair of dice on the drumhead.

"You must all throw the dice while blindfolded," García de Tejado informed them. "The unfortunate one who casts the lowest number must die." The pale prisoners stood as far away from the drum as they could, staring open-eyed at the dice as if they were rattlesnakes poised to strike. García de Tejado cleared his throat again, but no one stepped forward to test his luck.

"Let's throw in the order of our ages," Fero said, his voice hollow. "The oldest first." The others all glanced at Ephraim Blackburn. Ellis thought of all the dangers they'd faced before. Nothing equalled staking their lives on one throw of the dice while blindfolded.

Ephraim Blackburn knelt prayerfully beside the drum. A soldier tied a blindfold around his head and placed the crystal cup in his trembling hands. He shouldn't have to do this, Ellis thought. He came with Nolan, but didn't even fire on Spanish troops. All eyes were on the drumhead as Blackburn cast the dice. He immediately arose and lifted the blindfold, wincing when he saw he'd thrown a four. Swallowing hard, a look of resignation on his ashen face, he stepped back to make room for Luciano, who took his place by the drum. Ellis watched Luciano roll a seven and exhale deeply. Joseph Reed cast an eleven and involuntarily smiled. When he glanced around and saw Blackburn's somber face the smile vanished.

Fero threw an eight, Cooley an eleven, Jonah Waters a seven. Ellis wiped his moist palms on his trousers and knelt while the soldier fixed the blindfold. He cast the dice and arose, almost afraid to look. He'd rolled a five. Duncan followed with a six. The last was William Danlin, who cast a seven.

Solemn, black-robed priests immediately swarmed around Blackburn, clucking sympathetically and muttering Latin phrases. He gazed at his companions, his white hair crowning his somber face. "It's better this way, my friends," he said in a firm voice. "My death should buy your freedom." He started to go with the priests, but stopped and turned. "If any of you ever get to Natchez," he said, "tell my wife that I died, but don't tell her the circumstances." Then he was gone. Ellis felt a lump rise in his throat.

Two days later, the prisoners were ordered to the Plaza de los Urangos, where a large crowd had already gathered. Ellis caught his breath as he saw the newly built gallows, with the hangman's noose swaying in the light breeze. His face was sweating, but he suddenly felt cold when he saw Blackburn calmly mount the scaffold and stand under the noose. A soldier blindfolded him, then placed the halter over his head and tightened it around his neck. Ellis felt his skin crawl when he heard the roll of drums and Blackburn shot through the trap. A knot settled in Ellis' stomach, while he brushed away tears that streamed down his cheeks.

Three days later, Fero, Cooley, Ellis, and Danlin, the ones who'd been implicated in the plot to escape, were brought to the plaza. Tom House was too sick to move from his bed. Duncan saw a crowd gathering, and went to see what was happening. As he arrived, merchant Manuel Moreno was talking to Ellis.

"I have influential friends in Mexico City, my friend," he said. "I'm certain they can secure your release once you get there. I will write them immediately."

"Mexico City?" Duncan exclaimed. "Who's goin' there?"

Ellis nodded his head toward the other three prisoners. "The bad boys," he said. "The troublemakers."

The four prisoners were shackled and ordered to mount horses, then twenty-five cavalrymen surrounded them and they trotted away on the road to far-off Mexico City. Ellis glanced back at Duncan, wondering if they'd ever meet again.

Chapter Three

At every town or village along the way, the cavalry stopped for a time in the plaza and allowed the prisoners to walk about in irons. Curious men, women, and children crowded around them, for they'd never seen Americans. Women with shawls over their heads brought them bread and fruit, frowning and exclaiming over their shackles. "*Pobrecitos,*" they lamented.

After weeks of steady riding, the travelers stopped for the night at the village of Salamanca. As usual, the prisoners were allowed to stretch their legs, and chattering people thronged around them. A well-dressed, attractive young woman watched Ellis for a time, then shyly approached him. "Is it your wish to escape, *señor*?" she whispered in Spanish.

Surprised, Ellis looked at her, then shrugged. "It is," he replied, "but that's impossible. They'll find me again, and if they don't shoot me, they'll make me pay one way or another. I'll just have to take what comes."

"No *señor*," she said softly, her dark eyes flashing, "it *is* possible. I will return soon, and you will see." She hurried away.

"Who is that lady?" Ellis asked a portly villager, pointing at her. The man glanced at the retreating figure.

"That's María Baldonado," he replied. "Because of her

beauty a rich old *hacendado* married her not long ago. I don't know how many *haciendas* he owns, but more than enough."

Ellis stretched out on his mat, thinking about what she'd said, ignoring the curious people who came to stare at him. María returned shortly before sundown, followed by a tall dark-skinned man in a long blue cloak. She pushed her way through the crowd and knelt by Ellis. The tall man stood behind her, arms folded across his chest, staring off in the distance.

"He has files for cutting your shackles," she whispered. "You must go to the stables, where he will remove them. Then a man on the wall will lower a rope to pull you up and bring you to me. With me you'll be safe."

Ellis thought about it some more, recalling Manuel Moreno's assurance that his influential friends would secure his release. If I try to escape I may fail, and they won't be able to help me after that. Then he remembered the men who'd escaped at Nacogodoches, and the calamity that it had meant for the others.

"I can't do it," he told her solemnly. "It wouldn't be fair to my friends, for they'd surely suffer for it."

"Your first duty is to yourself," María said firmly. "God will take care of your friends. I have money and horses; you will have whatever you want without risk of recapture. I have *haciendas*—you can stay at any of them, and no one will ever know."

Ellis was rising on his elbows, ready to accept her offer, when a soldier called the prisoners to their evening meal. "Come to me early in the morning," María said, and told him where to find her.

Ellis thought of nothing else that night, and slept fitfully. One moment he was ready to go; the next he was sure it would be a mistake. If they recaptured him, or if her husband found out, no telling what would happen. In Mexico City, Moreno's friends would free him without such risks.

Still undecided, at daybreak he asked the officer in command of the cavalry for a soldier to accompany him to a shop, then hurried to the house where María waited by an open window, a gray shawl framing her oval face. Ellis gave the soldier a coin and told him to buy some spirits. "I'll wait for you here," he said.

"It's now or never," María told him. "There's no time to lose. I can hide you so you'll never be found."

"Are you absolutely sure?" he asked. "If they find me, they'll probably shoot me."

"Yes, yes," she said impatiently. "Trust me and have no fear. Soon we will be able to ride away together. Though I'm part Indian, I know you're too honorable to abandon me. But we must hurry!"

Ellis gazed at her lovely face, his thoughts racing. It just might work out, and if he wasn't discovered, they could make it to the States one day. He'd be proud to have her for his wife. While she fidgeted nervously, he thought again about Moreno's assurance. But supposing his friends failed? What then?

"Hurry!" María exclaimed.

"All right," he said, "I'll chance it." Just then, the soldier shouted, and Ellis turned to see him running toward them.

"The captain says to come *pronto*," he said, breathing hard. "They're ready to leave and are waiting for you. Don't make him angry at both of us."

Ellis turned to María, holding his hands out with palms upward in a gesture of resignation. "Adios, my lady," he said. "I'll never forget you." Then, as best he could in his shackles, he hurried after the soldier.

"Go with God, *señor*," María called after him, tears streaming down her face.

Another week of travel through the mountains brought them to the Valley of Mexico, and Ellis gazed down in awe at the splendid city. As soon as they free me, he thought, I'll go back and find María. The prisoners were immediately confined with several hundred other culprits. Ellis watched for Moreno's friends, wondering how long it would take them to obtain his release. The third day, a well-dressed young man came to see him.

"*Señor* Bean," he said, "Don Ramón Iglesias sent me to tell you he is working to free you, but it may take a month, maybe many months. He asks if you need money, and advises you to be patient." Ellis thanked him and shook his head. I have money, and being patient is what I do best, he thought, feeling elated. At least it won't be much longer.

A few days later, a guard ordered the four prisoners to follow him to the prison yard, where a troop of cavalry waited. A sergeant beckoned toward four saddled horses, and the prisoners mounted and accompanied the cavalry out of the city on a road leading southwest. Shocked at this unexpected development, Ellis spoke to the sergeant, who appeared friendly. "Where are you taking us?" he asked, his fears rising.

"To the Castle of San Diego at Acapulco," the sergeant replied, looking from one to another of the prisoners. "But you don't look like dangerous men to me."

I wonder what that means, Ellis thought. For one thing, he knew, it meant that Moreno's friends couldn't help him now. Damn. I should have gone with María when I had the chance.

In ten days, they reached the city of Chilpancingo, and several days later came out of the mountains and saw the white-washed houses of Acapulco gleaming below them on a narrow strip of land between the mountains and the white sand of the curving bay. Beyond was the Pacific Ocean, deep blue broken by white-caps rolling toward the beach. Ellis gazed at the magnificent sight, holding his breath in awe.

"I'm afraid this is your home now," the sergeant said, inclining his head toward the huge, star-shaped fortress of

San Diego, at the apex of a hill near the bay. It was bristling with cannons. "I hope it won't be forever. Good luck, *señor.*" Ellis saw that he was sincere, and felt his blood turn to ice.

As they rode down from the heights, Ellis felt like he had crawled under a heavy blanket, for the air grew hot and humid, and beads of sweat rolled down his face. Under the lush growth of many kinds of trees were countless varieties of ferns and plants with brilliant red or yellow flowers. Along the shore in the distance, tall coconut palms, their tops ringed with graceful fronds, stood like sentinels. Ellis gazed around him in amazement—he'd never seen anything like it before.

The troops and prisoners followed the trail winding down to the beach across the bay from the sleepy village of Acapulco. Ellis shaded his face with a shackled hand, for the reflection of the sun off the white houses hurt his eyes. The few people they met moved slowly, blinking in the bright sunlight as they stared at the prisoners. They looked up at the castle, then at the prisoners, and shook their heads, as if they knew they'd never see those bearded men again.

On up the hill by a winding road they went, until the castle loomed directly over them, much more forbidding than it seemed when they were looking down on it from the mountains. As they rode through the gate and across the drawbridge, Ellis gazed up at the awesome towers and felt fear. I'm glad I won't be alone, he thought.

The prisoners dismounted and stood stiffly while an officer read their names. When his name was called, Ellis stepped forward and a lieutenant beckoned him to follow. He looked back and saw the others weren't coming. At the side of the castle, the lieutenant stopped at a narrow door with a small opening in it. The hinges creaked as he opened the door and gestured for Ellis to enter. They creaked again as he closed and locked it.

Ellis stared at the cell in the dim light, a cubicle only three feet wide and seven feet long. At one end was a small grated window that let in a little air and light. He leaned down to peer through the opening in the door and saw a soldier standing guard. "Where are my friends?" Ellis asked him.

"Together in a big room." Ellis swore.

Before dark, the lieutenant returned, accompanied by a soldier carrying Ellis' blanket, old clothes, and a straw mat for a bed. The lieutenant handed Ellis a bowl with a piece of bread and a chunk of tough beef in it, and a pot of water. "Why can't I be with my friends?" Ellis asked.

The lieutenant hesitated before answering. "Colonel Carreño received a letter from a friend of his, an officer in Chihuahua," he replied. "I don't know what it said, but the colonel ordered us to take every precaution to see that you don't escape." Ellis scowled. The officer whose daughter he'd spurned must be gloating. He thought of María Baldonado, cursing himself for hesitating too long.

The next morning when the soldier came with food and water, and opened the door to inspect Ellis' shackles, he said nervously, "Colonel Carreño wants to see you." Ellis stood and faced the door, where a heavy-set man scowled at him. His mouth turned down at the corners, and his bushy mustache drooped around his mouth. His small, black eyes glittered like the eyes of a coiled rattlesnake. His lips curled and his nostrils wrinkled at the stench from the cell. Ellis shivered.

"So you're our *Señor* Bean," Carreño said, in a tone of contempt. "Make yourself comfortable. You won't be leaving as long as I'm governor of this castle." He turned and left. The soldier, who had been standing nervously to one side looked relieved.

"He looks like one mean son-of-a-bitch," Ellis said in Spanish. The soldier peered out the door to be sure Carreño was gone, then nodded his head vigorously and left, closing the door behind him.

Every day, the soldier who brought Ellis food and water

also checked his shackles to see that they were in place. Ellis still had the money he'd brought from Chihuahua. He took a peso from his pocket. "Will you buy me a knife?" he asked the soldier, handing him the coin.

"I'll bring it tonight," the soldier replied.

When he had the knife, Ellis tried to pick out the mortar between the huge stones of the outer wall, but soon realized it was hopeless. The days dragged by; Ellis thought only of being free again. It appeared that he'd never be released and would have to escape. But how?

One day, he noticed a white lizard that had crawled through the little window and was trying to catch flies. Out of curiosity, Ellis caught a fly, impaled it on a straw from his mat, and slowly held it up to the lizard's head. It eyed him suspiciously, but accepted the fly, and as many others as Ellis could catch. Every morning when the lizard crawled through the window, it sang like a frog to announce its arrival. From the time it turned light each day, Ellis listened eagerly for its song. He named the lizard Bill.

After some days, Bill became so tame Ellis could hold him in his hand and feed him scraps of beef. When he held Bill up to the light, the lizard was so transparent he could make out its bones. "You're just about the only friend I've got left in the world," he told it, and it cocked its head, staring at Ellis with shiny eyes. Bill became so tame that he even stayed with Ellis nights, but when the soldier came each day to inspect Ellis' shackles, the lizard hid under his blanket. He came out as soon as he heard the door close, and Ellis always picked him up. "Don't you worry about any of those soldiers," he said, stroking Bill's back. "If one ever tried to harm you, I'd strangle him."

When he'd been at Acapulco nearly a year, Ellis developed a fever, and the castle doctor ordered an Indian to carry him to the hospital. Now, he thought, if I ever get well, I'll find a way to escape. But at the hospital he was put in stocks—two logs with semicircular cuts in them that fit over his legs. While he was in the stocks, small biting insects called *chinces* nearly drove him mad by biting his legs, for there was no way he could get at them.

Many in Acapulco had been struck by the same fever, and the hospital was crowded. When men on each side of him died one night, and two more died the next morning, Ellis was sure his time had come, but he slowly recovered. He was fed only a little bread and gruel mornings, and soup and a chicken's head nights. As he recovered he was ravenously hungry, but the volume of his food wasn't increased.

One evening a monk with a shaved head brought Ellis his usual fare. Famished and feeling desperate, Ellis, who happened to be out of the stocks, arose. "Why is it that the only part of the chicken you ever give me is the head?" he growled.

"Eat it or go to Hell for more," the monk retorted. Enraged, Ellis flung his bowl, striking the monk's shaved head. While the monk howled in pain, Ellis threw his water pot at him but missed. Weakened by the fever, he fell back on his mat. A sergeant entered the room and put Ellis' neck in the stocks, where it remained for fifteen days. He regretted not killing the monk, for then they would have shot him and ended his troubles. While his neck was in the stocks the *chinces* bit the skin off it, leaving it raw.

When Ellis was released from the hospital, two soldiers armed only with sabers escorted him back to the castle. At the edge of town they came to a house where a woman sold beer. Ellis invited the soldiers to have some, and they gladly accepted. Determined to escape, Ellis asked one of the soldiers to accompany him to the garden behind the house. Catching him off guard, Ellis held his knife to the man's throat and seized his saber.

"What are you going to do?" the frightened soldier asked.

"I'm leaving. Why don't you come with me?"

"I will. If I don't Colonel Carreño will put me in your

place." Seeing that the soldier really didn't plan to accompany him, Ellis gave him a peso and told him to buy some bread for the journey. Then he fled to the woods before the soldier could return with others and arrest him. With the steel he used to strike fire, he removed the chains from his legs. He hid in the woods all day, listening to the birds and smelling the flowers. At night he slipped into town and bought bread, cheese, and a gourd of brandy. Two men in the shop were talking in English, so Ellis waited for them outside. They were Irishmen, and told him they were crewmen on a privateer that had just arrived from Peru.

"Will your captain talk to me?" Ellis asked.

"Come with us and we'll ask him," one of the men replied. They walked to the house where the captain was staying. He invited Ellis to his room.

"Are you Mexican?" he asked.

"No, American." The captain looked surprised.

"But you speak Spanish so well," he said.

"I've been a prisoner for years," Ellis told him, "Eight or nine, maybe more. I've lost track of time.

The captain shook his head sympathetically.

"Will you take me with you when you sail?" Ellis asked. "I've got to get away before they find me. I don't want to die in that hole."

"I'll take you, but I can't talk any longer now. Meet my men at the wharf tomorrow night. They'll take you out to the brig and hide you. We sail at noon."

After hiding in the woods all day and reveling in his freedom, Ellis met the two Irishmen at night, and once on board the brig they hid him in an empty water barrel. At last I'm going to get away, he thought, and anxiously waited for the brig to weigh anchor. Cramped and uncomfortable, he remained there all night as the ship rose and fell with the tide. At mid-morning he heard voices, and soon knew that a patrol had come to see if he was on board. Ellis held his breath and tried to make himself smaller. When he heard the patrol leave, he exhaled. Only a couple of hours more before we sail, he thought. He relaxed and tried not to think.

But the patrol returned, and Ellis shivered as he heard the clanking of swords and heavy footsteps on the deck. A voice said, "I know you're hiding a king's prisoner. Turn him over to us or you'll take his place." Ellis cursed under his breath as he heard the footsteps approaching.

"He's in that one," the Irish captain said. Soldiers removed the lid, dragged him out, and bound him hand and foot. Two of them picked him up and threw him down into their boat, bruising him badly but not breaking any bones. He wished they'd killed him.

When Ellis was back in his cell, Carreño ordered his arms and legs shackled. He was bitterly disappointed that he had come so close to escaping before being betrayed. At least I was free for a while and heard the birds sing, he thought. He looked for Bill. The white lizard had become wary again; it took Ellis a week to regain its confidence.

One morning a few months later, a captain and a sergeant came to bring food and inspect Ellis' shackles as usual. The captain remarked to the sergeant that he needed some rocks blasted. "We have men who can drill the holes," the sergeant replied, "but none to set the charges."

Seeing an opportunity to get out of his cell again, Ellis announced that he knew blasting. The captain ignored him, but a few days later, the sergeant told Ellis that Carreño had given orders for him to do the blasting. "If you behave, you can earn many privileges," the sergeant said. "Just don't try to escape." Ellis nodded as if agreeing, but his thoughts were on flight.

The shackles were replaced by a heavy chain around each ankle. By wrapping the chains around his waist, Ellis was able to walk under guard to the blasting site. He saw twenty soldiers guarding forty prisoners, and was astonished to recognize Nolan's old scout among them. "Luciano," he called, "why are you here?"

The old man's wrinkled face broke into a broad smile, and he came to give Ellis an *abrazo*. "It's good to see you, my friend," he said. "They called me a traitor to Spain for serving *Señor* Nolan—that's why I'm here." A soldier ordered him to get back to work.

Ellis made matches for igniting the blasting powder in the gallery of a house not far away. In the evening, he questioned the prisoners about escaping. They talked it over, and one of them said, "Some of us will go with you if you tell us when, and give the signal."

"Tomorrow afternoon, when you see me carry a basket of stones to the dump, get ready," Ellis replied, "but we must not flee until the soldiers are on the run. Each of you try to grab a soldier's gun."

As blaster, Ellis wasn't required to carry away the debris, but he loaded a basket with broken stones, hoisted it to his left shoulder, and carried it to the dump. A bored soldier stood there, yawning and watching the prisoners through half-closed eyes. Ellis paused beside him as if out of breath. He took a stone from the basket, knocked the soldier down, and seized his musket. The prisoners all threw rocks at the soldiers, who hastily retreated.

In the distance, Ellis saw reinforcements coming on the run, and most of the prisoners quickly scattered. Ellis and Luciano ran off together, both still in chains. Because the old man had difficulty keeping up with him, Ellis stopped and fired at their pursuers, who were gaining on them but who stopped momentarily.

"I'll hold them back while you get away," Ellis told Luciano. "Go and don't stop till you're in the woods. I'll join you there." Luciano ran ahead but soon returned with his hat full of rocks.

"What are you doing?" Ellis called, trying to conceal his irritation.

"I'm here to help you, my friend. See, I brought more stones."

Ellis glanced at the soldiers. "There are too many of them now," he exclaimed. "We've got to get into the woods." He fired a shot to slow the pursuers, while Luciano showered them with rocks. The soldiers knelt and fired a volley. When he looked around for Luciano, Ellis was shocked to see him stretched out on the ground, grimacing in pain.

"They've shattered my thigh," the old man gasped. "You must save yourself, but shoot me first. I'd rather be dead than a prisoner." Ellis looked at him sorrowfully, but couldn't bring himself to carry out his request. With bullets whistling around him, he fled, but the heavy chains slowed him down and he was soon recaptured and taken before Governor Carreño.

"Aha," he said. "So you tried to escape but we outwitted you. I assure you that you'll never leave here again. Not alive, anyway." He ordered Ellis chained to a huge mulatto and placed in a room with twenty other prisoners. The mulatto scowled, but said nothing to Ellis. At night, when they lay on mats, the prisoner next to Ellis touched his shoulder. Ellis turned.

"The colonel told that man he'll let him out early if he takes care of you," the man whispered. "He told him to beat you whenever he wants to."

"*Muchas gracias, amigo,*" Ellis whispered. He lay back, determined to settle affairs with the mulatto at the first opportunity.

The next morning they were taken out to the castle yard to eat breakfast. As Ellis reached for a piece of bread, the mulatto jerked on the chain, throwing him to the ground. Ellis saw a bull's skull with one horn attached to it near him. Grabbing it, he arose and struck the mulatto on the head with it, knocking him down. Ellis stood over him, striking him again and again with all his strength, while the mulatto bellowed for the guards.

They rushed in and seized the skull from Ellis' hands. The mulatto begged them to free him. Carreño ordered the two separated and Ellis flogged, and a wheel put around his neck. The officer didn't carry out the order to flog him, but he did have the wheel put around his neck. The wheel was so large Ellis couldn't reach the rim, and he couldn't stand or kneel, grimacing in pain as his muscles protested. He saw Carreño walk by and look into the room with an expression of satisfaction on his face. After four hours the officer ordered the wheel removed and took Ellis to his cell, again in double shackles.

Ellis was saddened by Luciano's likely death, and bitterly disappointed that he'd failed to escape again. I'd give my life for a chance to kill Carreño, he thought. He looked around in the unaccustomed dim light for the lizard. "Bill," he called, "come here," but the lizard didn't appear.

The next morning he saw the lizard crawling down the wall and reached for it as usual, eager to hold and stroke it. But when he held out his hand for the lizard to crawl on it, Bill backed away. Ellis gave it a few scraps of beef, but whenever he tried to hold it, it ran. He patiently set out to win its confidence again, and after four or five days, he was greatly relieved when it crawled on his hand and cocked its head at him while he talked to it.

Later, Ellis began twisting a small cord out of the palmetto leaves in his mat. In four or five days he had a string about thirty feet long. On tiptoe, he looked out the small window and watched until he saw a woman walking by. "Hello," he called in Spanish. "Wait a minute."

The woman stopped. "I can't see you," she said.

"I'm a prisoner," he told her. "Will you do me a favor?"

"What is it?"

"I want some *aguardiente*. I'll lower a string for it." When she agreed, he tossed some money through the window.

After she had gone, Ellis tied the string to his arm, feeling like a lazy fisherman waiting for a bite. He felt a tug on it, and the woman said, "You can pull it up now." He carefully pulled on the string, until a cow's bladder came safely through the small window. It was filled with *aguardiente*.

Ellis took a sip of the powerful liquor, then lay back on his mat. After half an hour he heard his cell door open, although it wasn't time for food and inspection. He quickly hid the bladder in his water pot and put his old hat over it. An elderly priest entered.

"My son," he said, "an officer of the guard told me you have tamed a lizard, and I came to see if it's true." Ellis took Bill out from under his blanket, where he was hiding, talked to him and stroked his back. The old priest was delighted.

"Man has the power to do anything he sets his mind to," he said. He gave Ellis a few coins and left. Ellis pondered his words. I'm going to get away from here, he thought. It can be done somehow, and I'm going to do it.

One morning late in 1810, a captain opened the cell door and stood in the doorway, eying Ellis a moment before speaking. "Brigands and desperadoes under Padre Hidalgo have stirred up an Indian *tumulto*," he said. "All prisoners who agree to serve in the army to help crush those monsters will be released." He paused, while Ellis tried to comprehend his message. He had no love for the army, but anything was better than this. "Is it your wish to serve?" the captain continued, looking at the tiny cell and wrinkling his nose in disgust.

"Yes, even getting killed would be better than rotting here."

Chapter Four

As he clanked through the cell door in his shackles, Ellis stopped and turned, looking up at the wall. "Goodbye, friend," he said. "This time I won't be back." The officer stared at him, bent over, and peered up at the cell wall, wrinkling his nose at the stench. Seeing no one, he shook his head as if he should have known that all prisoners were a bit loco, then led the way to where others were gathering. When a soldier removed the shackles from his arms, Ellis held up his scarred wrists. He'd become so accustomed to the weight of the irons that his arms seemed to float up toward his face.

William Danlin, bearded and long-haired, and still limping from the old arrow wound, hurried to Ellis and shook hands with him. "Ellis," he exclaimed, "I'm sure glad to see you again, and I know Cooley will be. I never had a chance to tell you before, but Fero is no friend of yours. When he and Tom House and I were fixin' to escape, Tom and I wanted to include you and Duncan. Fero wouldn't hear of it, but he never said why."

"Thanks. I'll steer clear of him."

A soldier handed each of them cotton pants, shirts, and leather sandals; another issued muskets. Blinking his eyes in the sunlight, Ellis marched with the other prisoners to army barracks near the town, where they were placed in two local militia companies. They were drilled on the parade ground for hours in the heat and dust. Weak from the months of confinement, Ellis collapsed on his mat at the end of each day, sure he'd never be able to rise again. By the end of two weeks of daily drilling, however, he felt strong and was eager to see the last of Acapulco.

With a company of uniformed regular troops, who acted as if they couldn't even see the shabby citizen soldiers, the two militia companies boarded small ships that tacked their way up the coast to the mouth of a river. The only time I was ever on a ship, Ellis thought, as he gazed at the ocean and sniffed the salt air, I was hiding in a barrel. This is better. When they landed and he took a few steps, his legs felt peculiarly unsteady, and he noticed that others also staggered a little. Captain Nicolás Cosío lined them up under coconut palms.

"Men, we have reports that the monster Morelos is somewhere inland, not many miles from here," he told them. "No doubt he'll try to ambush us, so we must locate his camp before we march. Who will volunteer to find it?"

Ellis, Danlin, and six Mexican militiamen from Acapulco responded, and set out upstream among the palms along the river. There was no breeze, and the heat was oppressive. Ellis wiped the sweat from his face. "Who is this monster we're looking for?" he asked a short, swarthy militiaman who walked at his side.

"He is Padre José María Morelos," the man answered, "but he is no monster, *señor*. He is a good man, a patriot who wants to free our land from Spain. When the revolution began, Padre Hidalgo sent him here with only twenty-five men. Now they say he has a small army. The only title he will accept is 'Servant of the Nation.'"

"Then we must warn him that the royalists are coming."

"*Seguro*. That's why we're here."

After several hours of plodding inland, the sweating men came to a farm that had many fowls of various kinds. The hungry militiamen bargained with the farmer for a few chickens, then lit a fire.

"You wait here while I locate the camp," Ellis told them. "No need for all of us to go." They gladly agreed. Danlin limped toward Ellis, intending to accompany him.

"You stay here and rest your foot," Ellis told him. "I'll come or send word when I find him." He walked on alone.

In half an hour, Ellis came to a trail leading through tall broad-leafed trees and flowering vines away from the river. He followed it a short distance, startling large green-and-yellow birds that raucously scolded him as they flew away. Ellis heard voices and crouched on the blanket of leaves in the underbrush until forty or fifty men were near. Among them he recognized several former prisoners, and knew they'd deserted to the patriots. When he stepped out and hailed them, they greeted him as a friend, and led him to the rebel camp. There he saw at least five hundred men of all colors, mostly Indians and mestizos, but also blacks and mulattoes. He looked around for their leader, wondering what sort of a man he might be.

"Where's Morelos?" he asked. One of the ragged men pointed to a group standing in the shade of a huge tree, but Ellis could see only their backs. He walked up and peered over the shoulders of the nearest men, but saw no one who looked like he might be the commander of such a motley army. In the center of the circle, a heavy-set individual, who was little more than five feet tall, was speaking in a low, almost musical voice. His features were coarse, his lips thick, his face marked with moles. His eyes and skin were brown, his eyebrows thick and joined above his nose, on which was a large scar. His face reflected boundless energy and uncompromising determination. Covering his head was a brightly colored kerchief. A slender chain around his neck held a small silver crucifix.

He must be the chaplain, Ellis thought, wondering which

of the others was Morelos. All but one of the men around the short man left. He looked at Ellis with raised eyebrows, his glance searching. "How can I help you?" he asked.

"Excuse me," Ellis stammered. "I was told that General Morelos was here, but. . . ."

"I've been a general only a short time," Morelos said, his tone both grave and amused. "I'm afraid I'll never look like one." He smiled, and Ellis instantly felt drawn to him. "Why do you want to see me?"

"I was a prisoner in the San Diego Castle," Ellis replied. "They let us out to fight in the royalist army. We landed at the mouth of the river, and eight of us volunteered to find your camp for them, but really so we could warn you they are coming." He told Morelos where Danlin and the others were waiting. Morelos sent the man at his side to bring them in, then faced Ellis again.

"I'm not surprised they have come," he said. "I expected that. Thanks to you, they won't take us by surprise. What will you do now?"

"Right now, all I can think about is getting back to the States somehow," Ellis answered. "I've been a Spanish prisoner for ten years."

Morelos sighed. "Ten years," he said. "Maybe you're fortunate. We've been prisoners of Spain for nearly three hundred years. Now we intend to throw off our yokes, but the struggle promises to be long and bitter. Look at us!" He gestured toward the ragged men squatting in the shade, sharpening knives or machetes. "We have to fight them almost with our bare hands."

Ellis looked around and shook his head. How could this ragtag army led by a plucky little priest with no military training hope to defeat veteran Spanish troops? Their cause was hopeless—all were doomed to die in battle, or worse, be shot in the back as traitors.

"I don't see many guns," he admitted.

"No, and we have little powder for the few we have."
Ellis thought about that.

"If you have any sulfur and saltpeter," he said, "I can at
least make some gunpowder for you."

"We have a small supply of both. Make all you can."

Ellis got some of the women camp followers to grind the
saltpeter and sulfur on the stone *metates* they used for making
cornmeal. He mixed the powder, then approached Morelos
again. "If I go back to the royalists, I know I can get at least
seventy men to come over. They'll have guns, too." The
stocky priest looked at Ellis for a moment, and it seemed that
he was taking his measure as a man.

"Go ahead, Elias," he said, "for I trust you not to betray
us. But make it appear that you escaped. If they're the least
bit suspicious, they'll shoot you on the spot. They may,
anyway."

Ellis and Danlin slipped away that night, and the next day
told Cosío about their capture and lucky escape. The captain
looked at them through narrowed eyes. "They were going to
shoot us in the morning," Ellis explained. "We had to get
away." Cosío shrugged and ordered them to join the force of
regulars and militia again.

"You'll have your chance to get even," he said.

"I sure hope so," Ellis replied. They marched to Tres
Palos, closer to the rebel camp, where they joined a larger
force under Captain Francisco Paris, who was preparing to
attack the rebels.

Because none of the militia had uniforms, Paris sent Ellis
and others to shoot cranes so they could use the white feathers
to distinguish the militia from the rebels. Ellis slipped away
to a house where he found two women whose husbands he
suspected were with Morelos.

"I've got to get word to Morelos," he told them. One
cautiously nodded. "Tell him Elias said to send as many men
as he can to that abandoned house by the creek. I'll meet them

there tonight and we'll capture the royalist camp and artillery." He hoped Morelos wouldn't think it was a trap.

That night Ellis and two Mexicans, who were rebels at heart, slipped out of camp, knowing that the sentry guarding the artillery also favored the rebel cause. In the light of a full moon, they waited anxiously at the abandoned house, listening intently. Overhead, bats squeaked as they flitted after insects, and owls hooted mournfully. "I hope they come," Ellis said impatiently. "It's too good an opportunity to miss." The others agreed.

About midnight, Ellis heard the muffled sound of footsteps. He and the two Mexicans walked quietly toward the sound, straining their eyes in the moonlight. "Who is it?" Ellis called softly in Spanish.

Captain Miguel Avila cautiously approached, leaving the others behind. "Elias," he asked, "is that you?" Ellis stepped forward and shook hands with him.

"How many men?"

"About five hundred," Avila replied, "but only thirty-six have guns."

"No matter. If all goes right we shouldn't have to fire a shot." Ellis explained his plan. Then he and his two companions led the way across the shallow creek and through the grass to the hill where the sentry waited by the five cannon. Avila quietly ordered some of his men to swing the guns around and aim them at the sleeping royalist soldiers, while Ellis lit a small fire with flint and steel. When he had five sticks burning, he handed four of them to others, then held the last one above the touchhole of a cannon. The others stood with their matches poised over the remaining artillery pieces.

"Order them to surrender," Ellis told Avila.

When the royalist soldiers heard Avila's demand to surrender and saw the five men ready to fire the cannon, they leaped to their feet and held up their hands. The militia, camped at a distance, fled; most, Ellis was sure, would join the patriots the next day. In his underwear, Captain Paris quietly untied his horse, leaped to its back, and dashed away.

"Get their weapons," Avila ordered his men. When they had collected all of the muskets and sabers they could find, Avila armed his men and placed a heavy guard around the camp. The royalist soldiers lay down again.

In the morning, Ellis and Avila counted the captured weapons. In addition to the five artillery pieces were six hundred muskets, nearly as many sabers, and a large supply of gunpowder. Avila was elated. "Wait till Morelos sees this!" he exulted.

Morelos soon arrived, and he smiled broadly when he saw the captured arsenal. "Elias," he said, "I thank you for my first victory." The usually undemonstrative leader embraced Ellis and gripped his hand. "Hidalgo ordered me to raise an army and seize Acapulco," he continued. "With these weapons we can do it, but I still need your help." He looked at Ellis expectantly.

Ellis tugged at his earlobe as he thought about it. If the rebels took the castle, it would mean capturing or killing Carreño. That prospect made his pulse quicken. "You can count on me," he replied, "at least until you take Acapulco. I've got some scores to settle there."

"Good. Your rank is captain of Engineers."

The rebel army immediately set out through the mountains on the way to Acapulco. As he looked down on the Castle of San Diego, Ellis thought of his years in the tiny cell, and wondered if Bill was still there. "If it wasn't for my pet lizard, I'd blow it up with my own hands," he said.

"We need to have it in our possession," Morelos countered. "With it we can control the whole southern coast. We must take it, not destroy it."

"But how can we possibly do that?" Avila asked. "It looks impregnable."

"Perhaps not," Morelos said knowingly. "Call the officers here."

When they were assembled, Morelos took a letter from his pocket and read it to them. It was from Major Pepe Gago, commander of artillery at the castle. "There is a conspiracy to surrender the castle to the insurgents," Gago had written. "On the night of February 7, we will raise a lantern to the top of the flagstaff. Form all of your men in the space before the drawbridge so they will be ready to rush in the moment we lower it and open the gate. We will fill the touchholes with tallow so the cannon cannot be fired."

"What do you think of that?" the smiling Morelos asked, folding the letter and pocketing it. Most were delighted at the prospect of gaining such a valuable prize without battle or siege.

"It sounds too good to be true," Avila remarked.

"It *is* too good to be true," Ellis interjected. "It's a trap. If we go where he says, they'll have a bunch of cannon trained on the spot and slaughter us."

"Oh, no," Morelos replied. "It can't be a trap. We'll do as he says. The castle is worth much risk." Ellis frowned, but said nothing more.

On the night of February 7 Morelos marched six hundred men to Las Iguanas, which overlooked the grim fortress. He split the troops into two divisions, one under Avila, the other under Ellis. "We'll do as he directed," Ellis said to Morelos, "but I request permission to place my men as I see fit."

Morelos agreed. They waited, straining their eyes at the castle, but midnight came and still no light appeared. "He lied," Avila yawned. "We might as well give up."

"Have patience," Morelos said. "Let's wait a little longer."

About four in the morning, Ellis saw a small, faint light over the castle. "There it is!" he exclaimed, and the others stared as the tiny light slowly rose to the top of the flagpole.

"Get into position," Morelos ordered.

Ellis marched his division to the side of the castle opposite the place Gago had told them to assemble. Avila and his men waited at a distance as a reserve. Ellis sent a man to inform Gago that they were in position by the drawbridge.

"Watch what happens now," he told his men. All flinched and held their ears when a tremendous roar went up and the earth trembled as fifty cannon fired on the space by the drawbridge. The cannon continued to shower the spot with grapeshot for half an hour, while Ellis, Avila, and their men withdrew into the mountains.

"If we'd been where he wanted us," Ellis told Morelos, "not one of us would be alive."

"We'll return the favor one day," Morelos said grimly. "I hope it's soon."

From the heights of Las Iguanas, they bombarded the castle for nine days with the cannon captured at Tres Palos. The following morning, a large force Carreño had sent during the night charged the insurgents and captured all but one artillery piece. Morelos hastily withdrew to the village of El Veladero, which was higher and more easily defended, but the loss of four cannon hurt.

In the first week of May, Morelos left Avila holding El Veladero and marched toward the little town of Chilpancingo, a key point on the road to Mexico City. On the way, a mounted scout galloped up. "The royalists are coming this way," he said. "We should meet them in the morning."

Morelos and Ellis rode ahead, looking for a defensive position. They found a deep ravine with steep sides that could be crossed only in a few places. Early the next morning, Morelos placed his army there, and they soon saw the royalists approaching in the distance. He sent Ellis with three hundred men on a roundabout march through the woods. Out of sight of the royalists, they crossed the ravine and waited until the two armies clashed, then charged the enemy rear. The royalists panicked and fled, while the rebels crossed the ravine as quickly as they could in pursuit. Many of them were Indians, who had centuries of grievances to avenge against all Spaniards. They pursued the royalists as far as they could run, hacking at them with machetes. Ellis overtook them on horseback.

"Capture them, don't kill them," he shouted, but few heeded him. As he knew, captured royalists might be exchanged for rebel prisoners.

The next day the rebels entered Chilpancingo, which surrendered without resistance. Morelos soon heard that a royalist force was preparing to move against Avila at Veladero, and sent Ellis with fifty mounted men to reconnoiter. The royalists were camped ten miles away, but had made no threatening move. At El Veladero, Ellis learned from an Acapulco woman that Governor Carreño was leading an attack on a rebel stronghold south of the town.

With reinforcements from El Veladero, Ellis hastened to the rescue. He prepared an Indian-style ambush where the road wound through bluffs, then sent a small force to fire on the enemy and fall back, luring the royalists into his trap. The ruse was successful, for five hundred royalist troops rushed headlong after the decoy party. Ellis watched with grim satisfaction as the last of the royalists came under the bluffs. Men fired down on them from front and rear—they couldn't go forward and they couldn't retreat.

Through the thick clouds of smoke that wafted over the royalists, Ellis glimpsed the heavy-set Carreño on his horse, waving his sword and trying to rally his men. Heart pounding, Ellis raced along the bluff to get closer. If I had my long rifle, he thought, I'd kill him for sure. When he was even with Carreño , who was about seventy-five yards below him, Ellis knelt and aimed his musket, waiting for Carreño to check his nervously prancing horse. When Carreño turned toward him, Ellis grimly squeezed the trigger. Carreño flinched, clutched his breast, and swayed in the saddle. I hit the son of a bitch! Ellis exulted. Two officers, seeing Carreño in trouble, dashed to his rescue while Ellis hastily reloaded. One rode alongside Carreño, holding him in the saddle, while the other led his horse away at a trot. Ellis fired at Carreño's back, but couldn't tell if he'd hit him. By the time the survivors extricated themselves, they had lost more than three hundred killed or captured.

The royalist force that had been threatening Avila at El Veladero suddenly marched toward Chilpancingo, and Ellis and his mounted men hurried there to warn Morelos. At the village of Tixtla, Nicolás Bravo and his men blocked the royalists' path, but after a fierce battle the rebels were low on ammunition. Morelos hastened to the rescue, circling around Tixtla to attack from the rear while Bravo's men charged the front. A desperate battle ensued, for the royalists stubbornly held their ground until a sudden rain shower drenched the gunpowder of both sides. Aware that the royalists had lost the advantage of their superior guns, the rebels unsheathed their machetes and charged, routing the enemy.

Morelos followed the royalists to Chilapa, where they had sought refuge with the garrison there. When royalists came out and attacked, they were repulsed with heavy losses— among the captives was Major Gago. "You thought to butcher us with your trick," Ellis said coldly to the pale Gago.

"I was only following orders," he replied.

Morelos questioned Gago for a few hours to learn what he could about royalist plans. When he was finished, he arose, gave a flick of his hand, and walked away. Rebel soldiers dragged Gago to a tree, stood him against it, then, while he begged for his life, shot him.

"The rainy season has begun," Morelos said, glancing up at the dark sky as they entered Chilapa. "No more fighting for a while. I'm going to stay here and train recruits, but I want you to go back to Chilpancingo. Sulfur and saltpeter are mined near there. Make all the powder you can; we'll be ready to use it when the rains stop." The two towns were less than twenty miles apart.

Ellis found an unused barn and repaired the roof to keep out rain. Eight Indian women came daily to grind the sulfur and saltpeter Morelos' men brought from the mines. Ellis mixed the powder and stored it in barrels, kegs, goatskin bags, anything he could find that would keep it dry.

When Morelos sent for him one day, Ellis left work and rode through the steady rain to the house where Morelos lived in Chilapa. "Come in and dry your clothes, Elías," Morelos said. His eyelids drooped and his usually bright eyes were dull.

"What's the matter?" Ellis asked anxiously. "Are you sick?"

Morelos gingerly put his palm on his throbbing temple. "It's not malaria this time," he replied. "It's another of those cursed headaches. But that's not why I sent for you." He sat weakly in a chair and looked sadly up at Ellis, who still stood, his dripping clothes forming little pools of water on the tile floor.

"Elías, I received terrible news. General Calleja badly defeated Hidalgo and drove him north. At Saltillo, he and Allende turned over what was left of the army to Rayón, then set out with a small force and a pack train of silver on their way to the United States to buy arms and recruit men. They never got to Texas, for the turncoat Elizondo betrayed them. All have been executed." He sighed deeply and put both hands over his face.

"Now we need help from the United States more than ever," he continued, lowering his hands. "Do you think if we offer Texas in exchange for arms and men, your government will send them?"

Ellis took off his wet jacket and hung it on a chair. "Everybody wants Texas, and I'll bet most Americans would like to see Mexico independent," he replied. "I think it might work." He wondered who Morelos would send.

Morelos pushed the kerchief up around his forehead to loosen it. "If I didn't need you here, I'd ask you to go," he said. "I'm going to send Major Fero and Mariano Tabares."

Ellis frowned. "I think Tabares would like to take your place," he said, "and I don't know how far I'd trust Fero."

Morelos shrugged. "Rayón and a lot of others would like to replace me," he said, "but I don't have much choice. Tabares has served well, and Fero was an American army officer. I have to trust them." Ellis bit his lip but said nothing.

Because the royalists controlled the sea, the two men set out over land for Rayón's headquarters at Zitácuaro, in the mountains west of Mexico City, on their long ride to the United States. Ellis returned to Chilpancingo.

A little over a month later, Ellis was astonished to see Fero and Tabares ride into Chilpancingo. "What are you doing here?" he asked. "I thought. . . ."

"General Rayón commissioned me a brigadier general and *Señor* Fero a colonel and sent us here," Tabares replied, while Fero scowled. "We're not under Morelos now." Ellis stared at them as if he couldn't believe his ears.

"The revolution has too many leaders," Fero growled. "It needs only one. Rayón." They rode on toward the coast. As soon as they were out of town, Ellis hurried to Chilapa.

"Elias," Morelos said when Ellis dismounted, "you were right not to trust those two. They've abandoned their mission and gone over to Rayón."

"I know. I came to tell you they rode through Chilpancingo on their way to the coast."

Morelos looked shocked. "To the coast? I wish now I'd arrested them. When I refused to recognize their commissions from Rayón, both were angry. I thought they'd go back to him. I must warm Avila to be on his guard."

A few weeks later, Morelos grimly rode into Chilpancingo with one hundred well-armed men at his back, and stopped to see Ellis. "Avila says that Fero and Tabares are at El Veladero, trying to get the blacks in our army to rise up and butcher the whites. I've got to stop them." He touched his spurs to his horse and trotted on.

A week later he returned, looking almost cheerful. "All is quiet now," he told Ellis, "but if I hadn't gotten there when I did. . . ." He shook his head.

"Where are they?"

"Where they'll never cause trouble again."

"They had it coming," Ellis said.

Leaving Ellis in Chilpancingo making powder, in November Morelos began his second campaign. Ellis, wishing he could be with him, eagerly waited for news. "After we took Tlapa," Morelos wrote, "we marched on Chiutla. I had to take it, for Mateo Mizutu was there, and he'd sworn to kill me. He even had a cannon named 'Kill Morelos.' They fought like fury, but our brave men couldn't be stopped. He offered me fifty thousand pesos to spare his life. I would have turned down a million."

Early in 1812 Ellis learned that royalist General Calleja had routed Rayón at Zitácuaro and scattered his army. In March Calleja, with eight thousand troops, besieged Morelos' army of four thousand in Cuautla. In early May a rebel officer wearily rode into Chilpancingo and found Ellis at his powder mill.

"The army and the citizens tried to slip away one night," he gasped. "Calleja pursued us and slaughtered everyone without mercy, even the families. Morelos barely escaped— many men gave their lives so he wouldn't be captured. He told us before we marched that if we were scattered, to meet him at Izúcar. He wants you there."

Taking half of the troops guarding Chilpancingo, Ellis hurried to Izúcar with all the available guns and a pack train with two thousand pounds of powder. He was greatly relieved to find Morelos there, but shocked at the sight of his hollow cheeks. His clothes, once tight, hung on him like flour sacks on a post.

"We tried to hold out until the rains began," he weakly explained. "That would have forced them to leave. But the rains were late, and we ran out of food. There wasn't another rat or lizard left." He paused, looking chagrined. "Friends in Mexico City say that Calleja told the viceroy he would abandon the siege in another day or two."

"Rotten luck," Ellis said. "Cooley and Danlin were with you. Do you know if they escaped?"

Morelos shook his head. "Cooley was out foraging when a royalist patrol caught him. They undoubtedly shot him. I don't know about Danlin."

"What will you do now?" Ellis asked, wondering if Morelos was so discouraged he'd accept the viceroy's offer of pardon to any insurgent who laid down his arms.

Morelos' sunken eyes flashed. "Why, keep fighting, of course. One defeat, even a disaster like this, doesn't mean the war is lost. The viceroy ordered Calleja to destroy me, but here I am. I won't stop till we're free. Or until I'm dead," he added, lowering his voice. "But you're not a Mexican. If you want to leave I'll understand."

Ellis gazed at the little rebel leader with unconcealed admiration. "I'm with you," he vowed, "to the end. As long as there are royalists to kill, I'm staying."

"Thank you, my friend," Morelos said hoarsely. "I will never give up."

The rebel soldiers who had escaped during the attack straggled into Chiutla, where Morelos had moved. Many men, most with only machetes for weapons, came from the countryside, eager to serve under Morelos. When a large force had been gathered and trained briefly they marched to Chilapa, which the royalists had reoccupied after Morelos left. The royalist commander refused to surrender. As he boldly led an infantry charge, Ellis recalled his fright when the Spaniards attacked Nolan's fort, and smiled. The sound of enemy gunfire was no longer terrifying. The garrison surrendered after a brief resistance.

After forcing the royalists to abandon the siege of Huajuacán, Morelos marched to the rich city of Tehuacán, the trade center for the provinces of Puebla, Oaxaca, and Veracruz. Ellis beamed and Morelos almost smiled as cheering citizens lined the streets and church bells pealed. Since the city was within striking distance of the Veracruz–Mexico City road, and a strategic base for campaigns against Mexico City, Veracruz, or Oaxaca, Morelos made it his headquarters.

On learning that most of the royal troops at Orizaba had been withdrawn to escort a large pack train from Perote to Veracruz, Morelos marched there with eight hundred men. Against little resistance, they seized the king's tobacco warehouse, helped themselves to all they could carry, then set fire to the rest.

"That cuts one of the king's purse strings," Morelos remarked, nodding his head toward the clouds of tobacco smoke that billowed about them. Tobacco was a much resented royal monopoly.

They returned to Tehuacán in high spirits, confident there were no royalists in the area. But the much larger pack train escort, on learning of the attack on Orizaba, had hastily marched to intercept them. Surprised, Morelos' men quickly formed two lines, but the enemy cavalry and grenadiers drove the first line back to the second. After a fierce fight, the outnumbered rebel soldiers broke and fled, with difficulty saving most of their artillery. Ellis, along with Morelos and other officers, put spurs to their horses and escaped, with musket balls whistling about them.

"We took a real flogging," Ellis remarked when they reached Tehuacán.

"That we did," Morelos admitted, his expression grave.

"Other than destroying the king's tobacco, we have accomplished little this year, and the enemy grows more confident." He paused, looking thoughtful, then continued.

"We must strike the enemy where it hurts and give new life to our cause," he said. "I'm going to gather our forces and take Oaxaca. But tell no one where we're going. The enemy has spies everywhere."

He called in Victor Bravo and his division from the Mixteca, and the warrior priest Mariano Matamoros and his troops from Izúcar. Fighting men come in all shapes and sizes, Ellis thought. The Bravos were tall, muscular men, the sons of an *hacendado*. Matamoros was small and thin, with a pockmarked face and blue eyes. He had, for one his size, a surprisingly powerful voice. Morelos considered him his left arm and Hermenegildo Galeana his right arm.

Shortly before they marched, Manuel Mier y Terán, a handsome young graduate of the School of Mines, rode up on a fine horse and offered his services. He was tall and slender, with light skin, brown hair, black eyes, and a neatly trimmed mustache. Morelos welcomed him warmly and gave him the rank of colonel of Engineers.

Ellis, now a major of Engineers, but without any formal training, looked over his new commander wondering how, at twenty-nine, it would be to serve under an officer who couldn't be more than twenty. Mier y Terán was obviously a member of a prominent creole family, an aristocrat accustomed to comforts. How will he react the first time he hears enemy gunfire? Ellis wondered. Then, recalling the attack on Nolan's fort, he smiled wryly. Probably the same way I did. I didn't quite pee my pants, but it was a close call. Mier appeared to be affable as well as intelligent, and dedicated to Mexican independence. Ellis decided to reserve judgment.

The rebel army, now nearly five thousand strong, headed into the rugged mountains that lay between Tehuacán and Oaxaca. As his stomach protested its emptiness, Ellis plodded up the steep roads on foot, for there weren't enough horses and mules to haul the artillery and carry sufficient provisions—all were on half-rations. As he looked around at the Mexicans from nearly every walk of life who were willingly risking their lives and sacrificing their comforts for Morelos and independence, Ellis felt warm and forgot his hunger.

After nearly two weeks of hard-going, they descended to the fertile plains that surrounded Oaxaca on November 24. Ellis gazed in admiration at the huge fig trees, the orchards, and vineyards—Oaxaca was a garden spot. They stopped at an *hacienda* a few miles from the city and made camp in a field, while Morelos sent royalist commander Gonazález Saravia a demand to surrender. He refused.

The next morning, Morelos divided his force into six columns, leaving one to guard the camp, two to cut off escape routes, and holding one in reserve. With one column, Colonel Ramón Sesma attacked the fort, which was surrounded by a moat and connected to the city by a drawbridge. Ellis and Mier each commanded an infantry company in the column under Galeana and Matamoros, who sent them to capture the gate at the Marquesado Street entrance. The two led a spirited charge and opened the gate, allowing the rest of the column to rush through it. They drove the royalists back to the plaza. Ellis no longer wondered how the youthful colonel would do under enemy fire—Mier was a born warrior.

In the attack on the fort, Manuel Félix Fernández, who later changed his name to Guadalupe Victoria, plunged into the moat, determined to swim across and lower the drawbridge. He was immediately bogged down in thick mud, and had to be pulled out. After two hours of fighting, the royalists hauled down their flag.

Knowing Oaxaca was a rich enemy stronghold, the rebel troops for once ignored Morelos' injunction against looting, and plundered the shops and homes of Spaniards. Morelos immediately ordered the political prisoners released. Ellis felt sick when he saw the wretched, half-starved men, but Morelos was outraged. He had them lifted to the backs of horses and paraded throughout the city to give the people a taste of royalist brutality. Then he ordered four of the royalist commanders shot.

Morelos soon formed a town council of creoles, or Spanish Mexicans, and extended patriot control over the surrounding area. Mier took charge of the royalist armory, while Ellis opened a powder factory.

In January 1813 they learned that ruthless General Calleja had been named viceroy. Early the next month, Morelos left Colonel Rocha and Ellis with one thousand troops to hold Oaxaca, and set out with the rest for Acapulco. Along the way, he sent columns under his lieutenants to seize strategic towns. He wrote that he'd taken Acapulco and besieged the Castle San Diego. Its temporary governor, he added, was a Captain Vélez. Ellis smiled grimly when he read that.

"If I didn't kill Carreño," he said, "at least I put him out of action."

"I wish Morelos would just leave troops to pin down the garrison and get on with the campaign," Rocha remarked, looking worried. "Every day the siege lasts means the enemy is that much stronger. The Spaniards here are boasting that Spain is sending three thousand soldiers who fought Napoleon. We should be closing in on Mexico City, not wasting time on Acapulco. That could lead to our undoing." His expression became gloomier. "I'm not a prophet," he said, " but for the first time I have a bad feeling about the revolution." Ellis said nothing, wishing Morelos would send for him.

Chapter Five

Ellis waited anxiously for news of Morelos. He knew that in June, while the siege of San Diego Castle went on, Morelos had invited all rebel-held provinces to send delegates to a congress in Chilpancingo in September, for Oaxaca had elected a delegate. In August news came that San Diego Castle had finally surrendered, after a siege of seven months. Morelos had granted generous surrender terms, then hurried to Chilpancingo. Ellis also heard that three thousand Spanish troops had landed at Veracruz, but his confidence in Morelos remained unshaken. Mier y Terán, he knew, had won several victories. Why do I have to stay here making gunpowder when my friends are fighting the enemy? It was frustrating.

The next news of Morelos made a knot form in his stomach. Late in December, with a large army, Morelos had attacked Valladolid, a strategic city Rayón had tried to take earlier. Learning of his march, Calleja had rushed powerful reinforcements there, and they repulsed the patriots with heavy losses. Before they could regroup, Agustín de Iturbide slipped out after dark with three hundred cavalry. His surprise attack had thrown the patriots into such confusion they fired on one another. The royalist cavalry swept through Morelos' camp and only the desperate resistance of his men saved him from capture. The patriot soldiers were so demoralized they fled.

Unable to check their flight, the officers spiked the cannon and followed, with the enemy in hot pursuit.

A few days later, early in January 1814, the royalists overtook them and forced them to make a stand even though they were without cannon. The royalist artillery decimated the patriot ranks, and a number of officers, including the able Matamoros, were captured. Morelos offered to exchange two hundred Spanish prisoners for him, but the royalists took him to Valladolid and shot him. Morelos ordered Acapulco burned and abandoned after the royalists captured the forts at El Veladero. The siege had been a waste of time. Ellis groaned aloud when he read the bad news. Rocha's fears had been justified.

A messenger from Morelos brought a letter promoting Ellis to colonel and ordering Rocha to march with eight hundred men, leaving two hundred with Ellis and Captain Simón Méndez. "Things look bad, Elias," Rocha said when they shook hands. "The siege gave Calleja time to destroy all rebel armies in the north; now he's concentrating his forces on the south. When they come here, as they surely will, save your men and all the powder you can carry. Try to get it to Morelos. If he still has an army, that is," he added.

In March a rebel courier dashed into Oaxaca. What now? Ellis wondered, as the man's lathered horse slid to a stop.

"The enemy is coming," the rider panted. "At least one thousand men, maybe more."

"Where is Morelos?"

"Who knows? The last I heard he was at Apatzingán with the congress. By now he could be anywhere. Or nowhere."

Ellis ordered his men to pack the mules with powder and two thousand pesos, all the money available. He frowned at the sight of royalist sympathizers joyfully preparing to welcome the approaching army. With his two hundred men and the pack train, Ellis headed north, carefully avoiding the oncoming enemy column, and not stopping to rest. In the mountains they came upon a camp of nearly one hundred ragged, bearded men. Brigands by the look of them, Ellis thought. Their stocky leader approached, eying the pack train, then the soldiers.

"Where are you going?" he asked.

"To Morelos." The bandit chief glanced again at the weary pack mules, and at the soldiers, who held their muskets ready. He spat.

"You're wasting your time," he told Ellis. "Lots of us have given up; many more have also accepted pardons and now fight for the king. You're as likely to be killed by former friends as by enemies. You'd do better to throw in with us."

"Doing what?"

"Knocking off Spanish pack trains."

Ellis appeared to consider that, then shook his head. "I promised to get this powder to Morelos," he said. "I've got to try."

The bandit leader couldn't conceal his irritation. "Fighting is useless, I tell you," he growled, his voice rising. "The revolution is dead. They'll catch Morelos sooner or later, if they haven't already."

"Maybe so," Ellis admitted, "but as long as he lives there's hope. I aim to find him." He signalled to his men to ride on. They continued pushing hard for several days, until they rode into the village of Cuicatlán.

An old man with a white beard arose from a bench and shuffled into the dusty street toward Ellis, who stopped his horse and leaned toward him.

"Without asking," the old man said quietly, "I know you are patriots." Ellis nodded, while the other villagers stared at the soldiers and weary mules.

"Rayón is near," the old man continued, his voice so low it was barely audible. "The enemy are also not far away, so take care, *señor*. They have spies even here. Be careful who you trust."

"Thanks, my friend," Ellis said softly. "I'm glad to know there's at least one patriot army left." He straightened in his saddle and rode on, stopping after they had crossed a stream to let the mules rest and graze. He sent scouts to watch for the enemy and a man to find Rayón.

The man returned an hour later. "The enemy are on his trail, so he's got to keep moving," he reported. "They're sure to see our tracks, too. Some of the villagers may have already gone to tell them about us. We had better get out of here *pronto*."

Ellis glanced at the tired mules dejectedly nibbling grass, and wished he hadn't pushed them so hard. His mind raced. We've got two choices—run or fight. The only way we can escape is to head into the mountains, but the mules would never make it. That means we'd have to abandon all this powder. His face felt hot at the thought of the enemy gloating over his powder supply. No, by God! That won't do. We'll fight!

He sent the man back to Rayón with a terse message. "I intend to make a stand. If you can't come, send all the men you can spare."

Ellis ordered the packers to take the mules a mile or two ahead and let them graze. Then he and Méndez looked for a defensive position. The creek the enemy cavalry would have to cross had high banks, which meant that crossing it would take several minutes. At one side was a low rise; facing the crossing was a small hill. Ellis placed Méndez and fifty men out of sight behind the rise. "Don't fire a shot until they're in the creek," he ordered. With the rest of his men he waited halfway up the low hill, in easy musket shot of the crossing. Once in the creek, the enemy would face a crossfire.

The messenger to Rayón rode up. "How many men is he sending?" Ellis asked.

"None. He says to save what you can and leave immediately." Ellis cursed. He saw one of his scouts dashing up. No time to worry about Rayón now, he thought.

"Enemy coming," the scout shouted. "Be here in minutes."

Ellis waited with his men on the hillside in full view of the crossing. His mouth was dry but he felt no fear when a hundred or more cavalrymen trotted up to the creek and checked their horses. When they saw Ellis had no artillery, they laughed scornfully and brandished their lances.

Come on! Come on! Ellis thought, fearing they might wait for infantry and artillery before attacking. But with a shout, they urged their horses down the steep bank and plunged into the stream.

"Fire!" Ellis shouted, and his and Méndez' men poured a deadly crossfire into the cavalry, emptying many saddles as the horses floundered in the water. Ellis pulled all of his men to the crest of the hill, where they knelt and aimed their muskets. The surviving cavalrymen spurred their mounts up the bank and came on. They met such a withering fire that halfway up the hill they broke and fled. Ellis gave a shout of triumph while his men cheered.

They caught the riderless cavalry horses and hurried after the pack train. A few hours later, a messenger from Rayón overtook them and handed Ellis a note.

"You must join forces with me," Rayón had written.

He didn't come when I needed help, Ellis thought. He probably wouldn't another time. Not wanting a confrontation with Rayón, he stalled.

"Tell him I'll meet him at the Llanos de Apán in a week," he told the messenger, who rode away. Then Ellis and his men continued on their way, traveling slowly to spare the mules.

Several days later, Ellis saw a rider approaching from the north, and wondered if he might be a courier. He wasn't in uniform, which could mean that he was a patriot. Ellis and the rider eyed each other cautiously.

"Are you an Americano?" the rider asked. Ellis nodded.

"At least I used to be," he said. "I've been here so long

I'm as much Mexican as American. You're looking for an Americano?'' The man cautiously admitted that he was.

"Patriot or royalist?''

"Patriot," the man said, barely above a whisper.

"That's what we are," Ellis told him. The man exhaled deeply and looked relieved.

"I guess there's not many of us left," Ellis added. "What's his name?''

"Colonel Bean.''

"You've found him. Got a message for me?'' The courier withdrew a letter that had been concealed under the skirt of his saddle.

"It's from Morelos," he said. "I was afraid the enemy would find it and shoot me.''

Ellis read the letter with difficulty, for although he spoke Spanish fairly well, he'd had little practice reading it.

"My friend Elias," it began, "we have suffered serious reverses, and many of our former friends have gone over to the enemy. One of them will probably kill me, but that's not why I write. We now have a constitution and a congress that has declared our independence. These actions make our cause respectable in the eyes of the world, even if we must hide in the mountains like wild beasts. But unless we receive help soon, I fear we cannot last much longer. I call on you for one last favor to save our cause. Go to your countrymen and persuade them, beg them if you must, to send us arms. Then get men and invade Texas, for that will draw the enemy away from us. I am counting on you not to fail. Go with God. Morelos.''

Ellis' hands trembled so the letter rattled. In a voice that sounded strange, he said to the courier, "Tell him I'll do my best and that I'm on my way. Take this pack train to him.'' He kept two of the mules and their loads in case he met other patriots who needed powder. The two mules brayed mournfully as the others disappeared.

The two thousand pesos he'd brought from Oaxaca weren't enough to buy many guns. There were, he knew, many wealthy planters around Tehuacán who respected Morelos. Leaving his men with Captain Méndez, he hurried there. Mier y Terán, now a brigadier general, greeted him warmly, then together they raised ten thousand pesos in a few days. Ellis returned to his men, then headed for the Gulf coast, anxious to be on his way to New Orleans.

At Puente del Rey, he found the fearless Guadalupe Victoria with a few hundred men but little ammunition. Ellis gave him most of his powder. "I'd make more for you," he told Guadalupe Victoria, "but Morelos sent me to get help in the States. I've got to find a ship."

"Go to Nautla," Guadalupe Victoria advised him. "Philipio still holds out there, so it's safe at least for the moment."

Ellis hurried to the little fishing village north of Veracruz, where the black patriot leader, Philipio, welcomed him. "Lafitte's ships from around New Orleans put in here from time to time," he said when Ellis told him about his mission. "I'm sure one of them will take you."

After anxiously scanning the horizon for five days, Ellis and Philipio saw a schooner sailing south past Nautla. Philipio studied it through a small eyeglass.

"That's *El Tigre*, one of Lafitte's ships," he said. "I'm sure of it."

Ellis and his men signalled to the vessel, and Ellis was elated when the crew lowered the white sails. But no boat came ashore. Ellis watched and waved his arms, but the crew finally raised the sails, and the schooner glided on toward Veracruz. Ellis' arms sagged by his sides and he exhaled deeply, feeling limp, defeated.

"Don't give up," Philipio consoled him. "She'll probably stop on her way north."

The next morning, Philipio's shore guard reported seeing a small schooner that appeared to be adrift at the mouth of a river half a mile from Nautla. Ellis loaded his men in three *piraguas*, then rowed to the little vessel and boarded it. There was no crew on it. They sailed it to Nautla; below decks they found a welcome supply of flour and dried beef.

"I don't know anything about sailing," Ellis remarked, "but maybe you can persuade some of these fisherman to get me to New Orleans in her." He looked expectantly at Philipio.

The black leader shook his head. "No, Elias," he replied, "she's only a coaster. She has neither compass nor sextant. She has to stay in sight of land."

"Damn. I wouldn't know how to use them anyway."

The following day, they saw two sails coming north, close to the shore. "The one in the lead is *El Tigre*," Philipio said. "The other is a brig, and it looks like it's after her."

They watched, spellbound, as the brig ran up English colors just before opening fire on the smaller vessel. The schooner sailed swiftly around the brig and shot away its mainmast, then lay to. The brig lowered two longboats and sent them toward *El Tigre* with a boarding party. Ellis held his breath as the schooner's guns sank one of the boats and badly damaged the other. The brig sent a launch to pick the men from the water, then limped south in defeat. *El Tigre* continued on to the north, still close to shore. Ellis and his men signalled frantically and waved their arms in vain.

Deeply discouraged, Ellis slept poorly that night, imagining Morelos surrounded by enemies and desperately looking for help from America. In the morning, a woman who had come down the coast with eggs and poultry to sell told him she'd seen a vessel near the shore a few miles away. It wasn't moving, she said, and its deck was covered with men.

"It's probably royalists from Tampico after us," Ellis said. "We'd better keep them from landing." Philipio agreed. Ellis and his men hurried up the coast until they saw the motionless vessel, its sails furled. Ellis hid his troops and sent five unarmed men to the beach to hail those on board.

He heard them shouting and the men on the ship replying, then one of the five returned. "It's *El Tigre*," he told Ellis. "They're sending a boat ashore now that they know we're not royalists." Ellis hastened to the beach as the boat approached, and was delighted to see that one of the men who stepped ashore was an American.

"What are you doing here?" Ellis asked him.

The American smiled ruefully. "I could ask you the same question," he replied. "You saw us whip the English brig yesterday?" Ellis nodded. "The Spaniards at Veracruz offered the captain two thousand pesos to capture or sink us. Well, after we ran him off, we had to celebrate." He pursed his lips. "We overdid it," he sheepishly admitted. "No one was paying attention to where we were headed, and we ran aground on that damned reef."

Ellis sent some of his men for the little schooner, and they took *El Tigre's* crew to Nautla. From the American, Ellis learned that the U.S. and Britain had been at war for two years.

"I'm on my way to get help for the patriots," Ellis said. "With a war going on, it's not a good time for that, but I've got to try." He waited impatiently for ten days while *El Tigre's* crew prepared the little schooner for the long voyage. Then, taking as many of *El Tigre's* crew as the schooner could carry, they sailed from Nautla.

Several weeks later, they landed at the Lafittes' headquarters on Grand Terre, a long, low island that lay across Barataria Bay. Jean and Pierre Lafitte, who had come from Haiti, were smugglers and privateers—some called them pirates. They had a large house, a fleet of ships, and a number of warehouses. Ellis left his schooner with them and set out from the bay with an old Frenchman as guide. He led the way through alligator-infested marshes and bayous, under huge trees that were festooned with Spanish moss. Ellis was greatly relieved when they emerged into the sunlight at the Mississippi, nine miles above New Orleans. The old Frenchman left him and returned to Barataria.

After walking along the bank for half an hour, Ellis came to a plantation where an overseer and a gang of slaves were clearing land. When he explained his need to get to New Orleans, the overseer had a slave row him there. Walking past shops owned by Frenchmen, Spaniards, and Americans, Ellis found the government house and called on Governor Claiborne, whose fine clothes and neatly trimmed hair and beard contrasted sharply with Ellis' shaggy appearance.

"I may not look like a Mexican agent," Ellis admitted, "but Morelos sent me here to get arms for the patriots. After that, he wants me to organize an invasion of Texas to give him some breathing room."

Claiborne held his quill pen in his right hand and stroked the end of the feather with his left while he looked Ellis over. "There's no law against giving or selling arms to the insurgents," he said evenly, " but organizing an expedition against another country on American soil is a crime." Ellis frowned.

"I hear there's already been an expedition to Texas," he said.

"That was organized in the Neutral Ground, where we have no jurisdiction, and I'm partly to blame for not trying to stop it," Claiborne replied. "The federal government doesn't intend for it to happen again. It caused a lot of unpleasant diplomatic exchanges and ugly charges of government complicity." He leaned back in his chair, still toying with his quill pen.

"As you'll soon know if you don't already," he continued, "there are a lot of men—Frenchmen, Mexicans, Americans— in New Orleans who are plotting to send expeditions against Texas and Tampico to help the patriots. General Humbert is one—he was an officer in the Napoleonic wars; now he claims to be a government agent, but everyone considers him a bit daft. Gutiérrez and Alvarez de Toledo invaded Texas in

1812; they had a falling out and lost most of their men as a result. I really don't expect any of them to do much, but I'm sure that if an expedition of Americans prepares to leave from New Orleans to invade Mexico, federal officials will intervene. Now if Mexican refugees in the Neutral Ground want to fight their way back into Texas, that's their business. The government will probably look the other way.''

Ellis thanked him for his frankness. On learning that General Humbert was taking a cargo of arms to Nautla in one of the Lafittes' ships, Ellis hoped the guns would get to Morelos. He headed for Natchitoches to look into the prospects of an invasion of Texas from the Neutral Ground between the Sabine and Arroyo Hondo. He found a number of dispirited Tejano refugees living a hand-to-mouth existence around Natchitoches and in the Neutral Ground, where their only occupation was smuggling. When he suggested another expedition to Texas, they shrugged. ''The royalists killed my father and brothers,'' one said. ''I barely escaped. None of us wants to go through that again.'' Feeling frustrated, Ellis returned to New Orleans.

Early in September, Humbert returned to New Orleans, bringing Juan Pablo Anaya, a follower of General Rosains, who was a Morelos partisan. He also brought Padre José Antonio Pedrazo, who represented Rayón. Rosains and Rayón were both fighting for Mexican independence, but they were bitter rivals. Anaya claimed to be Mexico's minister to the United States, which infuriated Pedrazo.

He angrily went to Spanish consul Diego Morphy and revealed Alvarez de Toledo's plan to attack Tampico while Gutiérrez led an expedition into Texas. Morphy protested to the government.

Because of the Lafittes' widespread smuggling activities, in mid-September, U.S. gunboats and troops captured their fleet and many of their men, while the rest went into hiding. Rumors of a British invasion of the gulf area brought General

Andrew Jackson to New Orleans on December 1, although his Kentucky and Tennessee riflemen remained at Baton Rouge, guarding the Mississippi. When a British fleet entered Lake Borgne on December 13, it was clear that their target was New Orleans. Jackson proclaimed martial law and ordered his troops from Baton Rouge to New Orleans.

Jackson found no fortifications worthy of the name, and the militiamen were without flints for their rifles. Aware of Jackson's need for flints and arms, the Lafittes, who had a secret warehouse well-stocked with military supplies, offered them along with their services and those of their men. Jackson, who a short time earlier had denounced them as "hellish banditti," gladly accepted the offer. He issued a proclamation of amnesty and ordered the prisoners released.

On December 23 Jackson made a night attack that slowed the British advance. Then he withdrew to a dry canal below New Orleans that ran from the east bank of the Mississippi to a cypress swamp. He set his men to converting the canal into breastworks. Ellis, whose father had known Jackson in Tennessee, offered to serve as an artilleryman. He and some of the Lafittes' gunners were assigned to one of the twenty-four-pounder cannon.

On January 1, 1815, the British attacked but, in a furious battle, were outgunned and withdrew to wait for reinforcements. Ellis and the others waited, sure they would return. On the morning of January 8, they heard bugles in the distance, and soon the British appeared again, more than five thousand strong against Jackson's four thousand five hundred. They headed for the breastworks, marching steadily in tight, compact columns. They're making it easy for us, Ellis thought.

He and the Lafitte gunners worked their cannon, showering the British with grapeshot, tearing gaping holes in the ranks. In the face of deadly rifle and artillery fire, the British withdrew to regroup. They immediately attacked again, with the same result. In half an hour the battle was over. Leaving seven hundred dead on the field, including their commander, Sir Edward Packenham, and two other generals, the British retreated. American losses were eight killed and thirteen wounded. No one on either side had known that two weeks earlier, peace had been made at Ghent.

As soon as the British sailed away, Ellis turned again to securing military aid for Morelos. The New Orleans Associates, a group of businessmen, among them the Lafittes, were willing to ship arms to Mexico, but only for a substantial profit. On February 8, Ellis sailed on their ship *Aguila* with all the arms he could obtain. He carried dispatches from Alvarez de Toledo to Morelos and the congress, asking for letters of marque to issue to privateers and for money to support an expedition to take Tampico. Alvarez de Toledo also urged that a port be kept open on the gulf coast and recommended sending a minister to negotiate a treaty with the United States.

The *Aguila* anchored at Boquilla de Piedras, where Guadalupe Victoria was in command. Ellis distributed arms to many of his men, then set out with a small party to deliver the rest to Morelos at Puruarán, six hundred miles away. They traveled cautiously, but saw no enemy patrols. They found Morelos with several hundred men.

"What news from the United States?" he asked, after warmly embracing Ellis.

Ellis delivered the dispatches and told him about the journey through enemy territory. "The U.S. and Britain have been at war," he explained. "Americans wish you well, but they haven't been in a position to help."

"What a pity!" Morelos exclaimed, disappointed. He read the letters from Alvarez de Toledo. "We will send a minister as he suggests, and all the money we have." He named Manuel de Herrera as minister to the United States. "Take him with you when you return, Elias," he said. "Also, take my son and put him in a Catholic school, for he can get no schooling here. And send us all the arms you can.''

Ellis, with thirteen thousand pesos from the congress, and Herrera with fifteen thousand for his mission to Washington, took Morelos' son, the thirteen-year-old Juan N. Almonte, and rode to Tehuacán, where Mier y Terán still held out.

''It's good to see you, my friend,'' he said, giving Ellis an *abrazo*. ''We're grateful for your help, even though ours may be a losing cause.''

Ellis looked at Mier's weathered face and the determined set of his jaw, amazed at how much he'd matured after a few years of war. Mier was, Morelos had told him, one of the most able patriot commanders. Even though he was discouraged about the patriots' prospects, Ellis knew that any royalist force that attacked him would meet its match.

With his two companions, Ellis rode on to Boquilla de Piedras, where they waited for weeks, anxiously watching for a sail to appear. Knowing that Morelos was counting on him, Ellis chafed at the delay, feeling helpless. He had nearly given up hope when Alvarez de Toledo arrived on the *Petit Milan* with a cargo of muskets the New Orleans Associates had sent. Their agent demanded immediate payment, but finally agreed to wait until they reached New Orleans. As soon as the arms were unloaded, Ellis, Herrera, and Almonte went on board, and the *Petit Milan* sailed.

For a month the ship tossed in stormy weather, giving Ellis a queasy stomach and making him eager to be ashore. When they finally reached New Orleans, a member of the Associates boarded, demanding immediate payment for the arms. Herrera reluctantly paid him, for he was left without funds for the trip to Washington, and in a melancholy mood.

After placing Almonte in a school, Ellis and Herrera met with the Associates to arrange for another shipment of arms in late November. The *Petit Milan* sailed again in January 1816, with Ellis and another shipment of arms on board. At

Boquilla de Piedras, he met Guadalupe Victoria, whose solemn expression alarmed him, for it was clear that something was amiss.

"Bad news, Elias," Guadalupe Victoria said. "Morelos was escorting the congress to Tehuacán, when one of the many royalist columns crossed their trail and attacked." Ellis caught his breath, dreading to hear what he feared was coming. "Morelos was trying to hold them off so the congress could escape," Guadalupe Victoria continued, "when he was captured by one of his former lieutenants. He should have abandoned the congress and escaped himself, for he was the only one they wanted. Once they had him, they didn't even follow the congress, and it went on to Tehuacán. They were a quarrelsome group and interfered with everything. They caused so much trouble that Mier finally ordered them to disperse. In the meantime, the royalists shot Morelos."

Ellis felt weak and sick at heart. The game little priest had been the symbol of the revolution, its pillar of strength. Now he was no more. If I hadn't failed him, Ellis thought bitterly, he might still be alive. He half-heartedly took the arms to Mier, for now even that seemed futile.

Mier's face was drawn with worry. "The end is in sight, I fear," he confessed. "So many of our men have gone over to the enemy, we no longer have reason to hope." Although he tried not to believe that, Ellis knew it was true.

"When you return," Mier continued, "I want you to take Magdalena Falfán de los Godos with you." Ellis frowned and started to protest, but Mier held up his hand. "Hers is a fine family," he said, "but they have lost everything in the revolution. An uncle has an *hacienda* near Jalapa. If there's any way you can get her there, he'll look after her. If you can't, take her to New Orleans." Before Ellis could say anything, Mier stepped into the adjoining room, then returned with Magdalena and introduced her.

Ellis, who had been almost resentful that Mier was saddling

him with one more unwanted responsibility, immediately brightened when he saw her. Magdalena was fair-skinned, with large, sparkling dark eyes, a beautiful oval face framed by black hair, and a well-proportioned figure. She offered a dainty hand to Ellis, who accepted it gingerly, and squeezed it as gently as if it had been made of glass. He held his breath, thrilled by her touch.

"You two get acquainted," Mier said, then left them. They sat, while Magdalena shyly looked at the floor. Ellis waited for her to speak, for he could think of nothing sensible to say and was afraid he'd babble like an idiot if he opened his mouth.

"I have heard much good about you, *señor*," she said in a low, musical voice that made Ellis tingle with delight. "General Mier says that you are a loyal friend of the revolution. I am pleased and proud to make your acquaintance." She shyly looked him in the face, then modestly lowered her eyes again.

Ellis smiled broadly, glowing in the praise of one so lovely. "Tell me about your family," he said, eager to hear her voice again.

"My father favored those who would make our country independent. He was open and frank about it, which was a mistake, but he couldn't be any other way. Troops came and arrested him and my mother and confiscated his property. They ignored me, but left me without means to support myself. I don't even know if my parents are still alive," she said, her voice quavering a little, her eyes filling with tears.

Ellis was beside himself with desire to comfort and reassure her, but he knew there was nothing he could truthfully say that would be encouraging. "I'm sorry," he mumbled. "I hope . . . ."

She quickly regained her composure, and her expression became determined. "We will be independent one day," she said firmly. "I'm sure of it. Hidalgo, Morelos, and all those other brave men did not give their lives in vain. If I were a man, I'd do the same thing." Seeing her expression and hearing her voice, Ellis knew that what she said was true.

He changed the subject. "Do you know how I happen to be here?" he asked. She shook her head. He told her about Nolan, the years in Chihuahua, and his imprisonment in Acapulco. She was enchanted with the story of his white lizard.

"He must still miss you," she said.

"Not as much as I miss him. In those days he was my only friend."

"How sad!" she exclaimed.

They spent a week walking around Tehuacán, admiring the city and talking. By the time they set out for Boquilla de Piedras, Ellis was madly in love, and the way Magdalena smiled at him gave him hope it wasn't one-sided. He couldn't take his eyes off her as they rode side by side. When she looked at him, he felt weak all over, but he got up his courage.

"Magdalena," he said, "I love you more than anyone in the world. Will you marry me? We can live in the States until it's safe to come back." He waited, red-faced and breathless.

She smiled and reached for his hand. "I've thought about that, too," she confessed, lowering her eyes and coloring at her boldness.

They came to a village with a small church and found the padre there, a ruddy-faced old man in a shabby habit that Ellis suspected he'd worn ever since he'd been ordained.

"Do you have a ring?" he asked Ellis.

"No. I'll get her one later."

The old padre shrugged and performed the ceremony. Ellis paid him and they rode on together as man and wife. Ellis felt like singing or shouting or firing his musket. They stopped for the night at an *hacienda*, where the *hacendado* and his gracious wife, recognizing that they were newlyweds, made them welcome.

The next day, Guadalupe Victoria rode up, accompanied by four men, and was astonished to see Ellis. "Elias," he said, "don't go to Boquilla de Piedras. The enemy overwhelmed us; these are all the men I have left. We were lucky to escape. I don't have a peso to my name."

"I have fourteen hundred pesos," Ellis told him. "Do you want to take them and make a fresh start?"

Guadalupe Victoria grimaced. "No," he wearily replied. "It's no use. Our friends have either gone over to the enemy or they're too discouraged to continue the struggle. Let's hide out in the mountains and wait for a better time."

Ellis had no wish to live like a hunted animal, knowing that the very men who gave them food might betray them. Besides, there was Magdalena. "No, I can't do that," he said.

The next day, Guadalupe Victoria and his men left for a mountain hideout near Córdoba. "When you come out of hiding and revive the revolution, I'll hear about it and join you," Ellis promised.

The *hacendado* had his peons butcher a steer and slice part of the meat into thin strips to dry in the sun, so Ellis and Magdalena would have food for the rest of their journey to the coast. Wishing they could stay there forever, Magdalena and Ellis were walking in the yard, hand-in-hand, when he saw a cloud of dust in the distance and knew at once that a royalist cavalry troop was coming.

"Someone must have told them I'm here," he said. He got his gun and powder horn. "You stay here and don't worry," he told her. "They'll shoot me if they catch me, but they won't harm you." He ran to the side of a nearby mountain before the cavalrymen arrived. From his hiding place he saw the soldiers catch his horses and gather up the beef strips that were drying on ropes. They took all of his money except two hundred pesos that Magdalena had hastily hidden.

After they left, Ellis warily returned. "We've got to get to the coast," he told the *hacendado*, "but they took our horses."

"Saddle two horses," the *hacendado* ordered one of his peons. When the horses were ready, Ellis shook hands with him. "Thanks for everything," he said. "If the royalists don't get me, we'll come back some day."

"My house is your house," the *hacendado* said.

As they rode toward the coast, Ellis was torn between the need to get Magdalena to a safe place and the urge to carry on the struggle for independence as Morelos would have wished. They rode steadily all day, stopping only briefly at noon. Ellis frequently looked back to see if they were being pursued. Aware of his concern, Magdalena also glanced back from time to time.

"If we can only make it to Nautla," Ellis said, "Philipio will look after us until a ship comes." They stopped for the night at a farm, where they were given food and a bed. The Mexican farmer fed the horses corn.

"Your horse needs at least two days' rest, *señor*," he told Ellis. "I'm afraid he'll give out otherwise. There's something wrong with him."

Ellis frowned, thinking of the cavalrymen who were undoubtedly grimly following their trail. "We can't take the time," he replied. "We'll have to chance it."

The farmer looked at the horse again and shook his head. "I hope your life doesn't depend on him, *señor*."

That's the trouble, Ellis thought. My life does depend on him. But with Magdalena in his arms that night he forgot for a short time the peril he was in.

They rode on early the next morning, walking and trotting their horses along the trail. About midday, Ellis heard a shout and looked back. He caught his breath, for a cavalry troop was approaching at a slow trot. They had obviously ridden hard, and their horses were worn down. Ellis and Magdalena urged their horses to a gallop, but after a mile Ellis' mount slowed down, then stopped, its sides heaving, unable to continue. Ellis glanced around desperately for a place to hide. There was none. Magdalena slipped from her horse and held out the reins. "Take him and save yourself, my husband," she exclaimed. "It's the only way. Hurry!"

Ellis dismounted, embraced her, then leaped to her horse's back. "Here," she said, handing him a silk handkerchief and a black mantilla. "Take these and don't forget me. Go with God."

After putting the keepsakes inside his shirt, Ellis dashed off. Over his shoulder he saw the cavalrymen stop their weary horses and stare after him. They had given up the pursuit. He rode on to Nautla, feeling empty without Magdalena by his side, wondering when he'd see her again.

Chapter Six

As he filed the rough edges of a new trigger he'd made for a cavalry carbine, Duncan McPherson gloomily supposed he should feel fortunate. His skill as a gunsmith had won him the unofficial post of armorer for two of the cavalry companies stationed at Chihuahua. He was treated as a competent craftsman by most of the officers and men, and he earned enough money to support himself. That was well and good, but he still wasn't free to leave, and he was virtually alone. His friend, Tom House, had died and he rarely saw any of the other Nolan men—most had married or moved to other towns.

Things could be worse, Duncan mused, but here I am nearly twenty-six, and it looks like I'll be here till I die. He wore the typical white cotton shirt, loose-fitting pantaloons, and *juaraches*, or sandals. But for his height, his blue eyes, his long blond hair streaked with brown, and his reddish beard, he looked like any Mexican artisan.

He did have one trusted friend, *mestizo* Sergeant Francisco Muñoz, who was about the same age but half a head shorter. He was stocky and powerful, with a bushy mustache and twinkling, mischievous eyes, at least when off duty. Like others of mixed Spanish-Indian ancestry, his skin was swarthy. He was, Duncan knew, an excellent cavalryman, or he'd never have made sergeant.

In the late fall of 1810, Spanish Major Franco, the only officer who was consistently hostile to Duncan, stalked into his shop, a small room off the cavalry barracks. From the lingering aroma, Duncan suspected that it had been a place where drunken soldiers forsook their sins and recovered their wits. Scowling, Franco thrust a pistol toward Duncan, who took it without looking up. He saw the hammer was bent.

"Fix it, *peón*," Franco snapped. Duncan laid it on his work-table, while Franco stood there still scowling, his trim mustache twitching.

"When do you need it?" Duncan asked, resisting the temptation to shove it down his throat.

"Immediately, you ass. Why do you think I brought it here myself?"

Duncan rubbed his finger along the bent hammer. "It's cracked," he said. "I'll have to replace it."

"All you need to do is put it in your vise and straighten it," Franco growled.

Duncan shrugged and put the hammer in his vise. When he tightened it, the hammer snapped. "I told you it was cracked," he said.

"You clumsy fool! You did that on purpose," Franco snarled. He stepped forward to slap him, but the look in Duncan's eyes stopped him. "I'll send for it tomorrow," he muttered. "See that you have it ready." He spun around and left.

Duncan was standing by his bench, still cursing in both Spanish and English when Muñoz entered a short time later, his eyes wide, his face animated. He looked at Duncan in surprise. "What's the matter?" he asked. "You look mad enough to kill."

"I am. That son of a bitch Franco was just here," he replied. Muñoz swore.

"That *Gachupín!*" he spat. "He hates all Americans. Of course he hates all Mexicans, too. But forget about him. We've had big news from the south. A padre named Hidalgo started an Indian *tumulto* in September, the biggest ever. They say it's spreading to the rest of the country," he said, extending his arms.

"What do they want?" Duncan asked, sitting again on his rough bench. Muñoz straddled it and sat facing him, unbuttoning his cavalry jacket to scratch his ribs.

"They say it started as a creole plot to declare independence at the annual fair, when so many people would be there they could overwhelm the *Gachupines*. But someone betrayed the plotters, and the viceroy ordered them arrested. One, an army officer named Allende, got wind of the arrests and rode to Dolores to warn Hidalgo. Instead of fleeing, Hidalgo called out the Indians. Although they had only clubs and *machetes* at first, they won several victories. Their war cry is 'Independence and death to the *Gachupines*,' but to them *Gachupines* are creoles as well as Spaniards from Spain." He paused to catch his breath, while Duncan stared at him and waited to hear more.

"What it means," Muñoz continued more calmly, his expression solemn, "is that what started as a creole movement for independence is now a war of Indians against the rest of the people. Creoles, even those who hoped for independence, now may have no choice but to fight for the Spaniards just to save their own skins, although some are still with Hidalgo."

"That's bad news," Duncan said, shaking his head. "Mexico should be independent. It's been a colony too long."

"We will be independent one day," Muñoz said, lowering his voice. "Maybe not this time, but the idea won't die." He went on to say that Hidalgo had sent Mariano Jiménez, a young creole mining engineer who'd proved a capable commander, to spread the revolution into Coahuila and Texas.

"That means among settlers, not Indians. If he succeeds, it will be a different kind of war after that," he added, "and it just might succeed." Duncan shrugged, for he couldn't see how it might affect him.

The next news Muñoz brought was that royalist General Calleja had crushed and scattered Hidalgo's Indian horde at Calderón. Hidalgo, Allende, and the rest of the officers were retreating northward with what was left of the army, but the disaster at Calderón discouraged the insurgents, and many had given up the fight.

"It probably will be easy for the royalists to stamp out the little fires before they can revive and spread," Muñoz said somberly. "I expect that General Salcedo will send some of us to Coahuila to help. Any change from garrison duty is usually welcome, but not this time. I don't like the idea of killing my countrymen for the *Gachupines*."

"I don't blame you. I'd be glad to fight for your people, but not against them."

A few days later Muñoz came again to see Duncan. "Both of our companies will march to Coahuila shortly to support Colonel Cordero," he told Duncan. "Since my troop is not at full strength, I have permission to take any of the Nolan men who are willing to serve, and of course, I want you. It may be the best chance you'll ever have to leave Chihuahua. What do you say?"

Duncan thought about it, his forehead wrinkled. If he served in the army, there'd be no excuse for holding him when the fighting was over. And once away from Chihuahua, he'd have a better chance to escape. The only drawback was the prospect of having to fight Mexican patriots, but that was a risk he'd have to take.

"I'm with you, *amigo*," he told the smiling Muñoz. "But I know nothing about fighting on horseback. Where I come from, we fight behind trees."

Muñoz chuckled at that. "It will take nearly a month to

reach Saltillo," he replied, "and in that time I can teach you enough to get by, then we can go on from there. Let's see the quartermaster and get you a uniform."

The quartermaster's clerk looked Duncan up and down and shook his head. "I don't know what I have that will fit you," he said. He went into a storeroom and returned with a blue shirt, jacket, and pants, as well as boots and a black hat. "These are the largest I could find," he said apologetically.

Duncan tried the pants first, and all three laughed when he pulled them up as far as he could, which wasn't nearly far enough. He got the shirt on with difficulty, but he couldn't move his arms forward, and the sleeves reached only to the middle of his forearms. He managed to button the jacket partway. He got the boots on after a struggle, and figured they'd stretch. Only the hat fit perfectly.

"I've never seen a soldier wearing only hat and boots," he said. "What can we do?"

Muñoz laughed, "That would make everyone notice you," he said, "but bring it along. I know a seamstress who can add inserts and make it fit. Then let's cut your hair."

The uniform was ready shortly before they marched a few days later, in mid-December. Duncan felt strange wearing a Spanish uniform and riding in a cavalry troop. Major Franco was in command, but if he recognized Duncan, he gave no sign. Duncan thought of the long ride from Saltillo to Chihuahua years ago, when Nolan's men were prisoners. All he remembered was crossing a desert that had seemed endless. The trail led across open sandy places, through rocky arroyos, and around or between hills and buttes, on and on, with more of the same. The vegetation was cactus and scraggly, oily bushes, but cottonwoods and willows flourished along streams and around waterholes. The only living creatures Duncan saw were occasional coyotes, jack rabbits, and scrawny buzzards watching the troops in hope that some of them would provide a feast.

When they were only a few days from Saltillo, a Spanish captain rode up at a trot, and the column halted while he reported to Franco. Muñoz' troop was first in line that day, close enough for Duncan to overhear most of what the captain said.

"Colonel Cordero's militia and a company of us regulars marched to meet the rebel Jiménez at Aguanueva," he explained. "The rebels had infected the militia with their lies, and Captain Elizondo and the lot of them defected to Jiménez. I was fortunate to escape, but they captured Colonel Cordero and then entered Saltillo. Hidalgo and Allende probably have joined them by now. Other rebels under Aranda control Monclova. Only Presidio Río Grande still holds out."

Duncan wiped the dust from around his eyes with a handkerchief, wondering what he'd gotten into. The officers talked among themselves for a few minutes, then Franco ordered the troops to march to Presidio Río Grande. There was no trail, so they strung out in a single file to avoid getting speared by cactus. A long cloud of dust hung over them.

Nearly a week later, the nervous presidio commander welcomed them, for he expected a rebel attack any day and was greatly relieved to have reinforcements. Riders passing from one town to another frequently stopped at the presidio to tell the latest news or rumors. With little to do except occasional patrols, Muñoz taught Duncan how to use a lance effectively.

At the end of January 1811, a party of royalist fugitives from San Antonio brought the bad news that a militia captain named Las Casas had arrested the governor—Colonel Salcedo—and Colonel Herrera, and sent them as prisoners to the rebel chieftains in Coahuila. Men from Saltillo reported that Jiménez had promoted Elizondo from captain to lieutenant colonel, but when Elizondo petitioned Allende to promote him to brigadier general, he had been refused.

Although he was sulking over his rejection, they said, Jiménez had sent him to guard Salcedo and Herrera on a *hacienda* near San Fernando.

Duncan was thrilled to know that all of Texas was in rebel hands. If he could elude the royalists and get to San Antonio, he could ride on to Natchitoches without difficulty. "What do you think?" he asked Muñoz. "Any chance I could make it to San Antonio?"

Muñoz shook his head. "I'm sure the Major would send both companies after you, and they'd overtake you and shoot you on sight. And if you ran into patriots while in a Spanish uniform, you can guess what they'd do. Those aren't very good choices," he added, his eyes twinkling.

"You're probably right as usual," Duncan admitted, frowning, "but . . . ."

"Be patient, my friend," Muñoz advised him. "Don't risk leaving until you're absolutely sure your way is clear. You're safe here, and there's no sense in getting yourself killed. Right now things are changing too fast."

Early in March, a courier from San Antonio brought word that royalists there had arrested Las Casas and restored control over Texas. "You sure gave me good advice," Duncan told Muñoz. "If I'd gotten to San Antonio, I'd have landed right in the middle of it." He drew his finger across his throat and grimaced.

Royalists from Saltillo reported that Hidalgo, Allende, and Jiménez had held a council of war and then turned over what was left of the army to Ignacio Rayón. It was rumored, they said, that the three were planning to head for the United States with about four hundred men to guard a pack train carrying silver bars for purchasing arms and recruiting men.

A messenger from San Fernando brought more startling news. Piqued at Allende's refusal to promote him, Elizondo had allowed Salcedo to win him back to the royalist side. He raised a militia company and at night, surprised rebel governor Aranda in Monclova, capturing him along with dispatches from Jiménez detailing plans for the expedition to the United States. Franco and the two cavalry companies hastened to Monclova. I'm on the wrong side, Duncan glumly thought, but what can I do about it?

In Monclova they joined Elizondo's militia, and Muñoz soon learned Elizondo's plans. "Jiménez doesn't know, of course, that Elizondo has changed sides again," he explained to Duncan. "He wrote Jiménez that he'd meet them with an honor guard at the Wells of Baján on March 21. That's the only water between Saltillo and Monclova. Elizondo is a slimy one. He recommended that they arrive in separate groups, not all at once, so there'll be enough water. If they do that, they haven't a chance."

"I don't like the smell of it," Duncan said, clenching his fists. "It's the lowest kind of treachery. Isn't there any way we can warn them?"

"No," Muñoz replied, "Elizondo has men watching the trail. There's nothing we can do, unfortunately. I wish there was."

On March 20 Elizondo, who was obviously gloating in anticipation, marched them along the desert trail to the Wells of Baján to set his trap. The trail from Saltillo wound around a low hill to the wells. In the morning, Elizondo posted fifty mounted militiamen in two lines to act as the honor guard, while the rest of the militia and the troops under Franco waited out of sight, ready to seize and disarm the unsuspecting rebels after they passed between the lines.

At mid-morning, the rebels began arriving in small groups. Duncan watched, feeling sick as they were easily disarmed. Hidalgo, who was riding in a carriage, looked shocked, as if he couldn't believe Elizondo was capable of such treachery. At dark, Colonel Salcedo arrived with several hundred more militiamen. There was now no possibility that the rebels could make a break with the slightest hope of success.

In the morning they herded the disconsolate prisoners back over the desert trail to Monclova. Then, leaving Herrera in command, Salcedo and the two cavalry companies set out with the rebel officers on the long journey to Chihuahua. As he rode with Muñoz and his troop, Duncan sadly observed the white-haired Hidalgo, whose pale countenance remained serene. Allende and Jiménez, both young men, were surely aware of the fate that awaited them, but they appeared to regret failing in their fight for independence more than having to face a firing squad. They wouldn't actually face it, Duncan knew, for they'd be forced to kneel facing a wall to be shot in the back as traitors. Duncan greatly admired them, and wished the rebels would come to their rescue. His own prospects weren't promising, for if the cavalry remained at Chihuahua, his chances of escaping were gone.

When they finally reached Chihuahua with the prisoners, General Salcedo smiled in grim satisfaction. He named his nephew, Colonel Salcedo, president of the military court that would try the culprits. The trials of the lower ranking officers began within two weeks. They were speedily found guilty, and executions immediately followed. In June, Allende and Jiménez were tried and shot, and on July 29 Hidalgo shared their fate. Duncan felt nauseated every time he heard the firing squad. The royalists called these men traitors and worse, but to Duncan they were patriots who deserved a better fate.

Duncan was greatly relieved when the two cavalry companies under Franco were ordered to escort Colonel Salcedo back to Monclova and then march to Saltillo, where Colonel Cordero was again in command. Saltillo was high enough that the nights were pleasantly cool, and although it was surrounded by desert, wherever there were irrigated farms Duncan saw flourishing orchards and green fields.

After the execution of Hidalgo and Allende, the royalists celebrated the end of the revolution, but rebels still controlled most of Nuevo León and Nuevo Santander to the east of Coahuila. In the south Morelos and other rebel leaders were winning victories. The revolution was not yet dead, but Elizondo had struck it a near-fatal blow.

Colonel Cordero, who was in his early fifties, was fairly tall and well-built, with a fair complexion and blue eyes. He was, Duncan learned, an ideal cavalryman and widely respected as a gallant and generous officer. His devotion to Spain and its monarch was obvious. Duncan had to admire him even though he was a staunch royalist who considered the rebels vile traitors to their king, not the heroic patriots their people regarded them.

No organized rebels remained in Coahuila, but since they still controlled most of Nuevo León and Neuvo Santander to the east, the cavalry patrolled the border to prevent them from infecting Coahuila again. Texas was still under royalist domination. Duncan glumly wondered if he'd ever have an opportunity to reach the States.

In the fall of 1812, a courier from Colonel Salcedo brought word that a long-expected invasion of Texas from the United States had begun, and the news caused a flurry of excitement. Four or five hundred Americans and Tejanos under the Mexican rebel, Bernardo Gutiérrez, and the former American army officer, Augustus William Magee, were besieged at La Bahía, and Salcedo called on other provinces for support. Only Colonel Cordero responded—he sent his best militia company and several barrels of gunpowder. Duncan was elated to learn of the invasion. If Americans conquered Texas, he had only to watch for a safe opportunity to join them. In the meantime he rode on cavalry patrols, and under Muñoz' tutelage, became a competent cavalryman.

Duncan was relieved, in fact, whenever the troop was sent on patrol. News that Americans had joined Gutiérrez in the invasion of Texas had infuriated the Spanish officers, especially Major Franco. Once afternoon when Duncan walked past the Major and other officers on his way to the barracks, Franco loudly proclaimed, "All Americanos in Mexico should be shot like the dogs they are!" Duncan knew the words were meant for him, but he kept walking as if he'd heard nothing.

Muñoz, who had also heard Franco, was troubled. "Watch your step around that *Gachupín, amigo*," he warned Duncan. "He wouldn't need much of an excuse to have you shot."

"I know," Duncan replied, slapping his hat against his leg to remove the dust. "I'm not goin' to give him an excuse, but I figure he won't be satisfied until he finds some way to do me in. I've got to get away somehow." But that was impossible.

In late April 1813, fugitives from San Antonio brought dire news for the royalists. Salcedo and Herrera had been forced to lift the siege of La Bahía and withdraw to San Antonio. The Gutiérrez–Magee army had followed and routed them, and it now controlled all of Texas. Resentful Tejanos, whose fathers or brothers Salcedo had executed simply because they had received rebel broadsides and admitted favoring independence, had seized Salcedo, Herrera, and a dozen other royalist officers and assassinated them. Later, other royalist fugitives from San Antonio reported that the Americans and Tejanos had fallen out over the killing of the prisoners, and that many Americans had left Texas in disgust. There goes my chance to escape, Duncan thought.

All of the officers were greatly aroused over the brutal murders, and Duncan shivered when he saw Franco glaring at him like he'd been responsible. A short time later, two infantrymen entered the barracks and marched up to Duncan.

"You must come with us," one said.

"Why?" Muñoz demanded to know. "He's in my troop."

"He's under arrest."

"What for and on whose orders?"

The soldier shrugged. "Who knows what for? Major Franco's orders."

Apprehensive over what the Major might have in store for him, Duncan walked between the two soldiers to the guardhouse, where he was thrown in with several sullen prisoners. They were fed a little gruel mornings and evenings, and given water. They could either stand or lie on filthy mats, for there were no benches. Duncan recalled the dungeon in San Luis Potosí and shuddered at the thought of being imprisoned and forgotten again. As the next few days passed, prisoners were released and others took their places. Muñoz came to see Duncan one afternoon, but there was no way they could speak in private.

"Courage, *amigo*," Muñoz said. "I'm doing what I can." Duncan shrugged. What could a *mestizo* sergeant do against a major from Spain? I'm doomed, he thought.

Nevertheless, a few days later, Duncan was released and allowed to return to the barracks. Overwhelmed by a feeling of relief, he bathed and washed his shirt in a nearby stream. Late in the afternoon, while he waited for his shirt to dry, Muñoz returned from a patrol.

"You did it," Duncan said, crushing his hand. "I never thought you could. Tell me how."

Muñoz looked up at him, but his eyes weren't twinkling. "Major Franco had you locked up for no stated reason," he said. "I suspect he was trying to drum up some charge that would have gotten you put away for good. It wasn't easy, but through Sergeant Castillos of headquarters company, I got word to one of Cordero's creole aides who dislikes the Major. Cordero called the Major in and told him all soldiers are needed, and none was to be punished for frivolous reasons." He paused and looked thoughtful. "Sooner or later the Major will figure out that I had something to do with it. Then we'll both have to watch out for him, but at least he'll leave you alone for the present."

Duncan put on his shirt, which was nearly dry. "We need to get to San Antonio," he said. Let's make a run for it while we can."

Muñoz' eyes opened wide. "Don't even consider it," he said. "The Major would like nothing better than to run us down and hang us. Besides, Arredondo has sent Colonel Elizondo with seven hundred militia to the Frío to watch the Americans, and we'd never get through. Arredondo has finished mopping up the patriots east of us, and he's preparing to march to Texas. And from what I hear, he doesn't take prisoners." Duncan frowned. He was almost willing to risk everything just to get away.

"Wait till you hear this!" Muñoz exclaimed a few days later. "Arredondo ordered Elizondo not to cross the Frío or to engage in battle for any reason, but fugitives from San Antonio told him the Americans had all left and the people would welcome him. So he disobeyed Arredondo and marched to San Antonio, then ordered the rebels to surrender Gutiérrez and other leaders. A few hundred royalists joined him, so he felt confident. But the Americans and Tejanos came out and thrashed him. He abandoned his artillery and everything else. I hear he wasn't so cocky when Arredondo got through with him." Remembering Elizondo's treachery to Hidalgo and the others, Duncan smiled grimly.

In August, they learned, Arredondo had marched into Texas with a large force that included a battalion or more of veteran troops from Spain. At the Medina he had prepared a strong position and waited. The Americans and Tejanos, after a gruelling march in sweltering heat that left them exhausted, had unwisely attacked him and been routed. As usual, Arredondo took no prisoners. His orders were to bayonet the wounded and shoot all who surrendered. Less than one hundred Americans escaped.

Duncan groaned on hearing of Arredondo's decisive victory and its consequences. In San Antonio he sent Elizondo and his cavalry after the families that had fled, while his own men rounded up all suspected rebels. Then, forcing their families to watch, he had more than three hundred shot without trials. Elizondo's troops had killed most of the men they overtook, but he forced a few of the prominent ones, along with the women and children, to walk back to San Antonio so Arredondo could have the pleasure of executing the men. A Spanish officer, maddened by the callous brutality, had fatally wounded Elizondo. Leaving San Antonio destitute and nearly depopulated, Arredondo had retired to Monterrey to establish his headquarters as commander of the Eastern Interior Provinces.

Arredondo's merciless sweep through Nuevo Santander and Nuevo León hadn't totally quenched the desire for independence in the two provinces. In mid-1814, an armed band under a *mestizo* named Valeriano captured an army pack train carrying guns and ammunition. Alarmed at the possibility of a revival of the revolution in the north, Cordero ordered Major Franco and the two cavalry companies to stamp out the uprising before it became dangerous.

The cavalry rode eastward to the region where the band had been reported, and circled the area. They made camp at the westernmost of two springs they saw, while scouts searched for the enemy. When they reported finding the rebel camp, Franco met with his officers. After he dismissed them, he sent an orderly for Muñoz and Duncan. Puzzled, they walked to where the Major waited and saluted him.

"I have an important mission for you," the Major said pleasantly, as if they were two of his most trusted men. "I want to arrange a meeting with the rebel leaders at the other spring we saw, so I can try to persuade them to disband. I want you to take them a letter under a flag of truce." He smiled. "I'm sure they know what a flag of truce is. Report to me after breakfast tomorrow." He dismissed them, and they returned to where the troop was bivouacked. They walked in silence, both thinking hard about the Major's orders.

"I doubt he'd have chosen us unless he thinks we're likely to be killed," Duncan said at last. "I can't see any other reason."

"You mean unless he's certain we'll be killed," Muñoz corrected him. "I'm going to talk to Sergeant Castillos; he's usually told, or figures out what's planned. But I can't let the Major see me talking to him." He didn't return until after dark; Duncan had already rolled up in his blankets, but he had difficulty sleeping. He listened to owls hooting mournfully in the cottonwoods, tossing restlessly and wishing he knew what Muñoz had learned.

Chapter Seven

After breakfast next morning they reported to Franco, who smiled when he saw that each of them carried a piece of white cloth tied to a stick. Muñoz also smiled, but Duncan saw nothing amusing. A scout described the way to the rebel camp, then the Major gave Muñoz an envelope.

"Take this to the rebel Valeriano," he said, "and bring me his reply." He smiled again, reminding Duncan of a cat playing with a helpless mouse.

Muñoz and Duncan saddled their horses and trotted off in the direction the scout had indicated. When they were well away from the camp, Muñoz stopped his horse and sat with both hands on the pommel of his saddle.

"Let me tell you what I learned," he said. "Of course, as you know, we're in real danger. The Major figured this one out so he's bound to win one way or the other." Duncan sat his horse, frowning and wondering how the Major had found a way to get them killed.

"In the first place," Muñoz continued, "if we ride into their camp in uniforms, even with these silly flags, they're almost certain to shoot us before we can say a word. If for any reason they don't, and Valeriano agrees to meet the Major at the spring, there'll be soldiers hiding nearby to shoot him down. The cavalry will be close enough to come to the

Major's rescue before the rebels can get him. So he will certainly get rid of either us or Valeriano. If he's lucky, maybe both.''

Duncan wiped the sweat from his forehead and exhaled. ''Damn,'' he said, ''I wasn't fixin' to die just yet. Couldn't we make it across Texas by keeping off the trails?''

''Without a pack mule and a month's supply of food, we'd starve to death if the Indians didn't save us the trouble. I have an idea that might catch the Major in his own snare, but only if we find someone who can persuade Valeriano to listen to us, someone who knows him, if possible. He's undoubtedly on friendly terms with the *rancheros* around here. If one of them will get him to hear us out, we may have a chance but it's risky. Convincing him is where the hair gets short.''

They crossed more prairie until they saw a small rancho and rode up to it. Dogs barked and a young *mestizo* woman, barefoot and wearing a loose cotton shift, came to the door of the hut holding a brown-skinned, naked infant in her arms. She gave them a black look when she saw they were soldiers.

''We need to talk to your husband,'' Muñoz told her.

''He's away,'' she said, not looking him in the face. ''I don't know when he'll be back. Tomorrow, maybe. Maybe not.''

''Are there other ranchos near here?'' Duncan asked.

''Who knows?'' she replied.

The two rode on. ''Soldiers aren't very welcome here,'' Muñoz remarked. ''After what Arredondo did to these people, small wonder. But we've got to get through to one of them. It's our only hope.''

A few miles farther on they saw another rancho and a corral holding a few horses. Nearby was a hut where the *ranchero* and his family lived. Dogs barked and children squealed as they rode up to the corral, where a young *mestizo ranchero* wearing one spur was saddling a cowpony. Seeing their uniforms, he scowled, but left his cowpony standing with the reins down and walked toward them. It was clear from his expression he knew that soldiers always meant trouble. "*Señores*?" he said, waiting, with hands on hips.

Muñoz showed him the letter. "We were sent to give this to Valeriano and wait for his answer," he said.

"Who is Valeriano?"

"I think you know. If you want to help him, hear me out," Muñoz said. "We don't know what's in the letter, but we're sure it's a trap. I have an idea how he can spring it on the *Gachupines*." He studied the young *ranchero's* face. "Believe me," he continued, "we want to help the patriots, not harm them."

The *ranchero* looked from one to the other, hesitating but no longer scowling. "How do I know I can trust you?"

"You don't, of course," Muñoz replied, "but let me explain. My *amigo* here is an Americano who has no love for the royalists. The *Gachupines* kept him a prisoner for ten years." Duncan held up his arms so the scars on his wrists were visible. The *ranchero* whistled. "The Major wants Valeriano to kill both of us," Muñoz added. "That's why he sent us with the letter. He also wants to kill Valeriano, so in a way we're in this together. We want to tell him how to turn the tables on the *Gachupines*. Otherwise we'd be heading for the Sabine right now. We didn't come here so Valeriano can kill us just to please the Major." He watched the *ranchero's* reaction, and saw that his words had been effective.

"What do you want of me?" he asked.

"Take us to Valeriano and get him to listen and trust us. We'll give you our guns so he can see we come as friends." He took his carbine out of its scabbard, while Duncan did the same. They handed their guns butt-first to the *ranchero*, who accepted them with some hesitation. "Will you do it?" Muñoz asked.

He nodded and tied the two carbines to his saddle. "I believe you," he said, "and you're lucky you found me, for I do know Valeriano. When they see me, they won't shoot you. At least not right away," he added as an afterthought. He mounted his cowpony. "Follow me," he said and led the way, while his wife and children watched anxiously from the doorway of their hut.

In about half an hour, they cautiously approached the rebel camp in a little valley, where many horses and mules grazed around an abandoned hut. Duncan held his breath, for at least fifty men seized their guns as the *ranchero* rode toward them, holding up his open hand. Duncan and Muñoz followed, with their flags of truce raised. Duncan felt foolish, for he was sure that holding up a handful of horse droppings would have meant as much to these men. Seeing the uniforms, the rebels scowled and fingered their guns. Gulping hard and desperately trying to keep from showing concern, Duncan glanced from one to another of the hostile faces, almost wincing at the hatred he saw in them. He wondered if it might not have been wiser to risk starving to death.

"Valeriano," the *ranchero* called, and untied the two carbines. A slender *mestizo* who appeared to be in his thirties walked toward them, smiling when he saw the *ranchero* holding the guns.

"You bring me prisoners?" he asked, accepting the carbines.

"No, *amigo*," the *ranchero* replied, and related what Muñoz had told him. "I trust them, and you should listen to what they have to say. I'm sure you'll be glad you did."

Muñoz held out the letter. "It's from Major Franco," he said. "He told us he wants to talk to you."

Valeriano frowned, but took the letter and opened it. From the way he looked at it Duncan knew he couldn't read. "Pablo," he called, "tell me what this says, *por favor*." An older man in white cotton shirt and pantaloons shuffled up to him and took the letter. Squinting his eyes, he read it haltingly.

"He wants you and your lieutenants to meet him at Dulce spring tomorrow an hour after sunrise," he said. "He will have two of his officers with him. He wants to offer you horses and money to stop fighting. His cavalry will stay in camp, so you'll be safe. To show his good faith, he will leave these two soldiers with you; if you aren't satisfied with what you see, you may kill them." Duncan shivered when he heard that. The tricky bastard, he thought. He told us to bring him Valeriano's reply. Damn him. He thought of everything.

"If you're willing to meet him," Pablo continued, "build a fire at the spring so he can see the smoke."

"Well, what about it? Valeriano asked Muñoz. "Why should I talk to him, and how do I know it's not a trap?"

"It *is* a trap," Muñoz replied calmly, "and that's why you should meet him." Duncan waited, his face bathed in sweat. "He's a *Gachupín*, and he wants you to kill both of us, but he also wants to kill you," Muñoz continued.

There was an ominous murmur among the rebels that reminded Duncan of a rattlesnake's warning—all appeared eager to oblige the Major. Duncan felt the hair rising on his arms. Valeriano held up his hand, and the murmuring ceased. Duncan exhaled.

"Let me explain how to catch him in his own trap," Muñoz said quickly, concealing his nervousness. The young *ranchero* looked at Valeriano, nodding his head vigorously.

"Do it," he said. The rebel leader hesitated. "I guess it won't hurt to listen to you," he agreed. "Without your guns you're not likely to shoot any of us." His men guffawed at that.

The *ranchero* turned his horse. "Good luck, *señores*," he said, then rode away.

Muñoz explained that at daybreak half a dozen soldiers would conceal themselves around the spring. The Major and two officers would arrive an hour later to meet Valeriano and his lieutenants. They would talk for a few minutes, then the Major would give a signal, and the soldiers would shoot the rebel leaders. The cavalry wouldn't be in camp, but would be close enough to hear the firing and dash up to prevent Valeriano's men from taking revenge on the Major.

"So what do you suggest?" Valeriano asked.

"Build the fire so he'll know you'll meet him. Have your men there well before daybreak," Muñoz answered. "When the soldiers arrive, seize them without firing a shot, and have some of your men hide. Then meet him. When he gives the signal, your men can shoot him. He'll think his own men killed him."

Valeriano, thinking about the plan, almost chuckled, then his face was serious. "I don't know," he said. "We'll have to think about it." He ordered Muñoz and Duncan into the abandoned hut and posted guards.

"I hope they do it," Duncan said. "I'd give anything to see the Major's face when he gives the signal." That was such a satisfying thought he momentarily forgot the danger they were in.

The afternoon seemed longer than usual. Late in the day a silent man with an impassive face gave them dried beef and water. Without mats or blankets, they tried unsuccessfully to sleep on the dirt floor. Duncan listened to squeaking rats scurrying around the hut and shivered, hoping no snakes were after them. Long before daybreak he listened intently for sounds indicating that the rebels were leaving for Dulce Spring to lay their trap, but he heard nothing and frowned.

At the first dim light the two prisoners stiffly arose, yawning, stretching their sore muscles, and rubbing their bloodshot eyes. Peering out the door, Duncan saw that the two guards were still there, but it wasn't light enough to see the camp clearly. At sunup a man brought more dried beef and water. Although hungry, they ate mechanically and without enthusiasm, then squatted on the dirt floor and waited. An hour or more passed.

"Did you hear that?" Duncan asked.

"No. What?"

"It sounded like distant thunder, or maybe gunfire. I wonder . . . ."

Some minutes later they heard shouts and hoofbeats, and forty or more horsemen clattered into the camp. "Our time has come," Muñoz remarked. "They either let us go or they shoot us." They stood nervously at the doorway, watching the men dismount. From their expressions Duncan couldn't tell if they were angry or jubilant.

Valeriano shouted, and the two guards ordered them to come out. They saw Valeriano limping toward them, and Duncan noticed a little blood on his pant leg. Oh, God, he thought, something must have gone wrong. He reluctantly followed Muñoz through the doorway, expecting to be riddled by a shower of bullets.

"Come here," Valeriano ordered, beckoning to them. They walked up to him. Duncan felt his heart pounding.

"What happened?" Muñoz asked, pointing to Valeriano's leg.

"Oh, just a scratch," the rebel leader replied. "One of the officers had a pistol in his pocket, and he got off a shot that nicked me before he went down. But it worked just like you said it would. The Major went down blaspheming, but you don't need to worry about him now. He's one good *Gachupín*. We left before the cavalry could get there. You can have your guns and leave."

"We can't let the army find us," Muñoz said. "They'll know we must have suggested this." He looked around the camp. "You must leave here right away," he said. "The scouts know where you are, and they'll surely come after you now. What will you do?"

"I know. We'll have to scatter immediately and return to our homes, but we were going to anyway. We thought that once we had a supply of guns, lots of men would join us. But Arredondo nearly wiped out many families, and most of those who survived want nothing more to do with the revolution."

"What do we do?" Duncan asked. "There's no place where we'll be safe."

"Come with me, both of you," Valeriano said. "I know a big *hacienda* where you'll have nothing to fear. The *hacendado* is a friend of the revolution; it's already cost him his oldest son. He'll see that no harm comes to you. We'll find you some clothes and get rid of your uniforms."

"And you?" Muñoz asked.

"I've got my own rancho north of the Rio Grande above Laredo. I'll be warned in plenty of time if anyone comes looking for me." Valeriano waved to his men as they rode away.

The Quiñones *hacienda* was in Nuevo Santander south of Laredo. Valeriano explained that it had been a royal grant in the mid-eighteenth century, when José de Escandón was extending Nuevo Santander to the Nueces and founding the towns of Laredo and Dolores on the Rio Grande. It is still in the same family, he told them, and *Don* Diego Quiñones, its present owner, is a great grandson of the founder.

From a distance across the prairie, the *hacienda* appeared to Duncan like a small village clustered around one big building. The two-story house of whitewashed adobe bricks gleamed in the sunshine. The surrounding huts of the *peóns* and *vaqueros* were of plain adobe. The closer they came to the house, the more impressive it appeared, and the more uneasy Muñoz became.

"This is no place for me," he said. "If I stay here I might end up a *peón*. That won't happen to Duncan because he's an Americano, not a *mestizo*." He turned to Valeriano. "Can I go to your rancho with you?"

"Of course. Arredondo made widows of many of the *rancheros*' wives. Maybe you'll find one to your liking. If not, my house is your house."

Muñoz waited in the courtyard while Valeriano introduced Duncan to *Don* Diego, a well-dressed, dignified gentleman whose hair and neatly trimmed beard were turning gray. "He's an Americano who came to Texas as a young fellow with *Señor* Nolan," Valeriano explained.

"Ah, so," *Don* Diego said, shaking hands with Duncan.

"He was a prisoner in Chihuahua," Valeriano continued, "until he joined a cavalry troop just to get away. A *Gachupín* major tried to get him killed, but he died in his own trap. We sprang it on him."

"Excellent!" *Don* Diego exclaimed.

"*Señor* McPherson must now hide from the royalists," Valeriano concluded.

"I'd be glad to live in a cow camp and work for my keep until it's safe for me to head for the States," Duncan assured *Don* Diego. "I don't want to be any trouble to you, but they'll surely shoot me if they find me."

Don Diego looked shocked. "You'll do nothing of the sort," he said. "You'll be a welcome guest. If you feel you must do something, my children have always wanted to learn to speak a little English. You may teach them if you wish." He beckoned to a barefoot *peón* to take Duncan's horse away, then prepared to usher him into the house.

"One moment, please," Duncan said. "I must say *adios* to a friend." He hurried to the courtyard, while Valeriano followed. Duncan gave Muñoz an *abrazo*, then shook hands with Valeriano.

"Good luck, *amigos*," he said. "I hope we'll meet again." They rode away while Duncan hurried back to *Don* Diego, who waited patiently at the door.

A young Indian servant girl in a loose cotton dress showed Duncan to his room, which was in an upstairs corner of the big house and had two shuttered windows. A wooden bed with a mattress filled with prairie hay stood in one corner. Near it was a chair and a brazier with a little charcoal in it for cold weather. A small table held a wash basin and a pitcher of water. A polished wooden crucifix hung on one wall.

When he went downstairs, Duncan had a feeling he was being watched, but he didn't turn his head. He heard giggles, and knew the eyes watching him weren't unfriendly. Before dinner, *Don* Diego introduced him to his wife, *Doña* Consuela, a plump, handsome woman whose braided hair was streaked with gray. She greeted Duncan warmly and made him welcome. Next he met twelve-year-old José and Carmencita, who was two years older than her brother. Knowing they were the ones who had watched him, Duncan was struck by the self-confident and easy manner with which they greeted him as an equal. That's a sign of their class, he decided.

"Where is Antonia?" *Don* Diego asked, a little impatiently.

"Here, Papa," a voice replied. Duncan turned and saw that she limped slightly as she approached. She wore sandals and a simple cotton dress trimmed with red; her black hair was tied in a ball at the back of her head. Her eyes were bright, her olive skin smooth. Although she may not be a stunning beauty, Duncan thought, she is surely attractive in her own way. He guessed her age as eighteen.

"*Señor* McPherson," *Don* Diego said, "my other daughter, Antonia. As you see, an unfortunate accident as a child has left her a little lame."

"Oh, Papa," Antonia said, lightly squeezing Duncan's outstretched hand and sending shivers up his arm. "A pleasure, *Señor* McPherson," she said in a melodic voice. "Papa's afraid no one will ever marry me. Papa says you speak Spanish very well, and English, too. I wish I could."

"Please call me Duncan, all of you," Duncan said, looking especially at José and Carmencita, who smiled. He turned to Antonia. "I haven't spoken English in so many years I'm afraid I've forgotten it," he said, "but if you want to learn it, I'll break my neck trying to remember."

She dimpled at that. "You Americans are such flatterers," she said, leading the way to the table. Duncan followed slowly, for he didn't know how to behave around such people and feared doing something outrageously wrong. He saw *Don* Diego stand behind his wife's chair and push it in for her, so he quickly did the same for Antonia, blushing madly. If she noticed, she was kind enough not to comment.

The next morning after breakfast, Antonia and her brother and sister took Duncan on a ride around the *hacienda*. His cavalry horse had been turned out so it wouldn't be found with the *vaqueros's* horses. His mount was one of *Don* Diego's fine Spanish horses that he raised in a well-guarded herd. It was a spirited bay with one white hoof and a star on its forehead. Duncan had never ridden so fine an animal. "He's your horse," *Don* Diego assured him. "No one else will ride him."

They saw *peones* working in the orchards, vineyards, and fields of corn and cotton, all irrigated by streams that ran across the *hacienda*. On the range they rode past corrals and sheep pens as well as grazing cattle and horses. Duncan gazed around in awe—it was like being in a little world. Out of the corner of his eye he saw Antonia watching him, a half-smile on her face. He realized she was smiling because of his pleasure and amazement, not in derision. He knew that he was lucky just to be among such people.

"We can't see it all in one day," Carmencita told him. "It will take at least a week. It's many, many leagues. I forget how many."

"I'm glad it will take more time," Duncan said, looking at Antonia. "The longer it takes the better." She smiled but said nothing.

Duncan taught the three of them to say a few sentences and many words in English, and they delighted each morning in greeting him in his own language. Carmencita often held his hand when they strolled in the gardens, and José stayed close by his side. After a few months they appeared to regard him as a beloved older brother, and their affection made him glow with delight. But Antonia—he couldn't look at her without his heart beating faster. I shouldn't have come here, he thought. Now I love her too much to want to leave, and I'm sure they'd never let her marry an American renegade like me, who may even have a price on his head. If I request permission to ask her to marry me, *Don* Diego will feel betrayed and order me out of the house. The thought gave him chills.

Yet *Don* Diego treated him almost like his own son, and they often discussed the few reports they received on the progress of the revolution. "In our war against England, we had important help from France," Duncan said. "If only the United States would send an army."

"Your country has been at war with England for two years," *Don* Diego told him. "Haven't you heard?" Duncan hadn't known that.

Don Diego enjoyed showing Duncan cattle, his fine Spanish horses, and his Merino sheep, and together they watched the *vaqueros* display their skills at roundup time. *Don* Diego had an old *vaquero* teach Duncan to use a rawhide riata skillfully. It was clear to Duncan that every member of the family regarded him almost as one of them, but he remained painfully conscious of the gulf that separated them from him.

In 1815 they learned that Morelos had been captured and executed, and that the only rebels left were a few bands in the mountains of the south, and they weren't expected to hold out much longer.

"That's a real disappointment," Duncan said. "I was hoping somehow they could hang on until the royalists gave up."

Don Diego looked somber. "I only hope I live to see us free," he said. "The *Gachupines* have lived at our expense and treated us as inferior for far too long. The revolutions in South America seem to be doing no better, but I know our day will come."

Valeriano came to see Duncan one day. "We learned from a deserter that the army reported you and Muñoz killed by rebels," he told Duncan. "I had to let you know they're not looking for you."

"That's good news," Duncan said, thanking him. "And how is my friend Muñoz?"

"He's married and has a rancho of his own. He doesn't worry about the royalists anymore. It's probably safe for you to leave, if you're careful."

I should be glad to hear that, Duncan thought, after Valeriano left, and yet I don't even want to think about leaving. But I know I'm foolish to stay here.

"You'll have to excuse me today," Antonia told him one morning a few days later. "A young man has asked my father for permission to pay court to me, and I must allow him to." She looked reproachfully at him. "I'm not getting any younger, you know. Most girls have been married several years by my age, but it seems no one has ever wanted to marry me before."

Duncan was shocked almost beyond words. "I understand," he mumbled, his face white. He left her, feeling crushed and empty. She must know I love her even though I've never told her, he thought, but how can I, a nobody, ask her to marry me?

He saddled his horse, then rode aimlessly all day, brooding and cursing his luck, not returning until late in the afternoon. *Doña* Consuela met him with a frown.

"You naughty boy," she said. "You haven't eaten all day."

"I forgot," he said lamely. "I just wasn't hungry."

"Ah, something is troubling you. Tell me about it."

He wanted badly to tell her, but was afraid to. "I was thinking that now I know the royalists aren't looking for me I mustn't stay here any longer," he blurted. "You've all been so kind to me, and I'm so fond of all of you, it made me sad to think about it." He paused and tried to appear mildly curious. "How did you like the young man who came to see Antonio?" he asked, his voice sounding strange.

Doña Consuela stared at him, a look of understanding on her face. "Oh, he's a nice young man from an old family," she replied, "but I hardly think that Antonia was smitten by him." Duncan's face brightened. "Of course with young girls, you never know," she added. Duncan frowned.

At dinner Antonia said little to anyone, and Duncan spoke only when addressed.

"What's wrong with everyone?" *Don* Diego asked, frowning and looking from one to another.

"Duncan has decided it's time for him to leave us," *Doña* Consuela answered, looking solemn.

"Oh, no!" Carmencita exclaimed, and José looked shocked. Antonia dropped her fork. "You mustn't!" Carmencita said firmly. Antonia stared at Duncan with a hurt expression on her face. *Don* Diego put down his knife and fork and leaned back.

"What utter nonsense!" he exclaimed. "Have we not made it clear we want you here? We have come to look on you as one of us." Duncan felt a lump rising in his throat.

"Yes, yes," *Doña* Consuela said.

"I wish I was," Duncan said hoarsely, "but unfortunately, I'm not." Antonia gave him a stony look. They finished the meal in silence, and before Duncan realized it, the others had quietly withdrawn, leaving him alone with Antonia. He felt hot, uncomfortable, and tongue-tied.

"Why do you want to leave? she asked. "Is it that you want to hurt me deeply, or do you have a sweetheart waiting for you?"

"Oh, no!" he stammered. "I adore you and wouldn't hurt you for the world." He cleared his throat. "It's just the thought of losing you, I mean seeing you marry someone else. I mean. . . ." His face turned crimson, and he breathed with difficulty. "I wish I was in a position to ask you," he confessed, "but I'm not. If the royalists ever find out I'm still alive, they'll likely shoot me. I'm a bad risk."

"I've waited months for you to say something," she told him. "I finally realized that either you have a sweetheart or you don't want me because I'm lame. Mother doesn't think it's that, but she can't understand you. Neither can Papa."

He gulped and swallowed hard, blushing even more to hear that they had all discussed him. He felt like an utter idiot. "Do you really mean you'd marry me? And they'd let you? I've dreamed about it, but dreams never come true," he stammered.

"Of course, you silly goose. Haven't you known that all along?" He put his trembling arms around her and kissed her.

Chapter Eight

When Ellis finally reached New Orleans on one of Jean Lafitte's schooners, he knew he'd been fortunate to escape with his life. Even so, his feeling of relief quickly gave way to a burning desire to throw himself once more into the struggle against the royalists. Until Mexico was independent, he could never hope to embrace his beloved Magdalena again.

When he stepped ashore after weeks on the tossing deck of a small ship, he reeled along the busy waterfront, carrying his blanket roll and watching keen-eyed men from Tennessee and Kentucky arrive on flatboats loaded with whiskey kegs and sacks of corn. Half-naked slaves, whose black skins glistened with sweat, slowly unloaded the cargoes for the Spanish, French, or American merchants who bought them. Then they broke up the empty flatboats for lumber.

With the comforting weight of coins in their pockets, the boatmen headed for the nearest saloons before starting the long journey upriver and along the Natchez Trace to Nashville. Ellis watched them, and sadly shook his head. If only they'd take a notion to fight for Mexico, he thought. A few thousand of them, armed with their deadly long rifles, could easily drive the royalists from the country.

New Orleans was still a nest of plotters, each jealously trying to launch his own expedition exclusive of control by others. Most grudgingly acknowledged the slender Cuban, Alvarez de Toledo, as the principal leader—both he and portly French General Humbert had at least delivered a few shipments of arms to the rebels. Alvarez de Toledo was preparing an expedition against Tampico; Humbert had a grandiose scheme for invading Veracruz with the help of his countrymen, the Lafitte brothers. Henry Perry of Connecticut, who had taken part in an earlier invasion of Texas, was determined to land on the Texas coast and capture the presidio at La Bahía.

In September 1815, shortly before Ellis reached New Orleans, James Madison had issued a presidential proclamation ordering citizens to refrain from taking part in illegal expeditions. Federal officers had been instructed to arrest those who persisted, and to seize their arms and ships. Most of the leaders had also been indicted for violating the neutrality laws, but there had been no move to bring them to trial, and it appeared none would be made.

The leaders, Ellis soon learned, were convinced that the proclamation and indictments were grudging gestures to placate the persistent Spanish minister Onís, and not a serious move to interfere with efforts to help the Mexican rebels. They continued to call openly for recruits. The leaders may have felt complacent about the government's intentions, but Ellis noticed that Americans appeared reluctant to risk arrest by joining any expedition to Mexico, and held back.

Ellis unwrapped Magdalena's mantilla and handkerchief and held them fondly in his hands, envisioning her lovely face when she insisted he take her horse and save his life. He ached to hold her in his arms, and his chest felt so tight he could hardly breathe. What can I do? he wondered in desperation. How can I get back to her? I've got to find a way.

A few days later, he sat on a bench glancing at a New Orleans newspaper someone had left there, when the name

Gutiérrez caught his eye. He remembered the stocky Mexican rebel with a bushy mustache who'd joined Jackson's force as a volunteer before the Battle of New Orleans, and vaguely recalled that he'd been involved in an expedition to Texas. Gutiérrez was advertising for volunteers to assemble in the Neutral Ground near Natchitoches for another invasion of Texas. Recalling that Morelos had urged him to invade Texas to draw the royalists north, Ellis headed upriver. It was too late to save Morelos, but perhaps there was still time to help the revolutionaries.

A week later, he stepped ashore from a little schooner among the towering pines around Natchitoches. The first person he recognized was Morelos' son, Juan Almonte, now a handsome lad of fifteen, who greeting him warmly.

"I asked about you at the school," Ellis told him. "They said you'd left, but didn't know where you were."

"I had to leave," Almonte replied. "No *dinero. Señor* Gutiérrez took me in, not that he's got much." He took Ellis to see the burly Gutiérrez, who welcomed him with an *abrazo*, delighted to have one of Morelos' former officers join him.

As Ellis and Almonte walked around the town, rubbing shoulders with frontiersmen in greasy buckskins and impassive Caddo Indians in breechcloths, Ellis asked about the earlier expedition Gutiérrez had led to Texas.

"I talked to a few of those who escaped," Almonte replied. "They told me that after they took San Antonio, Gutiérrez didn't stop the Tejanos from killing Governor Salcedo and the rest of the royalist officers." Ellis frowned. "The governor had executed some of their fathers or brothers just because they favored independence," Almonte quickly added, "so it wasn't surprising they retaliated when they had the chance. If they'd hanged your father or brother, what would you have done?" Ellis thought about it and was glad he hadn't been obliged to make that decision.

"The Americans in the army were outraged over killing officers who'd surrendered," Almonte continued. "As you well know, the royalists usually shot any patriot officer they captured, but the Americans didn't know about that, and found it hard to accept. Maybe it wouldn't have seemed so bad to them if the Tejanos had shot the prisoners. Instead, they cut their throats and left them wallowing in their own blood. The Americans had to bury them, and they were furious. Bad feelings arose between them and Gutiérrez as well as the Tejanos. A lot of Americans left San Antonio, but others took their places."

They walked slowly along the street, avoiding the worst of the mudholes. "After they controlled all of Texas, how did they lose it?" Ellis asked.

"About the time Arredondo's army crossed the Río Grande into Texas," Almonte replied, "the Americans forced Gutiérrez out and insisted that Alvarez de Toledo replace him, even though the Tejanos all favored Gutiérrez. Knowing that, Alvarez de Toledo reorganized the army, putting the Americans in one division, the Tejanos and Indians in the other. The men I talked to said that was a bad idea, for they'd fought well in mixed companies." They drew back to let a pair of roan oxen plod past drawing a creaky wagon.

"Some of the American officers had left," Almonte continued, "so Henry Perry was made colonel, and he commanded the troops when they routed Elizondo outside San Antonio. A week or two later scouts reported that Arredondo's army was at the Medina, and they marched to meet him. Alvarez de Toledo chose a good defensive position and ordered them to await Arredondo there. But Perry ignored him and marched the army through thick brush in the heat to the Medina, leaving the artillery far behind. Everyone wanted to go back to the place Alvarez had chosen, which was the sensible thing to do. But even though they were all worn down, Perry insisted on crossing the Medina and charging Arredondo's army, with all its cannon. It was a slaughter. Not many escaped, and Arredondo didn't take prisoners.''

Ellis whistled. "I wonder why Perry expects anyone to follow him after that,'' he said, shaking his head in bewilderment. "I'm dyin' for another crack at the royalists, but I don't aim to let someone throw me away.''

Although Gutiérrez advertised widely for recruits, only small parties came from time to time. They were looking for excitement or loot, Ellis suspected, and when it appeared they weren't likely to find either any time soon, most disappeared. Ellis was convinced, from their furtive looks when strangers appeared, that many of those who remained were hiding from enemies or the law. There were also bands of robbers, who found the Neutral Ground attractive because neither Spain nor the States had jurisdiction over it, but they avoided Gutiérrez and his recruits.

The number of men in the camp gradually grew to more than a hundred, and Ellis' hopes rose. If he and Gutiérrez could somehow take San Antonio, that would draw the royalists away from the rebels who still held out in the mountains of Guanajuato and the south. But they needed more men. Ellis ground his teeth in frustration.

While waiting for enough volunteers to arrive, Ellis and a dozen others earned a little money escorting pack trains of smuggled goods in both directions across the Neutral Ground, to protect the smugglers from bandits, not officials. Ellis learned from the Tejanos they met that the people of San Antonio, as well as the few companies of troops there, were daily on the verge of starvation. If we can just raise five hundred men, we can take all of Texas, he thought. He became familiar with the trails through the pines across the Neutral Ground and on to Nacogdoches. He burned to march there at the head of a few battalions of eagle-eyed frontiersmen armed with long rifles.

Late in 1816, Gutiérrez received a letter from a friend in New Orleans, and cursed when he read it. Alvarez de Toledo, who had been trying to launch an expedition to take Tampico, had written Spanish minister Onís to ask for a royal pardon. He'd kept it secret until he reached Philadelphia in August, but in the meantime he had given Diego Morphy, Spanish consul in New Orleans, complete information on all the plotters, their plans for helping the Mexican rebels, and the best ways to frustrate them. When Onís received the information Morphy relayed to him, then talked to Alvarez de Toledo, he demanded that the government take immediate and decisive action to prevent blatant violations of the treaty with Spain.

Other news arrived from the East at the same time. Spanish republican exile, Francisco Xavier Mina, who'd been a respected guerrilla leader against the French, had arrived at Baltimore with several ships and ample funds that English merchants had provided for organizing an expedition against Spanish America. Ellis expected to hear that federal officials, bowing to Onís' demands, had broken up Mina's expedition. It was rumored, however, that Mina had been allowed to recruit men and sail, but his destination was unknown.

The volunteers in the Neutral Ground rose to one hundred fifty, and Ellis watched anxiously for more. If that number would only double, he thought, we could at least take Nacogdoches, and one good scrap would bring a flock of American adventurers. Then one day a federal marshal in black coat and pants rode into Nacogdoches and asked for Gutiérrez. Ellis, wondering why he had come, took him to the rebel leader and served as interpreter.

"I have orders to look over your army," the marshal told Gutiérrez, who looked shocked. "Not to do anything, just to look at it and report," the marshal added.

"Come with me," Gutiérrez said, and the three of them

rode into the Neutral Ground to where the volunteers lived in shacks or crude tents. The men, many of them without guns, were stretched out in the shade or playing cards on blankets. Some of them took one look at the approaching marshal and faded away into the woods.

"There it is," Gutiérrez told the marshal, "my army, all of it. Fearsome, isn't it?" The marshal pushed his gray hat back, scratched his head, and smiled.

"The Spaniards claim you have a thousand men, all armed to the teeth," he said. "Their spies mustn't count very good."

"I wish we did have a thousand," Ellis said somberly. The marshal looked at him with raised eyebrows.

"Come to think of it," he admitted, "so do I. We should be helping the Mexicans. It's kind of our duty." He shook hands with them and rode away.

The next morning, Ellis and Almonte rode among the shacks and tents, while Ellis unobtrusively made a rough count. "Damn," he said. "At least half of them have skipped out. I figured we'd soon have enough to take Nacogdoches, and when word of that spread we'd get lots of help." His shoulders sagged. "Everything's against us." He thought of Magdalena and straightened up. "We just can't give up. We've got to keep on as long as there's a shred of hope."

"I hope I can go home some day," Almonte said wistfully.

"I hope we both can," Ellis added.

As the weeks turned into months, the hoped-for flood of volunteers never came. In desperation, Ellis thought of asking the Lafittes to put him ashore on the Mexican coast so he could slip past the royalists to Magdalena on her uncle's *hacienda*. "If I can get to the coast, do you think I'd have a prayer of making it to Jalapa?" he asked Gutiérrez.

The stocky Mexican tugged at his mustache, looked at Ellis' drawn face, and sadly shook his head. "Some rebel who has gone over to the royalists would surely recognize you sooner or later and turn you in," he said. "The

Gachupines will never forgive one who served Morelos loyally. You'd probably be shot before you ever saw your wife, and that would be small comfort to her." He paused, like he wanted to say no more, then forced himself to continue. "I hate to say this, but unless the revolution succeeds, you'll never see your wife again. Cruel though it sounds, you'd be better off to consider her dead and forget her."

Ellis was sunk in gloom early in 1817 when Gutiérrez received a letter from Manuel Herrera in New Orleans. Herrera had accompanied Ellis there three years earlier as Morelos' minister, but he'd never had enough money to continue the journey to Washington. "Mina is on Galveston Island with an expedition," Herrera wrote. "The privateer Luis Aury, who once served Bolívar, is there and claims to be rebel governor of Texas. Henry Perry and fifty men have joined Aury. If Mina is as good a fighter as they say, the royalists may be in for a surprise, although I don't know how many men he has." Gutiérrez wrote back, urging Herrera to keep him informed.

Ellis waited eagerly for more news of the expedition. If Mina was actually going to invade Mexico with enough men to take on the royalists, he wanted to be with him. But Herrera's next letter was discouraging—Aury and Mina had quarrelled, and it looked like they might not sail any time soon. Ellis shrugged. It was just one more disappointment, and he should have expected it. Without Aury's help and ships, Mina wasn't likely to get off Galveston Island.

There was no more news from Herrera until early April. Mina and Aury had reached an understanding, he said. Aury would command at sea, Mina on land. Mina had been in New Orleans buying large stocks of provisions and gunpowder, and it appeared that the expedition was ready to sail. Ellis embraced Gutiérrez and Almonte, then caught a ride to New Orleans on a little schooner. He fretted the whole way, fearful that he'd be too late.

He arrived in mid-April, and immediately found Herrera. "What's the news of Mina?" he asked eagerly.

"Some Mexicans think he's more interested in restoring the Spanish Constitution than freeing Mexico," Herrera replied. "I don't believe that, for by now he's probably in Nuevo Santander, and if he isn't already fighting the royalists, he soon will be."

"You mean they've already sailed?" Ellis was dumbfounded. "I wanted to go with him, but from what you said I was never sure they'd ever go." Herrera shrugged. Ellis stood there, jaw clenched, then his face relaxed. "Surely they'll take him supplies and reinforcements, won't they? Maybe I can still join him."

Herrera shook his head. "They should, of course," he replied, "but he may have to get along with what he can raise in Mexico. It seems that Aury is angry because Perry quit him and joined Mina. He may have washed his hands of them."

From Herrera Ellis learned later that Mina had landed three hundred fifty men and a large stock of provisions and extra guns a short distance up the Santander River. Seizing a small adobe fort at Soto la Marina, he made it his supply base. He had recruited and armed two hundred *rancheros* and repulsed several attacks, forcing the royalists to fall back temporarily and avoid him.

Fragmentary reports reached New Orleans from time to time by way of the Lafittes or Aury's privateers. Ellis eagerly devoured the news, trying to envision what was going on, still hoping that somehow he and others could join the expedition. He was thrilled to learn that Mina's reputation as a fearless and resourceful fighter was well deserved. Time after time, when his little force was surrounded and badly outnumbered, he'd led a daring charge that routed the enemy.

When Mina decided to leave one hundred men guarding his supply base and cut his way through royalist forces to the patriots holding Fort Sombrero in Guanajuato province, Perry protested. Even if Mina took the men from Soto la Marina, Perry insisted, his force would still be too small to invade central Mexico. When Mina persisted, Perry and his fifty men marched north to seize the presidio at La Bahía.

Mina and his men, Ellis learned later, had fought their way through the royalists to the rebels at Fort Sombrero. When seven hundred royalists laid siege to the fort, Mina had led three hundred men on a furious charge that killed, captured, or scattered the whole enemy column. Ellis heard the reports with delight—Mina, he was now certain, was the savior of the revolution, the man who would revive the rebels and lead them to complete victory. He was so eager to see Magdalena again that he convinced himself Mina was invincible, and chafed to join him. It didn't make sense that Americans weren't rushing help to him—he was sure that his friend Guadalupe Victoria and hundreds of Mexican patriots would come out of hiding and take up arms again. Under Mina they would be irresistible. He urged General Humbert to raise a force of Americans and hurry to Mina's support. He soon discovered that neither the portly Frenchman nor any of the other plotters in New Orleans was willing to place himself under a leader who cast as long a shadow as Mina.

Arredondo had sent two hundred cavalry on Perry's trail, then with sixteen hundred troops besieged Mina's supply base at Sota la Marina. Although his cannon pounded and pulverized the adobe walls day after day, the defenders fought so desperately and inflicted so many casualties on his troops that Arredondo finally offered them humane terms to surrender. They accepted, and Arredondo was stunned when only thirty-seven half-starved Americans staggered out to lay down their arms.

One of Perry's men limped up to Aury's outpost at Matagorda Bay and gasped out his story before collapsing. Late one afternoon, just as Perry ordered the presidio at La Bahía to surrender, Arredondo's cavalry overtook them. Perry's men found themselves caught in a deadly crossfire between the cavalry and the garrison, which came out to attack. Only the one man had been able to slip away after dark. He was sure there were no other survivors.

Ellis waited impatiently for more news of Mina's victories, confident he'd never be defeated, whatever the odds. He envisioned rebels by the score eagerly joining him in his triumphant march on Mexico City, and was ready to head for Jalapa the moment he heard that the royalists had been crushed. Unwrapping Magdalena's mantilla and handkerchief, he held them against his burning cheeks and thought of embracing her once more. A few more weeks, maybe a month or two, he was sure, and Mexico would be free. Then he and Magdalena would have a joyous reunion.

It was late December before Ellis could piece together the story of Mina's final campaign. The Mexican patriots had resented the fact that he was a Spaniard, a *Gachupín*, and many were jealous of his fame. Their support had been grudgingly given at best, and they had detached most of his original men to serve in other rebel units. Late in October, when Mina led a patriot force in a daring charge that carried to the center of the city of Guanajuato, he suddenly found himself almost alone. Enemy soldiers captured him, and the viceroy had ordered him shot. The royalists were again in control, and the rebels were hiding like rabbits in their burrows. The revolution was dead.

When he finally accepted the awful truth that the struggle was indeed over, and that he'd never see Magdalena again, Ellis felt the blood drain from his face, and his knees buckled. Breathing with difficulty and choking down a lump in his throat, he staggered to his cot and collapsed on it. Mina had raised his hopes to extraordinary heights. Now he plunged headlong to the depths of despair.

For days Ellis lay on his cot, racked by a burning fever, not caring if he lived or died, while Herrera nervously hovered over him. In his feverish mind Ellis saw himself struggling to get through royalist lines, his legs like sticks of wood, barely able to move. Behind him shouting enemy soldiers steadily gained on him. He saw Magdalena dressed in flowing white robes, waiting for him with arms outstretched. With a last convulsive effort he reached out to embrace her, when both fell in a hail of bullets.

Gradually the fever subsided, and Ellis' head cleared. He sadly recalled what Gutiérrez had advised. Unless the revolution succeeds, he'd said, you'll never see your wife again. You'd be better off to consider her dead and forget her. He's right, Ellis gloomily admitted. That's what the dream told me. There's nothing else I can do.

That spring of 1818, Ellis trudged upriver to Natchez, where he'd met Nolan eighteen years earlier. Then with a party of twenty-five boatmen, he headed up the Natchez Trace through the woods toward Nashville. Cutthroats lurked along the trail, ready to rob and murder any party not strong enough to defend itself, and Indians occasionally attacked the unwary. Ellis was on the way to visit his older half-brother, William Shaw, in White County, Tennessee, while trying to decide which way to turn. He'd written William he was coming and why.

Tennessee was no longer the wilderness Ellis remembered, for there were large, prosperous farms in many areas. White County, where Caney Fork entered the Cumberland, was one of these. William Shaw, a heavy-set man in his later forties, farmed and traded in livestock. He and his wife greeted Ellis warmly. "You're welcome to stay as long as you need to get your feet under you," William said when they shook hands.

William introduced Ellis to other farm families in the area, proudly announcing that he'd fought in both the Mexican Revolution and the battle of New Orleans. One neighbor was

Isaac Midkiff, a small gray-bearded man in his fifties who lived with his daughter Candace on a large farm he'd just purchased. She was a blue-eyed, doll-like girl who wore her blonde hair in braids tied with ribbons; because of her small size, Ellis assumed she was a child and hardly noticed her at first. He immediately took a liking to her father. When Isaac questioned him about the Mexican Revolution, Candace listened wide-eyed.

"I was let out of a stinkin' dungeon to fight the rebels," Ellis told them. "At the first opportunity I slipped away to Morelos. He was just raising an army and hadn't fought a battle—they had mostly clubs and *machetes* for weapons. I told Morelos I'd go back to the royalists and claim I'd escaped, then get a lot of the militia to join him, along with their guns. He warned me the royalists would likely shoot me, but luckily they didn't."

"That was dangerous!" Candace exclaimed, sitting up straight in her chair. "You might have been killed!" Ellis looked at her closely for the first time and was struck by her small, well-formed figure. She's no child, he thought. She's one good-looking woman, just kind of little.

"It *was* dangerous," he admitted, "but I got word to Morelos to have his men meet me at midnight by an abandoned house. There were about five hundred of them, but only thirty had guns, and I wasn't sure all of them would fire." He paused, as Candace stared at him, holding her breath.

"Go on," she said impatiently. "Tell us what happened."

"I led them to a hill by the camp where a sentry guarded the artillery. We got rid of him without a fuss, then turned the cannon on the Spanish soldiers and ordered them to surrender. When they saw the guns aimed at them, and us holding lit matches, they threw up their hands. The militia ran but joined Morelos the next day. He was one happy man, for it was his first victory, and now he had six cannon and hundreds of muskets as well as many more men."

That was the beginning. Ellis felt increasingly drawn to the Midkiff farm, where he enjoyed helping Isaac and regaling Candace with tales of his adventures. He was fascinated by her shapely, diminutive figure, and almost against his will gazed at her with lust in his heart. She's only eighteen, he thought, and I'm thirty-five. If we got married, there'd come a day when I couldn't get it up anymore and she'd still be . . . I'd be too jealous to live with if she even looked at another man. Anyway, I already got a wife. I can't marry her. I'd better clear out and let her find someone her own age. I'll move on next week or the one after for sure, he told himself, but without conviction.

In spite of his good intentions, Ellis continued to spend every day at the Midkiff farm, telling himself it was because of his warm friendship for Isaac. Seeing the tiny Candace made him forget the difference in their ages, for she gazed at him with doting eyes. She's waiting for me to ask her to marry, Ellis thought. If I don't get out of here something in me is going to explode.

One day as he sat on a kitchen stool while she prepared food, he noticed that she wore only a thin cotton dress with nothing under it. His eyes grew wide and his pulse quickened, for he could almost see through it wherever it was pressed against her body. When she casually walked to the open kitchen door, where the sunlight streamed in, and stood there feet apart, he could see every detail of her well-shaped body. His desire for her flamed so violently it was overpowering, and he was almost panting.

"Candy," he said huskily, "I want you badly." She turned and brightened. "Unfortunately I can't ask you to marry me." She looked shocked. "I was married for about a week in Mexico, and I don't even know if my wife is still alive. But I can't marry again without knowing. That's against the law."

Candace looked crushed, her expectations dashed, her

eyes moist. Ellis cleared his throat, then nervously continued. "Like I said, I want you, even if I can't marry you. If you're willing, we can live together as man and wife." Her blue eyes widened and her brow wrinkled. "I can get you a wedding ring and we can tell folks we're married." Her shocked expression faded, and she looked thoughtful. Ellis exhaled deeply. His face felt hot, and he tried to mask the fact that he could barely keep from tearing off her flimsy dress and ravishing her on the kitchen floor.

"I want you, too," she said softly, looking him in the face, "so bad it hurts. Some nights I can't sleep for wishing you were beside me." She paused and looked down. "What you ask isn't all I'd hoped for, but I'll think on it."

Ellis said no more, but waited eagerly for her decision. After another sleepless night, she made up her mind. "I just don't know how to tell Papa," she said, looking worried.

"I don't either," Ellis said, "but that's for me to do, not you. I wonder if I should unload his shotgun first."

When Isaac came in at noon, Ellis nervously cleared his throat. "Candace and I have a problem," he said. The kindly gray-bearded Isaac looked at him with raised eyebrows.

"Serious?" he asked. Ellis nodded.

"We want to get married, but. . . ." Isaac smiled. "But we can't because I was married in Mexico," Ellis hastily added. Isaac stared at him in surprise. Ellis screwed up his courage and plunged in. "We want to live together as man and wife," he blurted, his face flushed and perspiring. "If you agree I promise to treat her just like we're really married. I'd never abandon her." He was grateful that Isaac didn't look badly shocked or reach for the shotgun, which lay across two pegs in the wall.

Isaac looked intently from one to the other, stroking his beard thoughtfully. "You sure that's what you want, Candy?" he asked. She blushed in shame but nodded her head. "Well, since your mother is no longer here to object," he said, "I won't." Ellis felt a great wave of relief sweep over him. "By the way, daughter," Isaac added, "don't think you two are the first who have done this." Ellis felt like hugging him.

The Panic of 1819 hit Western farmers hard, for by the end of the year there was no money from unsold crops to pay mortgages or other debts. Shortly before the slump began, Isaac had sold several ox-teams and a dozen cattle on credit to raise money to pay his mortgage. He was unable to collect more than the first payments, for the purchasers' funds, like those of everyone else, had dried up. Isaac's face became set in a worried cast, and he looked like a man who was trying desperately to claw his way out of powerful quicksand that was slowly sucking him under.

Troubled by his expression, Candace asked one day, "Papa, are you worried about something, or aren't you feeling well?"

He gazed at her sadly. "I wanted to leave you a good farm," he told her, "but there's no money to be had and the bankers won't wait. By next year they'll foreclose and turn us out." He suddenly looked old and careworn.

"Don't worry about it, Papa," Candace said, hugging him. "We'll get along somehow." Ellis looked at Isaac, saddened to see him so forlorn.

"That's right," he said, trying to sound cheerful. "Arkansas has just been made a territory. There's lots of good grass there and woods enough so there's plenty of mast for hogs. I've seen it. Let's pack up and take the cattle and hogs there. We can squat on some good land and buy it when things get better. You've been workin' too hard at farmin' anyway. Raisin' stock ain't that much work."

Isaac's face brightened a little. "I guess we don't have much choice," he said. "We're lucky there's somewhere to go. At least we've got enough clothes and tools and stock to get us by for a few years. Maybe by then things will be better and I can collect what's owed me.''

In the spring of 1820, they loaded Isaac's big farm wagon, hitched two ox teams to it, and headed west. Candace rode in the wagon while Isaac walked beside the plodding oxen, goad in hand. On horseback, Ellis and two farm youths they'd hired drove the herd of about fifty beef cattle and more than twenty hogs. After a day or two of travel, the animals followed the wagon without trying to turn aside frequently. In a month of slow travel they reached the frontier town of Little Rock, where they rested a few days before continuing on to the southwest. Ellis was relieved to see that Isaac seemed excited about the move and was looking forward to raising cattle on the range.

In two more weeks they reached a little settlement of cabins, each with its own cornfield, where they stopped for a day. ''Are there more settlers beyond here?'' Ellis asked one of the men.

''Nope, leastwise not yet. This is kinda the end of the line,'' he replied.

''We're lookin' for a place where both cattle and hogs will do well,'' Ellis said. ''Any suggestions?''

'''Bout thirty mile on you come to Smackover Crick. It's real fine country, and ain't nobody nearer than us.''

They chose a spot near the creek but high enough to be safe if it overflowed. With the help of the two farm boys they built a cabin with a stone chimney and a loft. Then they built a corral, a smokehouse for curing ham and bacon, and a henhouse for the chickens Candace had brought in a crate on the wagon. The two farm lads returned to Tennessee. With the oxen, Ellis plowed ten acres of bottomland and planted corn, sweet potatoes, and a few rows of cotton.

Each morning they turned the cows out to graze, keeping the calves penned, knowing the cows would return at night. Before the calves nursed each evening, Candace got a little milk from each cow for making butter and cheese. To have something to trade or sell, Ellis and Isaac trained the four largest steers as oxen.

In mid-February 1821, Ellis carefully helped Candace into the wagon and headed for the nameless settlement they'd visited, where there were women who could help deliver her first child. There was no road to follow, only the tracks they'd made coming. Ellis watched Candace anxiously, fearful that the jolting wagon might cause her to give birth before they had help. He was greatly relieved when they reached the little settlement, and friendly women shooed him away and took charge. He wiped the sweat from his brow on his sleeve. Don't know what I'd done, he thought.

Ellis busied himself helping the men prepare fields for planting, grateful to have something to keep him occupied. Finally, on the morning of March 5, he was told that Candace was in labor, and he worked harder than usual that day. Late in the afternoon one of the women came out and called to him. "You have a fine son," she said. Candace named him Isaac.

Early in 1822, eight well-dressed horsemen with two pack mules rode up to the cabin from the east. Since it was late afternoon, Ellis invited them to make camp and gave them a ham from the smokehouse as an inducement. Starved for news of the rest of the country, he and Isaac visited with them while they ate.

"We're on the way to Texas for a look-see," the leader explained. He looked to be in his thirties, and from his appearance it was clear that he earned his living by using his brains, not his muscles. "Now that Mexico is independent and Stephen F. Austin is advertising for colonists, we figured we'd better see what the prospects are in Texas for making money in land."

"Mexico independent!" Ellis exclaimed. "We hadn't

heard that. Of course we don't get much news out here. When did it happen?''

"About a year ago an officer named Iturbide or something like that got together with some of the rebels. It took them the rest of the year to get all of the Spanish troops out of the country.''

"This Austin fellow you mentioned, who's he?'' Ellis wanted to know.

"His father went to San Antonio a couple of years ago and got what they call an *empresario* contract to bring three hundred families to Texas. He died and left the contract to his son Stephen. Everyone who goes gets a lot of free land; the *empresario* gets thirty or forty thousand acres for each one hundred families he brings. Mexico is real generous with its land, which I can't say for the U.S. Anyway, we want to check on its quality.''

"I was there once over twenty years ago,'' Ellis told him. "What I saw was damn fine land.''

When Ellis crawled into bed, Candace was already asleep. He lay on his back with both hands under his head, staring up in the dark. If he'd known Mexico would soon be independent, he'd have waited, but there'd been no way to foresee that. His thoughts went back to his days with Morelos and his moments with Magdalena, whom he'd earlier banished from his mind. That was all in the dimly remembered past, like it had been in a former life or had happened to someone else. He could look back on it now with detachment, like something he'd read about, not something that had happened to him.

Texas was another matter. He'd been promised a league of land—4,428 acres—for serving in the revolutionary army. He'd forgotten that, too; the rebel army had been defeated, so it hadn't been worth remembering. Now it came back to him, and he wondered if Mexico would make good on that promise. He thought of owning nearly forty-five hundred acres, and tried to figure just how long it would take to ride over them. Let's see, he thought, a section is six hundred forty acres, and that's a heap of land, a square mile. A league must be at least six sections. Imagine me owning all that. I'd be rich, at least in land.

When the horsemen rode on in the morning, Ellis and Isaac watched until they were out of sight. "Isaac," Ellis said, "I was promised a league of land, nearly forty-five hundred acres, for fighting in the revolution. Let's go to Texas and try to collect. If they won't give it to me, we can go on to Austin's colony and get land there."

"I like it fine here," Isaac replied, "but forty-five hundred acres!" He whistled. "Let's do it. But first you go back to White County this summer and collect what's owed me. I'd go but for my rheumatism. Times are better now, and they should be able to pay, though they probably won't admit it. Otherwise, I'll never see my money, and we can use all you can pry loose from them."

One morning that summer, Ellis kissed Candace goodbye and shook hands with Isaac, then rode off on his way to Tennessee. In his saddlebags was a letter from Isaac authorizing him to collect the debts. At Memphis he fell in with a distinguished-looking gentleman and his party, who were on their way to Columbia. His name, the man told him, was Sterling C. Robertson, and he lived in Nashville. Some of his friends had heard about a colony in Texas and were curious. Did Ellis know anything about it?

Ellis told him about his experiences in Texas and the Mexican Revolution. "I'm on my way to White County to collect some debts for my father-in-law," he added. "Then we're all headin' for Texas to get the land they promised me for serving in the revolutionary army. Tell your friends Texas is worth lookin' into for sure."

It took him three weeks to collect the money owned Isaac, but he refused to quit until he had it all, in cash, animals, guns, or tools. Then it took another week to sell or trade everything he didn't want to keep or couldn't take with him. By the time he left he had more than three hundred dollars in his saddlebags. Feeling satisfied with himself, he rode steadily, eager to get back and head for Texas.

When he finally reached the cabin and dismounted, Candace ran out to him. "What took you so long?" she asked, her voice trembling.

"Collecting the money was like pulling teeth. I came as fast I could. What's wrong?"

"It's Papa. He's so sick and I didn't know what do." The tears fell. Ellis put his arms around her and she pressed her head against his chest.

"I'm sorry," he mumbled, and hurried in to see Isaac, who lay on the bed staring at the ceiling. His face was gaunt, his breathing labored. He weakly held out his hand, and Ellis gently squeezed it.

"I'm glad you're back," Isaac said, his voice barely audible. "I didn't want to leave without saying goodbye. Did you have any luck?"

"It wasn't easy, but I got it all," Ellis assured him. The sense of satisfaction he'd felt had left him. Isaac half-smiled and closed his eyes. He didn't open them again. They buried him near the cabin, and Ellis rolled a big boulder from the creek for a headstone.

A few months later, in January 1823, Ellis hired two youths from the little settlement to herd the cattle and hogs, then loaded the wagon with all their possessions. Before he helped Candace and little Isaac into the wagon, they walked to the grave, and Ellis removed his battered hat. "Goodbye, old friend," he said. "I wish you could have come with us." Candace wept.

They traveled slowly south into Louisiana, and in February ferried the wagon and animals across the Red River at Natchitoches. "This is familiar country," Ellis told Candace as the oxen plodded on to Gaines Ferry at the Sabine. "I don't know why, but I'm as excited about getting back to Texas as I was comin' here with Nolan. And I was just a kid then."

They traveled on through the growing settlement at Ayish Bayou to Nacogdoches. Ellis pointed to the Old Stone Fort. "I was a prisoner there a long time ago," he told Candace. "That was after they killed Nolan."

"I wonder you wanted to come back here," she said.

Ellis found *alcalde* Luis Procela, a small, wrinkled old Tejano, in the cubbyhole that served as his office. "*Señor*," he said, rising to his feet, "what can I do for you?"

"I served under Morelos in the revolution," Ellis told him. "I was promised a league of land, and I've come to get it. What do I have to do?"

"All you need do is find some unclaimed land and have it surveyed. I'll send in your papers, and after they verify your service, your title will eventually get here. Things move slow—we're so far away they forget we exist, so it may take a year or two. But no one else can claim the land."

"Any suggestions where to look?" Ellis asked. Procela's wrinkled brow became all furrows.

"Almost anywhere to the south or west it's mostly unclaimed," he replied. "You might look out west toward the Neches, around Mound Prairie. No one has filed there, and the land is excellent. The Indians used to have cornfields there. People believe they built those mounds, but I wouldn't know about that." He gave Ellis directions. "It's under thirty miles," he added.

They saw the largest mound from several miles away across the prairie; it was oval-shaped and nearly thirty feet high. Nearby were two smaller mounds, and a mile and a half beyond them was the Neches. Lines of trees marked the courses of several streams that crossed the prairie to the river. Ellis was thrilled.

"What do you think, Candy? I only wish your father could have seen it. Look at the grass!"

She wrinkled her tiny nose. "Except for those little piles of dirt, it's kind of flat. Aren't there any mountains out here? I've never lived where I couldn't see mountains. It just doesn't seem right."

Ellis chuckled. "You'll get used to it, and those mounds will look bigger each year." He picked up Isaac, who stood beside Candace holding her hand, and they climbed the largest mound to gaze around. "Just look," Ellis said. "About as far as you can see will all be ours: In the morning I'll put the boys to cutting logs for the cabin, then go to town and arrange for a survey before someone beats us to it."

With little to do but watch his livestock grow and increase, Ellis often spent two or three days at a time in Nacogdoches, getting accustomed to the feeling of being a big land owner. He followed events in Mexico as best he could, questioning newcomers who arrived almost daily and reading the newspapers they brought, no matter how old. The *alcalde* received reports and occasionally newspapers from Mexico City that officials in San Antonio sent with a courier every month or two. Even though the reports were several months old by the time they reached Nacogdoches, Ellis welcomed them. Much of the news was about Emperor Agustín Iturbide. When Ellis first heard that Mexico had an emperor, he spat in disgust. Morelos and the other martyrs hadn't given their lives to take Mexico away from one king only to give it to another.

The news from Mexico made it clear that Iturbide wasn't likely to last long, and Ellis found some satisfaction in that. Iturbide had quarrelled with the congress, then ordered it to disperse and replaced it with a junta of his own. After squandering huge sums on the coronation, his government had no money left to pay its generals, and they turned their backs on Iturbide. Seizing this opportunity, a disgruntled officer named Antonio López de Santa Anna had led an uprising against the Emperor, who abdicated in the spring of 1823. Good riddance, Ellis thought, recalling that Iturbide had badly defeated Morelos at Valladolid.

The following August, everyone was relieved when Stephen F. Austin finally returned to his colony after a year in Mexico City getting his *empresario* contract reconfirmed. The contract his father had received, having been made before Mexican independence, was no longer valid. Iturbide's threadbare empire had passed a colonization law, but Austin was sure all imperial laws would be revoked, so he had to stay. Finally he appealed to the congress. Displaying its confidence in him, it reconfirmed his contract, then rescinded the imperial colonization law. The other men seeking *empresario* grants would have to wait until the republican government enacted its own law. The same month that Austin returned, Candace gave birth to Louiza Jane.

Ellis and other Americans were elated when the Mexican Republic adopted a federal constitution in the fall of 1824. It was largely the work of the liberal priest, Miguel Ramos Arizpe, who had been guided in part by the outline of the U.S. Constitution Austin gave him, in part by the Spanish Constitution of 1812. Ellis was even more delighted to learn that the election had placed his companions of revolutionary days in power. Guadalupe Victoria was President, Nicolás Bravo was Vice President, and Mier y Terán was Minister of War and Navy. "If I ever need a favor from the government," he told Candace, "I know where to go."

Early the following year, the *alcalde* announced that the congress had combined Coahuila and Texas into the State of Coahuila y Texas—neither had sufficient population to qualify as a state. The capital was at Saltillo, hundreds of miles away, but Texas would be governed from San Antonio by a *jefe político*, or political chief, José Antonio Saucedo.

The new Mexican constitution authorized the states to regulate immigration, except that no foreigners would be allowed to settle within thirty leagues of the border or coast. Coahuila y Texas adopted a state constitution in February 1825, and the state legislature quickly enacted a generous colonization law. Any family could acquire a league of grazing land and a *labor* (177 acres) of farm land, on its own or as a member of an *empresario* colony. *Empresarios* would receive five leagues and five *labores* for each one hundred families they introduced.

Immediately after the state colonization law was announced, a number of men hurried to Saltillo to apply for *empresario* grants. There was much talk about Austin and the others—*empresarios* were important men, colony builders who would soon own enormous tracts of land.

"I wish Papa was here," Candace said wistfully one day. "He'd have made a wonderful *empresario*." Ellis agreed, and that started him thinking. He'd felt rich owning nearly forty-five hundred acres of good land. If he were an *empresario*, what he had now would be a trifle, for he'd eventually own thousands upon thousands of acres, and men would speak of him in the same respectful tones they spoke of Austin. That thought made his head swim.

"With the friends I have in Mexico City," he remarked one day, "I don't see why I can't get an *empresario* contract." Candace stared at him in surprise, then frowned.

"Will you have to go there to get it?" she asked. He nodded.

"I'll go this summer," he said. She pursed her lips but made no reply.

Chapter Nine

Late that spring of 1825, Vidal Flores rode up to Ellis' ranch accompanied by a tall, bearded Anglo in a buckskin jacket and homespun pants. Vidal, a slender, handsome Tejano with a neatly trimmed mustache, had settled with his family on a nearby grant. Both riders were in their early thirties. Ellis, who was splitting pine logs for firewood, looked up when his hounds bayed.

"Here's a man who wants to talk to you," Vidal called in English as they dismounted. Ellis wiped the sweat from his forehead, then swung his axe with one hand so the blade stuck in a log. He appeared glad for an excuse to stop.

"I reckon you caught me doin' woman's work," he said, walking toward them. The Anglo in the buckskin jacket looked vaguely familiar, like someone he'd met years ago, but Ellis couldn't place him.

"I'm Micajah McPherson," the man said, extending his hand. "I'm hopin' you can tell me some news of Duncan."

"Micajah! You were just a little feller when Dunc and I left for Natchez." Ellis paused, his brow wrinkled. "Wish I had some news, but the last I knew Dunc was at Chihuahua, and that was about eighteen years ago. I heard they let all American prisoners leave in 1820. Maybe by then he'd got hitched and stayed put.'' He told them about his year in Acapulco and serving with Morelos.

Micajah gazed around at the corrals, and at the cattle and horses grazing in the distance. ''I like your place,'' he said. ''We're goin' to be neighbors, but Robert and William promised DeWitt they'd go to his colony, or they might have settled here too. Vidal and I are on the way to pick a spot for me right now.''

''How'd you two come to know each other?'' Ellis asked.

''We were both with Gutiérrez in '12. I knew from Lt. Pike's report that Nolan's men were in Chihuahua, and I had a silly notion that maybe I could rescue Dunc, so I joined the Gutiérrez-Magee army in the Neutral Ground. Damn near cost me my life; it would have but for Vidal.''

Candace came out of the cabin to see who the visitors were, and Ellis introduced her. After she returned to the cabin, he said, ''I'm headin' for Mexico City in a few weeks, and on the way I aim to visit Martín de León and Gutiérrez. Maybe one of them will know something about Duncan.'' He followed them a short distance after they'd mounted. ''I've got a wife in Mexico,'' he said. ''When the revolution died down I figured I'd never be able to go there again, so I hooked up with Candace. Now I'm goin' after a commission in the army and an *empresario* contract.''

''Good luck,'' Micajah said. ''I hope you get both.''

Early in June Ellis kissed the solemn-faced Candace, who held Louiza Jane in her arms, then chucked his daughter under the chin and patted the wistful Isaac on the head. ''I can't say how long it will take,'' he told Candace. ''They take their sweet time, and if you try to hurry them they sit on their hands. But I'll be back with the bacon one day. You can count on that.''

Candace brushed away a strand of blonde hair that had fallen across her face. ''Don't be any longer than you need to,'' she said, her lips quivering. ''It'll be hard on us bein' alone here.''

"Micajah and Vidal both said to call on them any time you need help," he replied. "And they'll check on you regular." Picking up the lead rope of his pack mule, he mounted his mustang cowpony. "Wish me luck," he said, and rode south, dragging the reluctant mule. A hundred yards away he turned and waved, then rode on without looking back again. Candace waved weakly, then her arm fell limply against her side.

Ellis rode among the scattered cabins at San Felipe hoping to see Stephen F. Austin, but the *empresario* was in San Antonio. When the *alcalde* learned that Ellis was on the way to Mexico City, he asked him for a favor. "While you're takin' care of your business," he said, "try to get the government to give Dr. Long's widow a pension. Long tried to free Texas, so it's kind of like he fought for the revolution."

"I've heard him called a filibuster," Ellis replied, "but I'll do what I can for her." He knew that Dr. Long had led an expedition to Texas about the time Mexico became independent, but had been captured at La Bahía and taken to Mexico City. Right after he was released someone killed him.

Ellis rode on to Victoria, the capital of Martín de León's colony, which had been settled mainly by families from Mexico. He found the affable León and introduced himself. "I was a colonel under Morelos," he said, "and for that they gave me a league near Nacogdoches. I have a wife in Jalapa, if she's still living, and I'm on my way to Mexico City to get my rank back and apply for an *empresario* contract. I figured you could give me some advice on how to go about it."

León took off his straw hat and scratched his head. "Just say you're a citizen with a Mexican wife and that you've established residence in Texas. Serving under Morelos should help, for some of his officers are in the government. They can't give you a contract—you have to apply to Saltillo for that—but their support will certainly do you no harm. By the way, how long have you been in Texas?"

Ellis gazed off in the distance as his mind roamed back over the years. "I first came here with Philip Nolan in 1800. After troops killed him, they held us at Nacogdoches and San Antonio for about six months. I came back a couple of years ago to claim my league."

"You were with Nolan? That's odd. One of my colonists was with him. You probably know him, name of McPherson."

Ellis laughed. "Duncan McPherson? You bet I know him. We left Tennessee together. I lost touch with him when they took me to Acapulco. His brothers are in Texas now. Where can I find him?"

León pointed the way to Duncan's *hacienda*; Ellis thanked him for his advice and rode there. He saw a fairly large adobe house and several small ones; beyond them were a stable, sheds, and two round pole corrals. He spotted a tall man in Mexican clothes and a high-peaked *sombrero* standing outside one of the corrals, his hands on the top rail and a booted foot on the bottom one. Ellis had to look twice to be sure the man was Duncan. Inside the corral two *vaqueros* with rawhide riatas were holding a struggling mustang. In the other corral were a few fine-looking Spanish horses.

Ellis rode up behind Duncan and dismounted. "Hey, Duncan!" he called. "Look who's here!"

Duncan turned and stared at him in amazement. His jaw dropped and a corn husk cigarette fell from his mouth. "Ellis! Is it really you?" They shook hands fiercely, both grinning with delight.

"You look like a real *hacendado* for sure," Ellis said, staring at Duncan's Mexican jacket and hat. "With your own *vaqueros* and everything."

"Come meet Antonia," Duncan said. "She's the reason for it." Ellis saw at once that she, like Magdalena, had the poise and dignity of the *hacendado* class. He noticed that she limped slightly as she came to greet him, but that didn't detract from her impressive appearance.

"My husband has mentioned you often," she told him in her musical voice. "He kept hoping you were alive and that he'd see you again. You two must have a good talk."

Ellis stayed a day, and they had their talk. He told Duncan his brothers were also in Texas and hoping to find him. Then he related what had happened in the years after he was taken to Acapulco. When he finished recounting his experiences while serving under Morelos, Duncan smiled sheepishly.

"While you fought for the rebels, I was on the other side," he admitted. "Joining the royalist cavalry was the only way I could get out of Chihuahua, and there were no rebels in the north I could join. But at the first opportunity I cut loose, and Antonia's folks sheltered me. That good deed cost them a daughter, for I couldn't help falling hard for her." He hugged Antonia and kissed her forehead, while she pretended to push him away and modestly turned her head.

"It ain't hard to see why," Ellis said.

Duncan released Antonia. "When we came here, her father let some of his *peón* families come with us," he continued, "and he set us up with cattle, sheep, and a few good Spanish horses. Because of the families, we qualified for four leagues and four *labores*." Ellis whistled.

"That's more than sixteen thousand acres." he said. "When they gave me one league I thought I was king of the mountain."

Ellis rode on the next morning. His league of land, which had seemed half as big as Tennessee and made him feel rich, now seemed small potatoes. Once he got an *empresario* contract and settled several hundred families on it, he'd own land beyond measure. The thought of it gave him gooseflesh.

He swam his horse and mule across the Rio Grande and continued on to the village of San Carlos in Nuevo Santander, which was now the Mexican state of Tamaulipas. He'd heard that Gutiérrez was commander general of what used to be the Eastern Interior Provinces, and expected to find him comfortably situated at last. San Carlos was a village of small adobe huts along a wide and dusty street. The only sign of life Ellis saw at first was a pack of scrawny curs snarling and snapping over a bitch in heat. San Carlos appeared anything but prosperous.

He found Gutiérrez at the barracks, his uniform hanging loosely on his once-bulky body. He can't be eating well, Ellis thought as they exchanged *abrazos*. He glanced around at the soldiers lounging in the shade. Their uniforms were shabby, and both they and their horses looked underfed.

"My pony and mule are kind of worn down," Ellis told Gutiérrez. "I was hopin' to swap them with you and maybe borrow a little *dinero*, but it don't look like you can spare either."

Gutiérrez shook his head slowly and pulled his empty pants pockets inside out. "You're right," he morosely admitted. "We haven't been paid for months, and we're barely hanging on. You know I'd help you if I could, but I can't even help my own family. I think the government has forgotten us."

Ellis decided it was useless even to ask Gutiérrez for a letter supporting his request for an *empresario* contract—it would probably embarrass him to have to confess that he didn't even have a sheet of paper. He cursed himself for not having followed the Camino Real through San Antonio and Laredo on down between the mountain ranges to the Valley of Mexico. He hadn't gotten what he'd come for, and now he had to cross the Sierra Madre Oriental, which would be hard on his animals and delay his getting to Mexico City.

He rode slowly south, then crossed the mountain range, which made it necessary to rest his horse and mule for a week. The only food he ate were the *tortillas* and *frijoles* that kind-hearted poor families shared with him. It was mid-October when he finally gazed down on Mexico City in the valley below. In the distance snow-capped Popocatépetl gleamed in the sun, and Ellis recalled that the first time he'd seen it he'd been in chains. His hopes rose as he rode past the Indian villages that surrounded the city. A little more time, he thought, and my day will surely come. He rode on through the city's gate to an establishment that dealt in horses and mules, and sold both animals and their saddles for the little that was offered. At least he'd have money for food and lodging for a week or two if he was frugal. Once he'd gotten what he came for, he could buy a good horse.

He shouldered his blanket roll and trudged toward the National Palace, where the government met, arriving in the area as the sun neared the mountaintops. Street vendors, mostly Indians, were offering fruits, *tortillas*, maize cakes, and roast ducks, their voices mingled and their cries almost unintelligible. Although the delicious aroma of the roast ducks almost overcame his determination to make his pittance last as long as necessary, Ellis bought only maize cakes, bananas, and a cup of *pulque*. He'd learned to like the nourishing drink of fermented maguey juice, which was the favorite of all classes in the city. The first time he'd tasted it he'd wrinkled his nose at the odor, but after a few sips he liked it. Now it warmed his stomach and made him feel almost contented. Then he entered a cheap inn and was ushered into a large room where fifteen or twenty others were preparing to sleep on mats on the dirty floor.

Ellis awoke at dawn to the shouts of the street vendors. The first was the *carbonero*, who sold charcoal, and whose cry, "*Carbón, señor?*" sounded like one unintelligible word. He was soon followed by a multitude of others hawking butter, salt beef, fruit, hot cakes, and *dulces*. Ellis arose, yawning and stretching his sore muscles. Leaving his blankets with a servant, he went to the street and bought a hot cake and fruit.

In mid-morning Ellis brushed bits of mud off his frayed buckskin jacket and ran his fingers through his shaggy hair.

Not much improvement, he thought, but there was nothing else he could do. He entered the National Palace, past guards who eyed him suspiciously but didn't challenge him, probably because he was an Americano, Ellis suspected. Then he walked the halls until he found the President's office. When he told the surprised male secretaries he wanted to see the President, they looked down their noses at him and asked him to wait outside. After several hours passed, he realized they had no intention of letting one so shabbily dressed in to see Guadalupe Victoria, so he gave up and hunted for the office of Mier y Terán, Minister of War and Navy. There the same thing happened.

Cursing under his breath, Ellis continued to prowl the halls, hoping for a chance meeting with either man. Several days later, when he was becoming discouraged and desperate, he saw a Captain López, now a colonel, who'd served under Mier at Tehuacán, and hailed him. López frowned when he saw the shabby figure, no doubt thinking that a *lépero* had accosted him for a handout. Then he recognized Ellis.

"Elias!" he exclaimed. "What brings you here?"

"I'm tryin' to see General Mier and get a commission in the army," he replied. "Dressed like this I can't get near him, but I have no money for clothes."

"Let me tell him you're here," López said, and left.

A few moments later the aristocratic Mier strode into the hall and gave Ellis an *abrazo*. "Come with me," he said, taking Ellis by the arm and leading him into his spacious office. As they passed the wide-eyed male secretaries, Mier said, "When *Señor* Beans wants to see me, show him in. We were comrades in arms under Morelos." Ellis felt like he'd just dreamed the world had come to an end and then awakened to find it alive and well.

Ellis related what had happened after he left Mier at Tehuacán, his marriage to Magdalena, his narrow escape from royalist cavalry, his months with Gutiérrez in the Neutral Ground, and his move to Texas. He made no mention of Candace. "I'm hoping you can give me the rank I held under Morelos," he concluded. "Then I aim to apply for an *empresario* grant."

The dignified Mier sat with both elbows on his polished desk, his hands touching at the fingertips while he gazed at Ellis. "Magdalena inherited her uncle's *hacienda*, Las Banderillas," he said. "I know she'll be delighted to see you." Then he changed the subject. "For your services to the revolution, Mexico is in your debt. You shall be a colonel again, and there's no reason you shouldn't also be an *empresario*. And while you're in the city, my house is your house." He called in a secretary, who stood stiffly with hands by his sides while Mier wrote a note and gave it to him. The young man left but soon returned and handed Mier an envelope, while Ellis wondered what was going on. Mier glanced at the envelope's contents, then held it out to Ellis.

"Here's a hundred *pesos*," he said. "Consider it a small token of Mexico's gratitude, and buy yourself suitable clothes. In the meantime, I'll start the process for getting your commission. Like everything else here, it will take at least a month. When that's taken care of, I know you're eager to get to Jalapa. But I intend to appoint you Indian agent for Texas, so you will need to return here by early March."

It was mid-December before Ellis was able to leave for Jalapa in the new uniform of a colonel. The coach set out before sunrise, but it made slow progress through the city gate. Entering the city were throngs of Indian men and women bent under enormous loads. Even burdened as they were, the men managed to doff their straw hats and show their white teeth to the passengers. Ellis watched them, marveling at their strength and their good nature; they seemed to have a cheerful smile for everyone. Also entering the city were long trains of pack mules following belled mares, small herds of steers, and flocks of bleating sheep.

The rough road crossed the fertile plains to the hills, where the vegetation changed as the elevation increased. The coach met or overtook pack trains and parties of horsemen. Despite the jolting ride, Ellis thought of seeing Magdalena at last, and smiled. As the coach ascended the mountains amid huge boulders and stunted firs, his mind roamed to the new uniform he wore and the application for an *empresario* contract he'd send to the governor of Coahuila y Texas on his return to Mexico City. Eager though he was to see Magdalena, he couldn't help thinking about becoming an *empresario* and owning many thousands of acres of Texas land. If it weren't for that, he thought, I'd be tempted to stay in Jalapa. Then he remembered Isaac Midkiff and his own promise not to abandon Candace. Anyway, I'm in the army, and Mier's sending me to Texas. I have no choice but to go.

After frequent changes of teams and jolting along for nearly a week, the coach stopped at Las Banderillas, a few miles from Jalapa. Ellis took his blanket roll, said *adios* to the other passengers, and stiffly alit. He gazed at the large stone house that was covered with vines and roses and surrounded by gardens. Beyond the house Ellis saw endless cultivated fields. All of it appeared to be well-managed.

Heart pounding, Ellis shouldered his blanket roll, walked as fast as his sore muscles permitted to the *hacienda* gate, and looked over it. He was thrilled to see Magdalena in the garden picking roses. She wore a white muslin dress and white satin slippers, reminding him of how she'd appeared in his awful dream. Hearing the heavy gate creaking on its hinges, she looked up and recognized Ellis. With a little cry of surprise mingled with joy, she dropped her flowers and hurried to him. He threw down his blanket roll and ran to embrace her. She was as lovely as he remembered her, only plumper.

For several days they talked from morning till night. Ellis told her about his months in the Neutral Ground, when he hoped to take part in an invasion of Texas, and his disappointment at missing Mina's expedition. He told her, too, of his appointment as Indian agent for Texas, and of his grand hope of becoming an *empresario* and owning a vast tract of land. She told him of her fears for him, not knowing if he'd escaped, and of her daily prayers for his safety.

Eager for everyone to see the husband she'd often talked about, Magdalena proudly took him on daily carriage rides around Jalapa, while one of her men drove the team. On every side were a multitude of flowers of many shapes and colors; roses grew so profusely on walls and along the streets, they faintly perfumed the air. A great variety of fruit trees flourished, many that Ellis didn't recognize. In the distance the snow-capped dome of Orizaba rose above a wreath of clouds like the peak of a white *sombrero*. Jalapa was, Ellis realized, a land of perpetual spring, where life was eternally delightful.

As the weeks passed, nevertheless, the inactivity made Ellis increasingly restless and eager to pursue his *empresario* grant. He would send off his application as soon as he returned to Mexico City to give the governor ample time to arrange it before Ellis reached Saltillo. That, he thought, might spare him from a month of waiting for the governor and his staff to get around to approving it.

"At least this is better than the first time we parted," Ellis told Magdalena as he prepared to board a coach. "There aren't any royalists trying to shoot me." He kissed her as she fought back tears. "I'll come see you as often as I can," he promised.

"Go with God," she huskily replied.

In Mexico City, Ellis met John Dunn Hunter, a white man who'd grown up among the Cherokees. Because of his prowess, they'd named him Hunter. When he was about eighteen—he didn't know when he'd been born, he said—he went to live in Missouri with a man named John Dunn, and had added his name to his Cherokee name. He'd had to relearn English, for he'd completely forgotten it. After living among the whites for ten years and writing a book about his life as an Indian, he'd gone to live again with the Cherokees who had settled in Texas. Mixed-blood chief Richard Fields had sent him to obtain a title to the lands in East Texas that had been promised the Cherokees when Fields was in Mexico City several years earlier.

Although Hunter was white by birth, his mannerisms reminded Ellis of the Cherokees he'd met in Nacogdoches. Since Ellis was to be Indian agent for Texas, he knew that Hunter could be of great help in getting on friendly terms with Fields and war chief Bowles, and perhaps the chieftains of other immigrant tribes like the Delawares, Shawnees, and Kickapoos.

"Mexican officials promised Fields they would set aside land for us," Hunter told Ellis. "They haven't done so, and now they're letting Americans settle in East Texas. We and the other tribes went to Texas to get away from Americans; if they keep coming, it will be the same story—sooner or later they'll force us to move again. We must have a title to protect our homes—it's either that or fight for them. The Cherokees are growing desperate; the officials Fields talked to when he was here are gone, and the new ones claim they know nothing about the agreement. If they refuse to give us a title, it won't take much to put the Cherokees into a mood for lifting scalps."

Ellis respected and admired Hunter, and the prospect of the Indian war he indicated was frightening. There were at least one thousand warriors among the immigrant tribes, and most had guns and knew how to use them. All had compelling reasons for resenting and distrusting whites, and as Indian agent, he'd be in the middle of any trouble. His assignment promised to be dangerous as well as difficult. He hoped that Mexican officials had the good sense to realize that the Cherokees' request wasn't one to be ignored or even delayed. They must send Hunter home with title in hand.

In early July, Ellis learned that the legislature of Coahuila y Texas was considering a bill to free all slaves in the state. Since there were none in Coahuila, or elsewhere in Mexico, for that matter, the proposed law was aimed at Texas planters. Ellis mentioned it to Guadalupe Victoria and asked for advice, for without slaves no cotton could be grown, and it was the only cash crop. The tall, lean old warrior, who'd been a lawyer before he joined Morelos, astutely suggested a way to get around the law. After his talk with Guadalupe Victoria, Ellis wrote Stephen F. Austin.

"I have not the honor of being acquainted with you." he began, "but I think it my duty to inform you as a friend that I heard about the proposed law in Saltillo that all slaves in Texas will be set free. I spoke to the President, as he is an old friend of mine, and he believes it will pass. But there is a way your settlers can get around it. That is to go in person to an *alcalde* and state how much each slave cost, and that when he repays it by labor there will be no charge against him. Say that he discounts it at so much a month, like pay for any hired hand. Then it will be the same as before, and will no more be noticed. Communicate this also to the men of Ayish Bayou, so they can take the same measure with their slaves. Do it as quickly as possible, before the law goes into effect, for then it may be too late.

"I have nothing else worth your attention. Please inform the widow Long that it is impossible for this government to allow her any pension, for her husband was not known as a general here, nor had he any commission from this government."

Ellis finally left Mexico City on July 21, heading up the Camino Real to Saltillo, itching to have his *empresario* contract in hand. He arrived in September, and met both the Baron of Bastrop, who represented Texas in the state legislature, and John B. Austin, the *empresario's* brother. They spoke of the grant Ellis had applied for, which was in the twenty-league border reserve between the Sabine and Nacogdoches, where it would be easy to attract families who came to Texas on their own. He should have an easy time fulfilling his contract there, they said, without the expense of advertising in newspapers. Aware that Ellis had served under Morelos, they were certain the contract was as good as his. Elated by their confidence, Ellis failed to notice the governor's excessive politeness while being quite vague, almost evasive, about when the contract might be confirmed. Instead of becoming suspicious, Ellis felt it was safe to go on to Texas without waiting for the governor to deliver the grant.

What Ellis didn't know was that listing Magdalena as his wife, rather than clearing the way for his contract, had raised serious obstacles. One of the officials in Saltillo who saw his application had been in Nacogdoches, and he felt sure that Ellis had a family there. About the time Ellis set out from Mexico City, the governor had instructed the political chief in San Antonio to investigate Ellis' marital status. Political Chief Saucedo then requested Austin to conduct an inquiry and to report the result.

In early August, while Ellis rode blissfully up the Camino Real, a man named Martin Allen testified in San Felipe. He'd known Ellis in Arkansas Territory and in the Nacogdoches district, he said. Ellis had a wife when he first saw him in Arkansas; he thought they had been married in Tennessee. The universal belief, he said, was that they were legally married. Ellis' father-in-law, Isaac Midkiff, was well known and had the character of a respectable and honorable man. Allen doubted that he would have permitted Bean to live with his daughter unless they were legally married. "This deponent thinks Bean to be an honest man," Allen concluded. "He is fond of boasting and telling large stories about his exploits in the Mexican revolution, and said he was a colonel in the army."

Candace meanwhile had been called before the *alcalde* of the Neches district. She feared that Ellis must be dead, and in that case, she wouldn't inherit his property if she admitted being his common law wife. "I was married to Ellis P. Bean in White County, State of Tennessee," she declared, "and I have two children by the aforesaid Bean. Their names are Isaac T. Bean, born in Arkansas Territory on March 5, 1821, and Louiza Jane, born on August 15, 1823, in the Province of Texas."

Ellis Bean whistled happily as he rode into San Antonio early in December. At forty-three he felt satisfied with the world and with his place in it, for he was not only a colonel in the Mexican army, but Indian agent for Texas. In Saltillo his application for an *empresario* contract seemed certain to be approved; his friends from revolutionary days were in power in Mexico City, and he swelled with pride at the thought of becoming another Stephen F. Austin. He wouldn't have felt so contented if he'd known that claiming Magdalena as his wife had ruined his chances of becoming an *empresario*. *Empresarios* were expected to lead exemplary lives. Bigamists failed to qualify.

In San Antonio Ellis learned that in November, Benjamin, the brother of *empresario* Haden Edwards had ridden into Nacogdoches with a party of followers and ousted *Alcalde* Samuel Norris, who had used his office to block Haden Edwards in ways that weren't legal. Knowing nothing about the Edwards colony, which had been established during his absence, Ellis was unconcerned. "I'll bet twenty-five *pesos* the *alcalde* won't be kept out of office for long or hindered in his work," he said to Saucedo. The political chief shook his head.

"Haden Edwards had a contract to bring eight hundred families to his grant around Nacogdoches," he said. "It took him three years and cost him much money to get it, and he wanted only wealthy colonists. But many poor families have lived there for several generations, and their rights had to be respected. Edwards ordered all who claimed land within his grant to produce titles. If they didn't, he threatened to sell their property. The old families naturally resented having a foreigner dispossess them just because their titles were never completed through no fault of their own." He paused.

"Edwards had no right to demand their titles or to sell any land at all," Saucedo added grimly. "I explained this to him and ordered him to desist, but complaints against him made it clear that he ignored my orders." Ellis looked shocked, for he knew that the other *empresarios*—Austin, León, and DeWitt—had been careful to follow instructions and obey Mexican laws.

"The Edwards brothers have shown only contempt for Mexican officials, even the governor," Saucedo continued. "From their actions I suspected they planned to secede one day, and I warned the governor. He has canceled their contract and ordered them expelled, but we have no troops in Nacogdoches to expel them. If you were there, what would you do about that? They're your former countrymen."

Ellis tugged at his earlobe as he pondered the question. "I'm a Mexican officer," he replied, "and I know my duty. I'd hate to have to fight Americans, but if they're in the wrong I'll do it." Saucedo stared at him, wondering what he'd do if he thought they were in the right. He left the question unasked, but he doubted the loyalty of all Anglos, except, perhaps, Austin and maybe DeWitt.

"It won't be necessary for you to expel them," he told Ellis. "In a few days Colonel Ahumada will march there with his troops, and I plan to accompany him." Ellis left immediately for San Felipe to talk to Austin.

When he reached the little village, he was shocked to learn that in mid-December a party of Edwards men had seized the Old Stone Fort, proclaimed the Republic of Fredonia, and ordered all Anglos to join them. He also learned that Hunter had returned from Mexico City without the promised land title, and the Cherokees were furious. The government would give them land as individual colonists, but not as a tribe.

Now aware that the situation in Nacogdoches was far more serious than he'd imagined possible, Ellis asked Austin for some of his militiamen and set out immediately with thirty-five of them. A few miles from Nacogdoches they met a grizzled frontiersman in greasy buckskins, who stopped his mustang pony.

"What's goin' on in town?" Ellis asked, wondering if he was an Edwards man. The rider frowned.

"Damned lot of foolishness, if you ask me," he replied. "Some Edwards men are holed up in the old fort, and right now they're dickerin' with the Injuns to get their support. They're offerin' to divide Texas into Injun and white territories along the Nacogdoches–San Antonio road." He squirted a stream of tobacco juice out of the corner of his mouth. "A lot of folks figger the Injuns would as leave lift white sculps as Meskin, and most are gettin' ready to head for the Sabine if they ain't done so already."

"Can't say I blame 'em for leaving," Ellis said. "There's at least a thousand bucks in the area and none of them have any reason to like Americans. How many Fredonians are there in town?"

"At first there were about two hundred, but they forced some of them to go with 'em, and those men left at the first opportunity. They're sure every American in Texas will gladly join them, but it seems folks around here don't cotton to that. Most are dead set agin 'em."

"Same with Austin and his people," Ellis said. "They're goin' to join the troops when they march this way." He glanced at his thirty-five men and shook his head. "If there's as many as you figure, we'd better find us some reinforcements before we go after 'em."

Knowing that if the Indians supported the Fredonians, whites would be killed or driven from East Texas, Ellis sent a man with messages for Fields and Hunter, who were both in Nacogdoches. He urged them not to get involved with the Fredonians, for that could lead to serious trouble for their people. While waiting for a reply, he penned a note to warn Austin. On the spur of the moment, he decided it sounded better to reverse his given names.

"There is one express rider going to your colony to make it rise up in arms, and today another will start," he wrote. "I hope you will keep a good lookout, for those villains count on you and your men. But I know you have more knowledge of things than to be led astray to save men from their crimes. They find themselves lost and will swim against the stream as long as they can. I have divided them so that I now have seventy men coming from Ayish Bayou to attack those that are in Nacogdoches. I have as yet no reply from Fields, but am waiting hourly for an answer. If I succeed in breaking him off, then the fire is out instantly, and I have little doubt but that I shall succeed. Watch out, for they are trying to seduce your colony. Your most sincere friend, Pedro Ellis Bean."

He anxiously sent another message, this time to war chief Bowles at the Cherokee village northwest of Nacogdoches. "If you try to set up an Indian state," he warned, "both the U. S. and Mexico will feel threatened, and they won't stop until they destroy it. This alliance could be the ruin of your people."

Soon after Ellis had reached the outskirts of Nacogdoches, he met Micajah. "We had a report from Mexico that you were dead," he told Ellis. "You were gone so long everyone was sure it was true. I believed it, and Candace believed it. Three days before we heard you were coming, she married

166

Martin Parmer. He left as soon as he knew she wasn't a widow after all.''

Ellis' face turned white, then red. "Parmer? I don't know him," he growled.

"He's one of the main Fredonian leaders," Micajah told him, "and he's one tough customer. Calls himself a ring-tailed panther, and I'd say that's about right. I'd hate to tangle with him, at close range, anyway.''

Ellis was mumbling, "damned faithless woman," when Micajah stopped him.

"Think about it, my friend. You've been with your other wife, and you knew you weren't a widower. Candace thought she was a widow, on her own with two small children. She did only what she had to do. I say forgive her and put the whole thing out of your mind.'' But Ellis continued muttering to himself.

He left Micajah and grimly rode to his ranch, where a pale-faced Candace greeted him apprehensively.

"I know all about it," he growled. "I suppose his pecker is a lot bigger than mine," he added, his face turning red. "Made you wish I really was dead, didn't it?''

Candace brushed the tears from her cheeks. "I was so lonely and desperate," she sobbed. "I thought you'd de-cided to stay with your Mexican wife, then a man who'd been in Mexico said you had died. The children and I were having such a hard time. How could we go on without a man?''

She looked so sad and contrite Ellis was touched. You're being an ass about this, he told himself. What she says is true and you know it. But try as hard as he might to forget and forgive, the thought of burly Martin Parmer in his bed enjoy-ing the doll-like Candace couldn't be banished from his mind.

Chapter Ten

The Fredonian revolt gave Ellis no time to brood over domestic affairs, for if an Indian war came, they might all be killed. A few days later, he wrote Austin concerning a letter he'd received from Elisha Roberts of Ayish Bayou. All of the men of the district, Roberts said, had planned to help put down the Fredonians until they learned that the Indians had joined them. Being so badly outnumbered by the Indians, married men of Ayish Bayou had taken their families across the Sabine.

"I wrote again to Richard Fields and Dr. Hunter," Ellis added. "Fields finally sent word it was too late. If he'd seen me a month sooner, he said, perhaps we might have come to terms. That is all the satisfaction he gave me."

In another letter, Ellis told Austin what he'd learned about the meeting of Indians and Fredonians in Nacogdoches. A man who attended it said that Hunter "pictured in strong and glowing language the gloomy alternative of abandoning their present abodes and returning within the limits of the United States or preparing to defend themselves against the whole power of the Mexican government by force of arms."

Chief Fields spoke next. He told of traveling to Mexico City to beg some land on which to settle his poor, orphan tribe. He stayed there a year, he said, and was promised the land. He returned and waited, but nothing was done. Recently he sold his cattle to raise money to send John Dunn Hunter to Mexico. "They said they knew nothing of this Richard Fields and treated him with contempt," he added. "I am a Red man, and a man of honor, and I can't be imposed on this way. We will lift our tomahawks and fight for land with all those friendly tribes that wish land. If I am beaten I will resign to my fate, and if not, I will hold our lands by the force of my red warriors."

"So, my dear sir," Ellis added, "the only way to stop this is to come forward and give them lands, or the country will be entirely lost. If we can break off the Indians, the thing is settled. Hurry Saucedo here and let him know what I write you."

Ellis also enclosed a certificate and asked Austin to translate it into Spanish. In it Candace, under oath before an *alcalde*, declared that she had claimed she was married to Ellis "to save the property of Ellis Peter Bean in her hands as she supposed that he would never return." When asked, "Were you ever lawfully married to Ellis Peter Bean?" she answered, "She never was." Ellis had insisted on her testifying because on her marriage to Parmer, her property became his. Ellis had learned about the inquiry into his marital status, and he hoped that the certificate would also revive his chances of becoming an *empresario*.

Greatly concerned over the threat of a devastating Indian war, Ellis continued to send men with conciliatory messages to the chiefs of the Shawnees, Delawares, Kickapoos, and Sacs, as well as the Cherokees. His warnings convinced war chief Bowles that it would be folly to join the Fredonians, and only thirty young Cherokee warriors joined the Edwards men. Perhaps on Bowles' orders, the Cherokees killed both Fields and Hunter for trying to involve them in a war with Mexico. The Kickapoos and other tribes hated and distrusted Americans too much to consider cooperating with the Fredonians, even though they were irate at Mexico for denying them land. But Ellis had no way of knowing this immediately.

On January 4, 1827, Ellis wrote again to inform Austin that he'd entered Nacogdoches "and found out those rascals were leaving. At this time there is only a guard of twelve men in the stone house. Hurry the troops on as fast as possible, for now is our time, before the Indians gather. I learned today that the Indians are divided, and it appears they won't be here very soon, but the troops must hurry all they can. Let the commander know the contents of my letter. Your friend and servant, Pedro Ellis Bean."

Saucedo, Colonel Ahumada, and the troops had been delayed in San Felipe for three weeks because of heavy rains that made the road a quagmire. Saucedo wrote Edwards that he was coming to Nacogdoches for the purpose of restoring order and hearing complaints against local officials. Although Edwards' contract had been canceled, he added, his colonists wouldn't be molested, and all who had taken part in the revolt would be pardoned if they laid down their arms. He sent this conciliatory letter to Ellis to deliver. Ellis added a note of his own.

"It is not too late," he wrote, "and we are able to forget past mistakes. You can gain much more by conciliation than by hostility." Edwards, who regarded any compromise as unmanly, spurned the offer.

At the same time Saucedo wrote Edwards, Austin wrote to Burril Thompson, a friend from Missouri who had settled on Edwards' grant. He again urged the Fredonians to meet with the political chief and respectfully explain their grievances against Norris and the others. Austin knew that Edwards had legitimate reasons for complaint, but his attitude and approach were wrong. He warned Thompson that two hundred troops were coming, and that two hundred fifty of his colonists were with them. "I am a Mexican officer," he concluded, "and I will sacrifice my life before I will fail in my duty or violate my oath of office."

After recruiting a force of seventy men, Ellis rode into Nacogdoches, and grimly searched for Parmer. He failed to find him, for the Fredonians were safely across the Sabine. When the troops and militia finally arrived, Nacogdoches was quiet. Colonel Ahumada and Saucedo both praised Ellis warmly for his success in restoring order. If Saucedo felt a little guilty about his earlier doubts, he discreetly refrained from revealing them. With the senseless revolt over, he issued a general amnesty proclamation, excluding only Parmer, who had been president of Fredonia. He also removed Norris from office, for his illegal acts had helped bring on the crisis. The outcome of the Fredonian affair revived state officials' confidence in the loyalty of the settlers, but to some in Mexico City the uprising was what they had expected, and they remained apprehensive about the rapidly growing numbers of Anglos in East Texas.

No matter what he was doing, Ellis couldn't keep his thoughts from returning to Parmer. "Just because I had business in Mexico was no excuse for you whoring with that man," he flung at Candace.

"You were gone so long," the diminutive Candace tearfully replied, "everyone said you were dead. I meant nothing wrong, and I couldn't be sorrier. He was here only two days. Why can't you forget about it?"

Ellis thought of Micajah's advice, and knew what he'd said was true. All widows, especially those with young children, needed to marry a man who would protect them and see to it they didn't go hungry. What kept him feeling tortured was the thought that his manhood had been exposed as inferior, and for that he'd like to kill Parmer. His injured pride was like a livid brand on his forehead for all to see, and that he could never forget.

In late January 1827, about the time it was clear that the

Fredonian revolt wouldn't erupt into an Indian war, Ellis received a letter from nephew Edmund Bean of Nashville. Times were hard and money scarce in Tennessee, he wrote, and he wanted to bring his family to Texas. What made him hesitate was that the papers were full of rumors of warfare between American settlers and Mexico. He asked about his prospects for acquiring land in Texas, and he wanted especially to know if Ellis expected war. Apparently aware that Ellis and Candace weren't legally married, he concluded by discreetly asking about Aunt Candace Midcalf. Spelling wasn't a Bean family attribute.

Ellis replied that Edmund could acquire a league (4,428 acres) of grazing land and a *labor* (177 acres) of farmland by paying fees that amounted to the modest sum of about two hundred dollars. American settlers had been well treated, he said, and most were content to live under Mexican rule. Except for the misguided Edwards and his men, who brought on their own troubles by scorning Mexican authority, there had been no friction between the Texians and Mexico. The vast majority of the settlers had opposed the Fredonians. Unless conditions changed drastically, he said, he foresaw no likelihood of conflict. "Mexico has been generous to them in every way, and they know it. As for me, after so many years in Mexico I'm as much Mexican as American. Your Aunt Candace is well," he concluded.

Before Saucedo and Ahumada returned to San Antonio, Ellis accompanied the colonel on a tour of the border area. They counted 168 families that had settled illegally in the twenty-league (about sixty miles) border reserve, where aliens were banned. Some families lived a hand-to-mouth existence in one-room cabins with dirt floors, but many had well-cultivated, prosperous plantations and comfortable houses. They saw a surprising number of cotton gins and grist mills, as well as wagon roads. Greatly impressed by the settlers' industry, and aware that they had opposed the

Fredonians, Ahumada promised to recommend that a commissioner be sent to grant them titles to the lands they'd developed.

After Saucedo and Ahumada left, Ellis resumed his duties as Indian agent. He made frequent visits to the chiefs of the immigrant tribes, which kept him in the saddle and away from home much of the time. He had to admit to himself, when he thought about it, that a widow with small children desperately needed a husband; under the circumstances, Candace did only what any woman would have done. He tried hard to put it out of his mind, but the thought of Parmer in bed with her for two nights continued to nettle him like a deep-seated, irritating rash.

With a well-traveled Delaware guide and a squad of cavalry from the small force Ahumada had left in the old Nacogdoches barracks, Ellis set out for the villages of the hostile Wacos and Tawakonis. An extra pack mule bore gifts from the Cherokees to the two tribes. They approached the Wacos cautiously, bearing a white flag and hoping the Indians would recognize it as a symbol of peaceful intent. They responded to the Delaware's hand signals and allowed the riders to enter their village, but their reception was cool. After a few days of talks in Spanish and sign language, the Wacos accepted a peace treaty and agreed to cease their raids. A few of them then accompanied Ellis and his party to the Tawakonies, who were also willing to make peace.

On his return to Nacogdoches, Ellis wrote Austin concerning the treaties, and assured him that his settlers could now treat the two tribes as friends. Some of them, he added, had even agreed to accompany him to San Antonio, and from there to Comanche camps, so he could try to make peace with them.

They met with only one small band under a chief named Wounded Bear, for no other Comanches were in the area. Although Wounded Bear was willing to talk peace, one of the Tawakonis who spoke Spanish took Ellis aside. "If you make peace with just this one band," he warned Ellis, "you are condemning them to death. Each band does what it wants, and none of the others will even know about this treaty. When others raid and a party of whites goes hunting Comanches, they're likely to come onto this band because it won't be trying to hide. To whites, all Comanches are enemies, so they will kill the peaceful warriors."

Realizing that what the Tawakoni said was true, Ellis broke off the peace talks with Wounded Bear. "When all the Comanches are willing to talk peace," he told the Comanche leader, "have the chiefs send word to the officers in San Antonio."

In June, Colonel José de las Piedras arrived as commander of the Nacogdoches garrison, bringing with him two hundred cavalrymen. Piedras, who was senior to Ellis, was humorless and strictly military in all actions. Ellis found him stiff-necked and inflexible, and he was soon unpopular with both Tejanos and Texians, who yearned for the opportunity to catch him away from his troops and cane him.

In March 1828, Ellis wrote Austin about a small party of filibusters under a Dr. Dayton, who claimed that two or three hundred more followers were coming. When they arrived, Dayton said, they would seize De León's fort. He recruited a few idlers in Nacogdoches, then left. Ellis doubted that more were coming, but warned Austin that the troublemakers appeared to be headed for his colony.

A month later Austin wrote to thank Ellis for the warning. Dayton had been in his colony trying to stir up trouble by telling men that the *empresario* should bear all of the expenses for settling them on their lands, and trying to recruit followers. Austin's men had seized Dayton and convicted him of disturbing the peace. After shaving his head, they'd stripped him to his drawers and tarred and feathered him. Then they ordered him to leave and not return. He appeared eager to comply, Austin wryly added.

With all but the Comanches at peace, Ellis took up buying and selling land, hoping to make money while waiting for an *empresario* contract. He maintained his ranch at Mound Prairie, and with a pair of slaves he'd traded for, he cultivated cotton as well as corn. His cattle, bearing his "B" brand and swallow fork cut in the right ear, now numbered nearly a thousand head. Each year he sold fat steers to men who drove them to New Orleans. On May 28 Candace gave birth to a son. She immediately named him Ellis, hoping that would be balm on Ellis' wounded pride. It was, but only briefly.

Early in June 1828, aristocratic General Manuel de Mier y Terán rode into Nacogdoches accompanied by Lt. José María Sánchez and several scientists. He immediately sent for Ellis.

"I'm inspecting the boundary and making a scientific survey," he explained after greeting Ellis warmly. "I'm also selecting sites for new presidios, and I want your opinion. After the Fredonian revolt, and with all the warlike Indians, we certainly need more garrisons than the ones at San Antonio, LaBahía, and Nacogdoches." Ellis agreed, but not wholeheartedly.

"There are Indian troubles on the frontiers," he admitted, "but I don't expect to see another foolish affair like that one. Everyone was against it."

"That may be true," Mier y Terán admitted, "but officials in Mexico City are still aroused over it. It confirmed the fears of many of them that the American government plans to seize Texas if we won't sell it, and they don't intend to allow that to happen."

"The ones who have titles to their lands are all satisfied and grateful to Mexico," Ellis assured him. "Austin once said that the worst thing that could happen would be for the U. S. to take over Texas and introduce its land policy."

Lt. Sánchez spoke up. "In my opinion, the spark that

ignites the torch that will consume Texas will be struck at San Felipe." Ellis tugged at his earlobe, then shook his head.

"You won't find a more loyal or reliable Mexican citizen than Stephen F. Austin," he replied, "and his colonists follow his lead. Remember that a lot of them helped put down the Fredonian revolt. Things would have to get pretty bad to change Austin's attitude. In my judgment, trouble is much more likely to start among those who can't get titles to their lands, and that includes the Cherokees and other tribes. Luckily for us, they listened to me and only a few of them joined the Fredonians."

"Nacogdoches doesn't look at all like San Felipe," Mier observed. "Straight streets with houses built of lumber, instead of log cabins that look like they'd been blown there in a storm and scattered every which way." He paused. "Speaking of storms," he continued, "the worst one I ever saw struck us at San Felipe. Lightning striking all around us, and the rain so heavy you couldn't see ten feet. And the wind!"

"Yes," Lt. Sánchez added, "and the river rose so high we were stuck there. We finally got an American to ferry us across, and that was a mistake. He was drunk and trying to steer the boat while two slaves rowed it. They must have been drunk, too, for they sang—it was more like howling than singing—the whole way. I thought I'd go mad before a floating log could swamp us. Somehow we made it across, but it was awful." Mier nodded and smiled at the thought of the wild boat ride.

Ellis took Mier y Terán through the piney woods to visit the chiefs of the Cherokees and other tribes who came to the meeting. "I'll do what I can to get you titles," Mier y Terán assured them, while they listened, their faces impassive. He also promised the squatters in the border area that he would urge the governor to send a commissioner to give them titles, as Colonel Ahumada had already recommended. Mier wrote the governor as promised. "I asked him to appoint you as *empresario* of the border reserve," he told Ellis, "so that you can see to it that the region is legally colonized." Ellis' hopes rose again.

Accompanied by Ellis, Mier y Terán chose a number of sites for new presidios, and he gave most of them Aztec names to emphasize that they were Mexican. Anáhuac was to be at the head of Galveston Bay, Tenoxtitlán, where the Nacogdoches–San Antonio road crossed the Brazos. Lipantitlán would be on the Nueces. The smaller posts were Terán on the lower Neches and Lavaca on the river of the same name. Later, a strong force would be stationed at Velasco near the mouth of the Brazos. These posts were strategically located for dominating the approaches to all of the settlements.

"Once these forts are constructed," Mier y Terán remarked, "we've got to build up Mexican or European settlements around every one of them. Either we occupy Texas soon or it will be overrun by Americans. They make industrious citizens and Mexico needs them, but it would be folly not to balance them with Mexicans or Europeans. They carry their constitutions in their heads, and if they ever become dissatisfied with the government, Texas is lost forever. A reconquest from a base eight hundred miles away would be impossible. Don't you agree?"

Ellis shrugged, feeling uncomfortable. "I reckon you're right about that," he admitted, "but Mexico has been generous to them, and I know most appreciate it. I guess some do resent having to change their religions."

"Since there aren't any priests among them," Mier y Terán responded, "I'm going to recommend that the government drop the religious requirement. It would be better to have any religion than none."

When Haden Edwards' contract was canceled, Ellis and the Mexican liberal Lorenzo de Zavala both applied for it.

Before Mier y Terán left Nacogdoches early in 1829, he gave Ellis permission to visit Magdalena for a month. Leaving Candace and the children in a house he'd built in Nacogdoches, Ellis took a riverboat to New Orleans and boarded a schooner for Veracruz. As they approached the port city, Ellis stared at the grim fortress, with its black and red walls, looming up on the island of San Juan de Ulúa. He thought of the Castle of San Diego in Acapulco and shuddered.

To Ellis, Veracruz appeared unimpressive, partly because of the hundreds of black *sopilotes*, or buzzards, soaring in search of dead animals or circling around one they'd found. Behind the port city were hills of red sand, which did nothing to improve his opinion of Veracruz.

The men on the streets wore the typical wide-bottomed trousers split up the side, broad-brimmed hats, and *serapes*. Many of the women wore black dresses and mantillas. Others wore *rebosos*, or scarves, over their heads. Everywhere Ellis saw *sopilotes* playing the role of street-cleaners, at least where carrion was concerned.

The coach jolted across the barren stretch, then entered the hills among a great variety of trees and vines. It passed through Indian villages, where women with their hair in braids and straw hats on their heads carried infants in slings on their backs. As the road climbed higher, the air became cooler, even cold.

Ellis recalled Jalapa's steep streets, the fine old houses and churches, and the ancient Franciscan convent. A few miles beyond Jalapa the coach stopped at Las Banderillas, and Ellis eagerly alit for a joyful reunion with Magdalena. During his month's stay, he told her of his success in quelling the Fredonian revolt and in making peace with the Indian tribes. "I've applied for the grant that Haden Edwards lost," he told her. "With General Mier's support, I should get it as well as the border reserve. When I get it I'll have to fulfill the contract. That will take a while, but it should make me wealthy."

She told him of her problems managing the *hacienda*, but with the vision of an *empresario* grant on his mind, he found it difficult to focus on them.

"When are you coming to stay?" she asked when his month was up and he prepared to leave.

"When I get things well in hand," he replied. "I don't know when that will be, but I promise you that one day I'll come for good." She wistfully watched him board the coach.

On his return to Nacogdoches, Ellis replied to an inquiry from Austin concerning a rumored Spanish invasion of Mexico from Cuba. He'd heard talk about it in New Orleans, he said, but the general view there was that if the Spanish troops left Cuba, the Cubans would immediately rebel. Most of the men he talked to thought that an invasion of Mexico was unlikely. He thanked Austin for sending him a copy of a state law that exempted colonists for twelve years from being sued for debts contracted before coming to Texas. He'd heard, he wrote, that American speculators were buying up the debts, expecting to use them to gain possession of valuable cotton plantations.

Ellis waited, hoping for good news from Saltillo, but in February, the state government decided that, although Ellis deserved to be rewarded for his services, his "personal difficulties" made it necessary to award the former Edwards grant to Zavala.

Disappointed again, Ellis still hoped Texas would be made a territory and that he would be named governor. But the Texians chose not to accept territorial status, for that would mean the federal government, not the state of Coahuila y Texas, would control all public lands. In the meantime, Ellis developed and leased a salt deposit. He also bought a league of land on Carrizo creek near Nacogdoches on which he built a house and sawmill. He lived alone in the house, while Candace and the children remained in Nacogdoches.

Political strife in Mexico would soon make Mexicans look back on the years of peace under Guadalupe Victoria with nostalgia. In 1828 Gómez Pedraza had been elected President, but Santa Anna led a revolt that ousted him in favor of old rebel Vicente Guerrero. King Ferdinand VII still regarded Mexico as a colony in rebellion, and the political strife offered an opportunity to intervene to restore order and to recover Mexico. He seized it.

Spanish troops from Cuba landed on the coast of Tamaulipas, but the admiral, who had quarrelled with the general, immediately abandoned them there and returned to Cuba. The troops seized the fortress at Tampico, where General Mier bottled them up until yellow fever decimated them. Santa Anna, smelling an opportunity for vainglory, hastened there without orders. With his usual luck, he arrived in time for the surrender but, when the Mexicans learned of the Spanish surrender, they erroneously gave Santa Anna credit for engineering it. With his encouragement, they bestowed on him the undeserved laurel of "Hero of Tampico."

Late in 1829, Vice-President Bustamante drove Guerrero from office, and in January 1830, proclaimed himself president. He named archconservative Lucas Alamán as Minister of the Interior, and his friend Mier y Terán, as commandant general of the Eastern Interior States, with headquarters at Matamoros. Although Bustamante was honest and well-intentioned, he was manipulated by more astute men, particularly Alamán.

Alamán's deep distrust of Americans had been reaffirmed by the Fredonian revolt, and he reminded the congress of the recommendation to colonize Texas with Europeans and Mexicans to offset the American settlers before it was too late. Alamán wanted no half measures. He urged military occupation and military rule over Texas, and the exclusion of immigrants from the United States. The congress complied by enacting the Law of April 6, 1830, which went far beyond the reasonable recommendations of Mier y Terán. It provided for a loan to cover the cost of bringing Mexican families to Texas and opened the coastal trade to foreign vessels for four years. It recognized existing slavery but prohibited the importation of slaves in the future. Article 11 banned further immigration from the United States and canceled all *empresario* contracts.

Fortunately for the Texians, Mier y Terán was named commissioner of colonization and administered the law. Aware that both Austin and DeWitt had introduced colonists who made desirable citizens, he canceled only the contracts of *empresarios* who had brought less than one hundred families and allowed the two men to continue bringing colonists to fulfill their contracts. Soon after the law was passed, many more troops were sent to Nacogdoches, San Antonio, and La Bahía, which had been renamed Goliad, an anagram for Hidalgo. Work on the new posts began immediately.

To soothe the Texians who viewed the law as an ugly turn in their relations with the government, the ever-prudent Austin tried to point out its presumed advantages in the *Texas Gazette*. The troops that were being sent would protect the colonists from the Indians, he wrote, and allowing foreign vessels in the coastal trade would provide them better access to markets. Viewing the law quite differently, most Texians resented it, for many had friends or relatives in the States who had been planning to move to Texas. Now the door was slammed shut in their faces. They were also alarmed by the troop build-up.

Because the number of troops in Nacogdoches increased to four hundred, Colonel Piedras arranged for building a larger *cuartel*, buying lumber from Ellis' sawmill on credit. Ellis was ordered to build the small post of Terán on the lower Neches, then to remain there as its commander, with a company of fifty men. Candace, who he now saw infrequently, remained in Nacogdoches.

It wasn't long before the new law's teeth were felt in East Texas. Both the state and federal governments had agreed earlier that the squatters there should be given titles even though many were in a restricted border area. The first commissioner who came in 1830 to issue titles was arrested on what were suspected to be trumped up charges of embezzlement and murder. The disappointed people of the border area urgently petitioned the state government to send another, and it complied. In January 1831, commissioner Francisco Madero published in the *Texas Gazette* his plan to issue titles to families that had arrived before April 6, 1830.

At the new presidio of Anáhuac at the head of Galveston Bay, Colonel John D. Bradburn saw the notice and arrested Madero and his surveyor on the grounds they were violating the Law of April 6. Bradburn was an irascible Kentuckian who fought in the Mexican Revolution and then later rejoined the Mexican army. Once more the East Texas settlers were disappointed and angry.

Mier y Terán had instructed presidio commanders to maintain cordial relations with the Texians and to cooperate with local officials. But while building his presidio, Bradburn had seized supplies from settlers, used their slaves without compensation, and harbored runaways. Later he arrested Patrick C. Jack for organizing a militia company to protect families against Indians, and lawyer William B. Travis for trying to recover runaway slaves for their owners. They and others were held indefinitely in the guardhouse without being formally charged or brought to trial. Finally, in June 1832, a small force of angry men under Patrick Jack's brother William set out from Brazoria to rescue the prisoners, by force if necessary. By the time they reached Anáhuac, their numbers had grown to 160.

When Bradburn refused to release the prisoners, the Texians attacked and seized a building. Bradburn then agreed to free the prisoners if the Texians withdrew. But when they set up camp at Turtle Bayou he sent calls for help to Colonel Piedras and to Colonel Ugartechea at Velasco, recovered a supply of gunpowder from the building the Texians had held, then defied them. At Turtle Bayou, the Texians drew up resolutions in which they declared their support of the constitution and the liberal party. Incensed by Bradburn's duplicity they sent calls for reinforcements, while John Austin, a friend but not a relative of the *empresario*, and others headed for Brazoria. Their purpose was to return with two cannon that the steamer *Ariel* had unloaded there to enable it to get across the bar at the mouth of the Brazos. While they were gone, the force at Anáhuac swelled to more than two hundred.

On receiving Bradburn's call for help, Colonel Piedras set out with part of his force and sent word to Ellis to join him. Hoping to restore peace without a confrontation with the Texians, Piedras sent Ellis and another officer to invite them to a conference. Seeing another Anglo in a Mexican uniform, some were suspicious of him, but he persuaded them to talk to Piedras. What they told him convinced Piedras that their grievances against Bradburn were justified. He promised to turn the prisoners over to civil authorities, to pay for property Bradburn had seized, and to persuade him to leave, promises he kept. The Texians soon disbanded. A few days later, the whole garrison at Anáhuac declared for Santa Anna and sailed for Mexico. Ellis was greatly relieved.

At Velasco, near the mouth of the Brazos, Colonel Ugartechea properly refused to permit John Austin and the others to sail past his post with cannon to be used against Mexican troops at Anáhuac. Early on June 25, John Austin and 112 Texians demanded that Ugartechea surrender and leave Texas with his garrison. Ugartechea refused. The next day, forty Texians moored a small armed schooner near the fort and opened fire, while the others attacked by land. The fighting continued all day, as Ugartechea's losses mounted. At the day's end he capitulated and agreed to leave Texas. A year or two later, he would be named commander at San Antonio.

At Nacogdoches the colonists were determined that Colonel Piedras should declare for Santa Anna and the Constitution of 1824, which his officers favored. Piedras stubbornly announced his support for Bustamante, and ordered the settlers to surrender their guns. Ellis, who disliked Piedras, encouraged men from Ayish Bayou to join those around Nacogdoches, who were gathering on Pine Hill east of the town, but he took no other action. They elected James W. Pollock of San Augustine as commander and sent a delegation to tell Piedras to join them against Bustamante or fight. He chose to fight. The Texians marched to the center of the town, where they repulsed a cavalry charge and took possession of houses around the square. That night they heard the whole garrison riding out of town.

The tall James Bowie, whose brother Rezin invented the famous Bowie knife, had migrated to San Antonio years earlier. There he'd married Ursula Veramendi, but after losing her and their child to cholera, he settled at Nacogdoches. An experienced fighter and born leader, he picked twenty men and dashed along the lower road to get ahead of the troops and check them at the Angelina crossing. When the advance party of troops reached the crossing the next morning, Bowie's men opened fire on them, and the whole force forted up in a house on a hill. The rest of the Texians soon arrived, and the firing kept up all day, while Mexican losses mounted. On the following morning, Piedras turned over command to Major Francisco Medina and was escorted away. Medina and the rest of the command quickly proclaimed Santa Anna and were soon on their way to Mexico.

Not long after this, Major Francisco Ruiz marched the Tenoxtitlán garrison to San Antonio over the protests of the settlers, who were left exposed to Indian raids. Only the garrisons at Goliad and San Antonio remained.

When Santa Anna pronounced against Bustamante, Mier y Terán supported the latter, for he distrusted Santa Anna and he was deeply disturbed by Mexico's continued instability. On learning of the troubles at Anáhuac, he wrote Austin, asking him to use his influence to quiet the discontent. "The affairs of Texas are understood by none but you and me, and we alone can regulate them. But there is no time to do more than calm the agitation, something that can readily be accomplished because the objects for which they contend are definite and well-defined."

In San Antonio de Padilla, where Iturbide had been executed when he tried to return from exile, Mier y Terán remarked to Colonel Díaz Noriega, "Things are in a bad way; the political horizon is ever more cloudy, and the net result will be the loss of Texas. I would give my whole life if Mexico could appreciate the beauty and fertility of that land, but no one will think of it." Gesturing toward the south, he added, "The men there have enough to think about in their own intrigues and ambitions."

"Sir, you'll probably receive a majority of the votes in the next election. As president, you can take steps to remedy the evils," Díaz Noriega said.

Mier y Terán snorted. "That's an insane idea," he said.

Santa Anna sent Colonel José Antonio Mexía to Matamoros to seize control from the Bustamante forces there, and Colonel Guerra withdrew his small garrison. At San Antonio de Padilla, Mier y Terán's depression overwhelmed him. Early one morning he donned his best uniform and buckled on his sword. Outside he stopped a corporal. "If your general should die, what would happen?" he asked.

"Someone would be sent to take your place, sir."

Lips twitching, Mier y Terán walked on. Behind what remained of a ruined church he placed the butt of his sword against the wall and the point over his heart and lunged against it. His body was placed in the same crypt that held Iturbide's remains.

When Colonel Mexía learned of the troubles at Anáhuac and Velasco, he feared it meant that a general rebellion had begun. Accompanied by Austin, who had been in Saltillo trying to persuade the state legislature to support repeal of the Law of April 6, Mexía sailed to the mouth of the Brazos with five hundred men. John Austin wrote him there, relating the Texians' grievances against Bradburn and explaining their actions. "The people," he wrote, "are Mexicans by adoption, are so in their hearts, and they will remain so. If the laws grant them the honorable title of citizens, that title should be respected, and they should be governed by the authorities established by the state constitution, not by the military."

Mexía was greeted everywhere with enthusiasm and support for the liberal cause. Satisfied that the Texians would remain loyal to the federal government, Mexía sailed for Mexico to continue the war against Bustamante.

On April 1, 1833, Texian delegates assembled at San Felipe to draft a petition for statehood for Texas. Among them was newly arrived Sam Houston, who had served under Andrew Jackson against the Creeks at Horseshoe Bend. Later he'd been elected governor of Tennessee, but an unfortunate marriage caused him to resign and live among the Cherokees, who called him "Big Drunk."

Lawyer David G. Burnet drafted the petition, while Houston and others prepared a state constitution. Because the delegates expected Santa Anna to approve the petition, they sent the proposed constitution along with it and other requests. Austin carried these documents to Mexico City.

At first Vice-President Gómez Farías treated Austin with suspicion and hostility. Austin, fearing that Texians might resort to violence if the petition were denied, in desperation wrote the San Antonio city council, urging it to take the lead in setting up a state government in defiance of the federal government. Then his relations with Gómez Farías and other officials became cordial, and when he was satisfied that he had done all he could, he set out for Texas. But the San Antonio city council had sent his intemperate letter to the government, and Austin was arrested in Saltillo and confined in the old Inquisition jail in Mexico City.

In late April 1834, Colonel Juan N. Almonte, the son of rebel leader Morelos, reached Nacogdoches and immediately called on Ellis. Vice-President Gómez Farías, who was confident that Texas was on the verge of revolt, had sent Almonte to take a census and prepare a statistical report. Secretly, he was to determine the Texians' ability to wage war, to identify leaders hostile to Mexico, and to devise methods to neutralize them long enough for the government to prepare for war.

Again Ellis faced a predicament. He'd helped Mier y Terán select sites for new military posts, which had made some Texians regard him with suspicion. I'm for both sides, Ellis thought, and that's a hell of a fix to be in. If this keeps up, neither side will trust me anymore. Maybe they don't already. Almonte visited him off and on for three months, and Ellis was able to convince him that most Texians were not at all eager to break away from Mexico.

Because of Austin's arrest, Almonte hesitated to visit San Felipe and other settlements in Austin's colonies. "Do you think they might attack me?" he asked.

Ellis shook his head. "There's absolutely no likelihood of that," he assured Almonte. With some trepidation, Almonte rode to San Felipe, where he was treated cordially. After visiting Brazoria, Matagorda, Harrisburg, and Velasco, he was satisfied that Mexican officials misunderstood the situation in Texas. In his report he praised the Texians for their industry and loyalty, recommended that the reforms they desired be granted, and urged that Austin be released from prison.

From his cell Austin had written friends in Texas urging them to remain calm about his arrest. "Any excitement will do me harm, and do great harm to Texas," he wrote. "Keep quiet and let me perish if that is to be my fate." The repeal of the Law of April 6, which had occurred before Austin's arrest, had pleased everyone, for after it went into effect nearly three thousand more Americans flocked to Texas. The legislature of Coahuila y Texas, possibly on Santa Anna's recommendation, enacted most of the reforms the Texians had urged. It divided Texas into three departments, each with its own political chief and delegate to the state legislature, and it created new municipalities at Matagorda and San Augustine, at Ayish Bayou. It also authorized a circuit court and trial by jury, but neither could be immediately implemented. The new departments were Brazos, with its capital of San Felipe, and Nacogdoches. The Texians were relieved, too, because the only garrisons remaining in Texas were the main one at San Antonio and one company at Goliad.

Texians were also pleased at first by provisions for the sale of public lands to raise funds for the penniless state government. The legislature was aware that Texas might soon become a state, which would end any opportunity to sell land there. To encourage sales, the legislature added the statement that no person should be molested for political or religious opinions, provided the public order was not disturbed, which in effect meant freedom of religion. As a result of these desired changes, Texians were generally contented, but they would soon be outraged at the scandalous speculation in enormous tracts of Texas land.

Ellis was greatly relieved at the easing of tension; it appeared that Texas was advancing steadily toward statehood and the management of its own affairs. The only shadows still hanging over Texians were the Indian troubles on the frontiers and Austin's continued confinement in Mexico City. But the colonists had followed Austin's advice and remained calm about that.

"It looked for a time like we'd have soldiers breathing down our necks wherever we went," Micajah remarked.

"If they ever get things straightened out down there, we may yet," Ellis replied, "though they say Santa Anna acted real friendly to Texas when Austin saw him."

"My father talked to General Mier y Terán when he was here," Vidal observed. "He said Santa Anna is a viper, and an ambitious one at that. The General predicted only trouble for Mexico as long as he's around. My father's friends in Mexico City say he's plotting to overthrow the federal constitution and replace it with a centralist one. If that ever happens, *cuidado*—take care."

Ellis tugged at his earlobe while Micajah scratched his head. "Right now it looks like things are goin' the way we want," Micajah said. "Everyone's satisfied with the constitution, and the state legislature gave us everything we asked for. All we lack is statehood, and if people keep a comin' from wherever, we'll be a sure enough state before much longer. Or don't you see it that way?" he asked Vidal.

"I'm not as wise as my father," Vidal replied. "He says Spaniards always trust their kings to be just. If there's injustice, it's the fault of officials, not the king. That's why Spaniards never overthrow their kings. But Mexicans don't feel that way about presidents, for they're not of royal blood and can't take the place of the king in men's minds. But kings must be legitimate—not like Iturbide. If he'd been a European prince. . . ."

"What're you tellin' us?" Ellis interrupted.

"Simply this. Mexico's troubles aren't over. They will continue, and they may either help or hurt Texas."

"Let's hope they help us more than they harm us," Micajah said, "since we can't do anything about them anyway."

Chapter Eleven

Over the years, Ellis had bought and sold a number of leagues of land as well as town lots in Nacogdoches. He'd traded for a slave couple, Dory and Vina, who bore five daughters and a son. He also acquired Bolton, a fine Kentucky thoroughbred stallion. Because he was looked on more as a prosperous country squire than as a Mexican officer, the area around his ranch became known as Bean's Prairie. That made him feel pretty good about himself, but it still rankled him that he wasn't an *empresario*.

Although he frequently thought of disposing of his property and joining Magdalena at Jalapa, Ellis was too caught up in his business ventures to abandon them completely. He was also too satisfied with life in East Texas to turn his back on it forever, and in any case he didn't want to leave until his children were grown up and independent. They still lived with Candace in the house he'd given her, and he supported them. He hoped to see Louiza Jane safely married before he left, for he was especially fond of his eleven-year-old freckle-faced daughter.

Ellis frequently visited them and his young nephew Sam Bean, who lived with them, although he and Candace had become little more than acquaintances. In December 1834, she applied to *empresario* David G. Burnet for a league of land, describing herself as a widow with three children. Although Ellis doted on Louiza Jane, he was also proud of his sons, and whenever he rounded up his cattle for branding calves or separating steers for market, they accompanied him. Micajah, Vidal, and other neighbors helped one another at such times. Ellis suffered increasingly from rheumatism, especially in winter, but despite the pain in his hands and shoulders, he remained active.

The only clouds on the Texas horizon in early 1835 were Santa Anna's machinations and his unpredictable intentions, and the continued confinement of Austin in Mexico City. Aware that Almonte had urged his release, Ellis expected to hear any day that Austin was back in San Felipe.

In March Colonel Ugartechea, now commander at San Antonio, instructed Ellis to persuade the Cherokees to wage war on the Comanches, who retaliated against the invaders of their hunting grounds. He was to promise them the powder and lead they needed, and to assure them they could keep the loot they captured, knowing that much of it had been stolen from settlers. Accompanied by his friend, William Goyens, the mulatto trader who was also on good terms with the Indians, Ellis visited war chief Bowles. After talking to his leading warriors, Bowles agreed to send them against the Comanches.

On his return to Nacogdoches, Ellis learned that the people of Goliad, mostly Tejanos, were aroused over an American trader who encouraged the Comanches to raid so he could trade for whatever they stole. Ellis put an end to the practice by threatening to send well-armed Cherokee warriors to attack all Comanches who came to his post.

Ellis found the news from Mexico ever more discouraging. In May, the congress, which was dominated by centralists, declared that it had the right to alter or replace the constitution, and the erstwhile federalist Santa Anna apparently agreed. That means they aim to throw out the federal constitution, Ellis thought. Every Texian will be up in arms if they do, and all Mexican federalists should be. But he soon discovered that only the states of Zacatecas and Coahuila y Texas had defied the government. Santa Anna was raising an army to subdue Zacatecas, and he'd named his brother-in-law, General Martín Perfecto de Cós, commander of the Eastern Interior States to deal with Coahuila y Texas.

Governor Viesca of Coahuila y Texas appealed for a hundred men from each of the three Texas departments to help defend the state government, now at Monclova. But because Texians were still seething over the scandalous sale of enormous tracts of Texas land to speculators for a few cents an acre, sales in which Viesca had a leading part, they scoffed at his request.

In July, William Roark rode to Ellis' ranch to tell him the latest news. The previous month, a military courier had delivered a letter from Cós to political chief James B. Miller in San Felipe. It was court week and, as usual, most of the families from the surrounding area were in town. When Miller read the letter and announced that Cós had dismissed the state legislature, arrested Viesca, and was himself acting governor, angry men immediately clamored to rescue the ex-governor. Several of them seized the courier's mail pouch and emptied it.

In it were letters from Cós and Ugartechea to Captain Antonio Tenorio, who had arrived at Anáhuac in January with a detachment of troops and a customs officer. Cós informed Tenorio that substantial reinforcements were coming to him by sea, and that Cós himself would soon land with troops to reinforce the garrison at San Antonio. Other units were marching there from the south, he added, and when they arrived he would arrest the agitators, expel all men who had entered Texas illegally, and disarm the settlers. Ugartechea wrote Tenorio that Santa Anna had thoroughly crushed Zacatecas, and his army would reassemble at Saltillo for the march to Texas. "These revolutionaries here will also be crushed," he grimly predicted, no doubt still smarting over his defeat at Velasco.

There was a lot of talk about rescuing Viesca, expelling Tenorio before more troops arrived, and preventing Cós from reaching San Antonio. A band of young men sailed for Anáhuac, and on the way elected lawyer William B. Travis as their commander. Captain Tenorio, unaware that more troops were coming, surrendered and agreed to leave Texas. Ellis groaned and his rheumatism flared up when Roark told him the startling news.

"The men in Austin's colonies are badly divided," Roark continued. From what he'd heard, when Travis and the others returned in triumph from Anáhuac, peace party meetings in all the settlements bitterly denounced them for trying to involve Texians in a war. "If Cós carries out his threats," Roark added soberly, "we'll be in big trouble, and who can all agree on to lead us? No one. Could be a lot of folks will be headin' for the Sabine." Ellis gloomily nodded, and tried to ease the pain by rubbing his gnarled hands together.

"Divided like they are," he said, "I can't see 'em puttin' up much of a fight." He tried to envision the different things that might happen, and to figure a way he could deal with each possibility. Mexico can send a large army, but if Cós succeeds in disarming one settlement after another, it won't be necessary. If, however, some Texians choose to resist, they'll likely be badly outnumbered and overpowered. And even though he felt sure his friends wouldn't turn against him, Ellis knew that some hothead might shoot him as a public service.

I could slip away to Mexico and wait there till it's over, he thought, then shook his head. If I do that, and by some miracle Texas becomes independent, maybe with U.S. help, they'd never let me come back. I'd lose everything I've worked for, and I might even be forced to fight Americans. I don't aim to do that, but if I threw in with the Texians and they lost I'd be in the same fix.

Unless Cós moderated his stand, he knew Texians would be forced to decide between knuckling under to military rule or taking on the Mexican army. Many of the Old Settlers had developed prosperous plantations, and it was clear they'd rather submit to whatever Mexico demanded than risk losing their land. It appeared, at least for the moment, that the peace party outnumbered the war party, although Cós could quickly change that by carrying out his threats. Hundreds of adventurers had entered Texas illegally after 1830, and many of them talked openly of annexing Texas to the U.S. They were, Ellis was sure, eager for a war, but could they win it? He saw little reason to believe that was likely.

He recalled how it had been in the early years, when Mexican officials had been generous to American settlers, giving them huge tracts of land and even allowing them to have slaves when slavery was illegal elsewhere in Mexico. They had been eager to see Texas become settled and prosperous, but that had changed after Bustamante seized power. Repeated U.S. attempts to purchase Texas had convinced him and other officials that the Americans intended to acquire Texas one way or another, and they were determined to prevent that from happening. And now Santa Anna was preparing to reduce Texians to the status of peons.

In late July, when William Roark stopped for the night on his way to San Antonio, Ellis asked him to deliver a letter to the commander there. He wrote Ugartechea to explain why he hadn't replied to official communications recently. He'd received no answers to his letters, he said, which convinced him his mail had been intercepted. ''I have thought it advisable to remain silent under the delicate circumstances. I avail myself of this opportunity to assure you that the majority of the inhabitants of this frontier refuse to take part in a revolution and have agreed to remain quiet, notwithstanding the inducements tendered them by the citizens of San Antonio and those of San Felipe, who have committed grave acts at Anáhuac. And in the vicinity of the Colorado, they have killed a mail courier.''

Whatever happened, Ellis was determined not to commit any overt act of disloyalty to Mexico, at least as long as it was governed under the Constitution of 1824. At the same time, however, he had no intention of helping Cós disarm Texians for supporting that constitution. He'd opposed the Fredonians even though they were Americans because they were clearly in the wrong, and most Texians opposed them for the same reason. If Texians became convinced they had to fight for the constitution and their rights as free men, that was quite another matter. He knew most would prefer to risk their lives rather than submit to oppressive military rule. He feared for the Mexico he knew and loved, for under Santa Anna its future appeared bleak.

Continuing to carry out his duties as Indian agent, in September Ellis wrote President Jackson that Benjamin Hawkins, who was half Creek, had ''informed me that a good speculation could be made out of the Creeks by persuading them to move to lands in this country, that a large sum of money could be obtained from them. I promptly assured him that no such thing could take place nor be permitted by me, as it was contrary to the laws of this republic and existing treaties with the United States.'' He condemned the avarice and cupidity of individuals who ''make a barter of human life,'' and he urged Jackson to prevent the emigration of the Creeks. He signed it ''Peter E. Bean, colonel of cavalry, commanding the eastern department.''

That same September, the welcome news reached Nacogdoches that Austin had returned to San Felipe after a year and a half in prison without ever having been brought to trial. Texians everywhere rejoiced, including those who previously had been critical of Austin. Here, at the most crucial moment, when the future of all was in the balance, was a leader that both parties respected and trusted. For troubled Texians it was like a sudden break in the blackest of clouds. The storm would still strike, but the sight of the sun was reassuring.

Austin immediately sent a circular to all settlements calling for the election of delegates to a consultation at Washington-on-the-Brazos for October 15. He also urged each settlement to send one delegate immediately to form a permanent council. His concluding words sent a thrill through the war party but struck the peace party like the frigid blast of a blue norther. "War," he said, "is our only recourse."

"That's sure to bring Austin's people around," Roark observed. "They've always followed his lead, and it would be madness not to now. With war certain, what you reckon on doin' when it starts?" he asked.

Ellis gazed off at the horizon, his brow furrowed, his thoughts troubled. "Elisha Roberts told me he aims to lay low and take no part on either side, and that sounds like good advice," Ellis replied. "It may cost me the trust of both Texians and Mexicans—if either still trust me—but it's what I got to do. I can't see any other way for me." He held out his arm, and patted the sleeve of his buckskin jacket. "I put away my uniform for good," he said.

In Nacogdoches to visit his children early in October, Ellis saw a rider lope into town waving one arm and shouting. Men quickly gathered around his sweating horse, which stood with lowered head and heaving sides. "The war has started!" the rider shouted. "Ugartechea sent a bunch of dragoons to Gonzales to take back the old cannon they given us. We sent out calls for help and stalled until enough men come, then we crossed the Guadalupe and run 'em off. It warn't much of a scrape, but we killed one and maybe nicked a few." He paused to catch his breath.

"Boys," he continued, "Cós has landed at Cópano and is headin' for San Antonio. As soon as enough men git to Gonzales they'll take after him and run him outa Texas. All you fellers with guns git movin' or you'll miss the fun."

It was bound to happen sooner or later, Ellis thought, but now that war had come, he felt suddenly old and weary. If they'd let Texians alone and not sent more troops, things might have been settled without a war. But Santa Anna appears set on bullying Texians into submission, and that won't work. I hope by some miracle the Texians can win, but the odds against them are too long to bet on it. Enough men could come from the States to swing it, but will they come in time? He doubted it.

The next morning Ellis stood with Sam Houston, who towered over him, while they and others watched the first party of men, Micajah and his son Angus among them, assemble near the Old Stone Fort. There were men of every description—young, old, and in between. Tall men in greasy buckskins straddled small, half-broken mustangs or nervous little Mexican mules, their long legs nearly reaching the ground. Beardless youths in homespuns perched on placid wagon horses. A woman tried to hand her husband a heavy coat, but he waved her away. "Won't take us all that long," he said. "We'll be home afore it gits cold."

"They may not look like an army," Sam Houston remarked, "but most are dead shots and they won't run from a scrap." He shook his shaggy head. "Cós must have over a thousand men and plenty of cannon. They can't attack a force like that without artillery, and they're not equipped for a siege. I hate to say it, but their chances of success are pretty slim. I'd go with 'em anyway if it wasn't for the consultation. I'm a delegate, and that's my first responsibility."

Ellis watched the warriors ride away, most obviously in high spirits, and recalled the day he and Duncan had set out from Natchez with Nolan's party thirty-five years earlier.

"Fightin' trained soldiers ain't like fightin' Indians," he observed. "Mexico has a few really well-trained battalions, but most of the rest are jailbirds. That doesn't mean they won't fight if they're cornered." Houston nodded.

Like everyone else, Ellis anxiously followed the bits of news, although he discreetly remained at his ranch most of the time, relying on friends to keep him informed. The Texians who gathered at Gonzales had elected Austin commander, he learned, and on October 12 they cheerfully set out for San Antonio. Two yoke of oxen hauled the little cannon that had precipitated the conflict, until it became too much trouble. Then they happily abandoned it, for they much preferred fighting with their deadly long rifles.

In a little over a week they neared San Antonio, where Tejanos informed them that the Mexican army, which numbered about twelve hundred, was entrenched behind barricades and had at least thirty cannon in place. Austin, Colonel Edward Burleson, and other officers glumly agreed that a siege was their only hope. On October 9, a party of Texians under George Collinsworth had captured the presidio at Goliad, which put them in a position to cut off supplies sent Cós by sea. If Austin's army could bear up under the boredom, inactivity, and shortage of provisions long enough, it seemed possible it could starve the Mexican garrison into surrendering.

On October 15, delegates to the consultation rode into Washington–on–the–Brazos, but it was soon clear that most were with the army. Lacking a quorum, they adjourned until November 1, leaving the permanent council to act for them.

The Texians at San Antonio were as poorly prepared for besieging Cós as his army was for withstanding a siege, but James Bowie and a party of Texians beat off a Mexican attack near Concepción mission and captured two cannon. Colonel J. C. Neill, an experienced artilleryman, took charge of them. Most supplies except whiskey were scarce, but

Erasmo Seguín and other Tejano ranchers kept the army supplied with beef. At least one hundred fifty men left to get winter clothing, but eager volunteers from the States, such as the Mobile Grays, swelled the army to more than a thousand.

In late November, William Roark brought Ellis news of the Consultation that met at Washington–on–the–Brazos on November 1. The delegates had chosen a provisional government consisting of governor, lieutenant governor, and council, but without specifying the powers of each. The governor was hot-tempered Henry Smith; James W. Robinson was lieutenant governor. They named Sam Houston commander of the Texian army yet to be raised, but the men at San Antonio were excluded from his command. "From what I hear," Roark said, "The governor is for the war party and all the rest are peace party men. That smells like trouble to me, for all must agree on what needs to be done if we're to survive. The council wants to attack Matamoros and cooperate with Mexican federalists in restoring the constitution. Does that make sense to you?"

Ellis took off his straw hat and ran his twisted fingers through his thinning hair. "The chances of cooperating with the Mexican federalists are at best slim to none," he replied. "If the council sends an expedition against Matamoros—" He shrugged. "That would unite all Mexicans against them. It's the worst thing they could do." When Roark told him that on October 3 the Mexican congress had replaced the federal constitution with a centralist one, Ellis threw up his hands. "Not even the peace party can accept that," he said.

Before mid-November, when the Consultation adjourned until March 1, 1836, the provisional government had named Austin, Branch T. Archer, and William H. Wharton as commissioners to seek aid in the States. Before he left San Antonio on November 25, Austin had ordered an attack, for he feared the army would abandon the siege after he was gone. The volunteers from the States, accustomed to choosing their own officers, refused to obey. Austin departed in disgust. The Texians and volunteers elected Colonel Edward Burleson to replace him as commander.

The news from San Antonio convinced Ellis that the siege would fail, for many Texians, bored by the lack of action, mounted their horses and rode away. None was under oath, and all felt it their right to come and go at will. Fortunately for Burleson, volunteers from the States continued to arrive and take the places of those who left.

When Samuel Maverick, a Texian who lived in San Antonio, escaped his captors and reported that the siege had greatly weakened the Mexican troops under Cós, Burleson ordered the men to prepare for an attack, and they eagerly complied. To their disappointment, however, the officers voted to lift the siege and go into winter quarters. Burleson was furious, but there was nothing he could do about it. The Texians were also angry, and nearly half of them left in disgust.

Only about five hundred remained in camp when Ben Milam returned from a scout. He had recently escaped after capture by Cós in Mexico, and he was outraged at the sight of the men preparing to abandon the siege. Accompanied by Frank W. Johnson, he stormed up to Burleson, who explained what had happened. He also favored an attack, Burleson said, and he told Milam to call for volunteers. About three hundred responded. Milam divided them into two columns, one under his command, the other under Johnson. Burleson held the rest in reserve.

Just before dawn on December 6, Colonel Neill made a diversionary attack on the Alamo with one of the captured cannon. Hearing the Mexican troops rush there, Milam and the others charged into San Antonio. They fought from house to house, driving steadily toward the military plaza. On the third day, when a sniper's bullet killed Milam, Johnson took over command and the fighting continued without interruption. On

December 9 Cós asked for terms. Not wanting to prolong the conflict, Burleson was generous, and Cós agreed to leave Texas. Although Mexican casualties had been heavy, the Texians lost only Milam and Captain Peacock. That convinced them they had nothing more to fear from Mexico, so most headed for home, leaving Colonel Neill and volunteers from the States at San Antonio.

Micajah soon returned to Nacogdoches, looking weary but contented. His blond hair reached his shoulders, and his square jaw was hidden by a reddish beard.

"I never expected you to pull it off," Ellis said. "Tell me about it."

"They're scrappy little fellers, I give 'em credit for that," Micajah replied, "but their guns and powder are inferior, and they ran out of grub because we held Goliad. We just kept after 'em until Cós knew he was whipped." He brushed hair out of his face. "Now that all Mexican troops are out of Texas, I'm wondering what's next. What's your guess?"

Ellis frowned and folded his arms across his chest. "If they think it's over, they're way off the mark," he replied. "They say Santa Anna really destroyed Zacatecas for opposing him, and my guess is he won't be satisfied as long as there's one cabin still standing in Texas. His army is already gathering in Saltillo, I hear, and don't forget Cós is his brother-in-law. I figure Santa Anna himself will come at the head of his army so they can enjoy their revenge together." He paused and looked Micajah in the eye. "Texians better start getting ready for a real war right now. If they don't, I hate to think what will happen."

Micajah looked surprised, then shrugged. "They won't do it," he said. "After beating at least three times their number, they can't believe Mexico will risk sending another army here. It'll take a real shock to make 'em think different."

"By then it could be too late," Ellis said somberly.

Weeks before the delegates gathered for the Consultation

at Washington–on–the–Brazos on March 1, 1836, Ellis was convinced their cause was already lost. Provisional Governor Smith and the council had quarrelled bitterly over the Matamoros expedition, which the council had approved over Smith's veto. Most of the volunteers from the States, who chafed at the inactivity, had eagerly joined the expedition, leaving Colonel Neill with only one hundred men to defend San Antonio. The council, bypassing Houston, had compounded its error by naming James W. Fannin and Frank W. Johnson separately to command the expedition. The two were competing for recruits, but most of the volunteers from the States were at Goliad with Fannin. The council, on its own authority, deposed the governor, but since late January it had ceased to function for lack of a quorum. Santa Anna's troops were poised to strike, while Texas had neither government nor army, and the independent volunteers were preparing to loot Matamoros. It appeared to Ellis that Texians were purposely inviting disaster.

Early in February 1836, Ellis was surprised to see Sam Houston in Nacogdoches. "I know I'm supposed to be in command," Houston explained, "but because Governor Smith supports me, the council undercut me. The governor furloughed me to make a treaty with the Cherokees to keep 'em neutral."

"Good idea," Ellis said. "If the Mexicans attack on one side and the Indians on the other. . . ." He shook his head. "I figure it'll be tough enough without that."

Houston looked grave. "Our only real hope is to make Santa Anna extend his supply lines to the breaking point while we muster an army. At that point we'll have a good chance of defeating 'em, but it won't be easy. I've sent Bowie to San Antonio with orders for Neill to blow up the Alamo and pull back."

Ellis declined Houston's invitation to accompany him to the Cherokee villages. "It would be better to take Goyens," he said. "If I go, and any of the Indians join the Mexicans, everyone will remember I'm a Mexican officer and hold me responsible."

Late in February, Ellis was astonished to learn that Neill had refused to blow up the Alamo and withdraw, and that Bowie had also vowed to "die in these ditches" rather than retreat. Then came a letter from Travis, who'd arrived there with thirty men. Neill had been called home because of illness in his family, and Bowie was incapacitated, leaving Travis in command of the 155 men there. His letter was addressed to the people of Texas and all Americans in the world. They had been under constant bombardment, Travis wrote, and more Mexican troops arrived daily. He expected Fannin and his volunteers to come from Goliad, but he called on Texians to rush to his aid, vowing never to surrender. In the following days other moving appeals from Travis reached the settlements, but Ellis saw no sign of response from the men around Nacogdoches. Many apparently couldn't believe the situation was serious; others were determined not to fight and risk losing their lands. Some, like Micajah, were with ranger companies protecting settlers from the Comanches. Ellis heard that thirty-two men from Gonzales had headed for the Alamo, and wondered if they'd been able to slip through Mexican lines.

On March 5 young Jim Allen set out for Gonzales with another desperate appeal from Travis, for he'd learned at last that Fannin wasn't coming. Copies of the letter were speedily carried to other settlements. Incredibly, the only Texians who'd responded to his repeated pleas were the thirty-two from Gonzales, but this time parties of men from many settlements set out for the Alamo. At Gonzales they learned that the Mexican army had completely surrounded the old mission, so they stopped there, cursing themselves for waiting too long.

The news that reached Nacogdoches in March was sketchy

and often contradictory, but wild, exaggerated rumors a-bounded. Ellis learned that on March 2, the Consultation at Washington–on–the–Brazos had declared Texas independent, but with six or seven thousand Mexican troops already north of the Rio Grande, it seemed a futile gesture. The delegates, said to be the ablest and most experienced men in Texas, had elected an interim government, with David G. Burnet as president and Mexican liberal Lorenzo de Zavala as vice-president. They named Houston commander of all armed forces, including the volunteers from the States. While a committee drew up a constitution, Houston hurried to Gonzales, where 370 Texians still waited. Two Tejanos from San Antonio brought the almost unbelievable news that on March 6, the day after Travis sent his final appeal, Santa Anna's army had overwhelmed the 187 Alamo defenders and slaughtered them to the last man.

Having learned of the Alamo's fall and that Mexican columns were on the march, the delegates to the Consultation hastily concluded their work in the early hours of March 17, then adjourned and departed. The interim government immediately left for Harrisburg. Their obvious haste spread panic among the families and triggered the Runaway Scrape. Without taking time to pack provisions or to don proper clothing, terrified women and children, accompanied by a few men and slaves, plodded miserably through mud, cold, and steady rain as if demons were after them.

There was no way of knowing where Houston's little army was after it burned and abandoned Gonzales, but Ellis heard that parties of Texians, at last fully aroused by the peril facing them, had grimly set out for the Colorado in search of it.

In April, even more shocking news arrived. Houston had ordered Fannin to abandon Goliad and march immediately to Victoria. Fannin, who was confident no Mexican troops would dare attack his force, waited nearly a week before marching. The delay gave able General José Urrea, who'd crossed the Rio Grande at Matamoros, time to intercept Fannin's column and force it to surrender. Urrea sent the prisoners, nearly all volunteers from the States, back to Goliad. There on Palm Sunday—March 27—on Santa Anna's direct order, they were marched out in three columns and halted. Infantrymen opened fire on them, while dragoons lanced those who fled. About twenty-five escaped to tell the story—Mexicans had rescued some of them; others had feigned death or made it to the woods, where Tejano families sheltered them.

When word of the shocking massacre at Goliad reached Nacogdoches, more men rushed off to join Houston. A delegation of citizens came to Ellis' ranch one day and took him into custody as a Mexican officer and an alien, then confined him in the Old Stone Fort. "It's for your own safety," William Roark told him. "Some men are so wild about what happened at Goliad they might think you're Santy Anny and shoot you." Ellis thanked him.

As he gazed around at the high stone walls, his thoughts turned back to the time Nolan's men had been held there in what seemed a lifetime ago, and shook his head. Then he'd been a captive of Spain, with no idea what was in store for him. Now he was a Mexican officer, and his own country-men had confined him in the same place, and again he wasn't sure what the future held. He thought of what was likely to happen when Santa Anna's army approached Nacogdoches and shuddered. Outraged Texians would probably riddle him with bullets just for having been a Mexican officer. That's a hell of a way to wind up, he thought.

As it turned out, his confinement was surprisingly brief. "Houston's army wiped out Santy Anny's column at San Jacinto and captured him," Roark told him one day. "Santy Anny ordered the rest of the army to leave Texas, and they're headin' for the Rio Grande with Colonel Rusk following 'em to see they cross it. He ordered you released on parole, but that means you're free. The war is over and Texas is independent.''

Ellis' jaw dropped. ''You mean Santa Anna ordered them to leave and they obeyed him?'' He could hardly believe his ears, but a great wave of relief swept over him, and he hoped he wasn't losing his mind. Texians had needed a miracle, and they got one when Santa Anna fell into their hands.

''Yes,'' Roark replied. ''If they'd marched immediately to San Jacinto they could have had an easy victory. Houston was down with a shattered ankle and his army was in such total confusion that any one of the Mexican columns could have made short work of it.'' He smiled broadly and waved his arms. ''It's the most unexpected, incredible ending imaginable,'' he continued. ''Of course we'll likely have to fight 'em again one day, but we should be better prepared another time. If we can just join the States in the meantime, we won't have to worry.''

Thinking he might soon leave for Jalapa, Ellis assigned his salt lick contract to another and sold his share in the land and mills south of Nacogdoches to Haden Edwards and James Carter. He also sold hundreds of acres of unimproved land to a score of buyers. Because he'd never been paid for the lumber he supplied on credit for building the barracks, he brought suit against Colonel Piedras as an abandoned debtor. ''Feeling fully satisfied that the said José de las Piedras, colonel, as aforesaid, will never return to this Republic,'' he wrote, ''and having no other means of obtaining justice and the demand due, I request a writ of attachment.'' The court granted it, and Ellis seized Piedras' properties, which included a valuable lot next to Frost Thorn's general store in Nacogdoches.

In November 1837 Candace married a man named Isaac Hix, but bad luck still dogged her. Shortly after her marriage, Hix was accused of horse-stealing. Apparently the charge was true, for Hix immediately disappeared, and Candace heard no more of him.

Ellis continued to live at his ranch and to serve unofficially as Indian agent to keep the immigrant tribes peaceful. On one occasion he visited the Cherokees to serve as a witness when his namesake, Little Bean, granted freedom to his slaves, Billa and Mina, in exchange for the eleven hundred dollars they'd earned. In March 1839, chief Bowles agreed to journey to the plains and negotiate with the Comanches, who were now anxious to make peace with the Texians.

That same month rangers killed an East Texas troublemaker named Manuel Flores near San Antonio. On his body they found a letter that made it clear Mexican officials were trying to enlist the help of the Indians in the reconquest of Texas. Mirabeau B. Lamar, who had succeeded Houston as president of the Texas Republic, seized this as a pretext for expelling all of the immigrant tribes. Houston angrily protested, and Ellis supported him, but the majority in East Texas agreed with Lamar that the Indians must go, for they had cleared and cultivated fertile lands that whites coveted. The Delawares and other small tribes gave up and departed, but the Cherokees refused to leave until their corn was ripe. In mid-July the Texian militia attacked them, killing Bowles and many others, and driving the survivors across the Red River.

Ellis shared Houston's outrage over the callous treatment of the Cherokees. Bowles had dissuaded the Cherokees from joining the Fredonians and kept the tribes neutral during the Texas Revolution. He had also sent his warriors against the Comanches, and had agreed to negotiate peace with them, but instead of gratitude, this was his reward.

A few years earlier, Ellis had written the story of his experiences under Nolan and Morelos. When young John H. Reagan visited him, Ellis showed him the manuscript and asked him to edit it and arrange for its publication. And because travel was difficult for him, Ellis urged him to go to Mexico City and collect his pay for his final years of military service, and on the way to deliver a letter to his wife. Reagan had to decline both requests, for he was in no position to oblige him.

In January 1841, Ellis was delighted when eighteen-year-old Louiza Jane married William Lacey, the son of the county clerk. Now, he thought, I have no excuse for not pulling up stakes, but he was so crippled by rheumatism that he dreaded the journey and kept putting it off. Except on warm days, he didn't even ride to Nacogdoches.

Finally he made up his mind to go. On April 12, 1843, he drew up his will, naming his nephew Sam Bean and cousin Dr. Jesse Bean as executors and guardians for his seventeen-year-old son, Ellis. Sam Bean was a short, heavy-set farmer in his twenties. Jesse was in his forties; a slender, dignified, honest physician with brown hair and eyes and a neatly trimmed beard.

"Why don't you transfer your property to them right now?" Jesse asked. "It's not likely you'll ever return, and that's the only sure way to see they get it."

Ellis looked embarrassed. "You're right, I know," he admitted, "but I just can't bring myself to close the door on comin' back here. Down there I'll have nothing to do, and I don't know for sure I can stand it." Jesse shook his head but said nothing more.

Ellis left his oldest son Isaac the undivided half of his headright of a league and a *labor* near the Trinity, as well as the slave girl Louiza. Louiza Jane would receive the slave girl Matilda, who was already in her possession. To his son Ellis he left his ranch and livestock, including his fine stallion Bolton, and also the old slaves Dory and Vina, their son, and three daughters.

He said goodbye to Louiza Jane, who wept to see him leave, then headed for Natchitoches, where he sold his horse and saddle before boarding a riverboat for the trip downstream to New Orleans. There he bought passage on a vessel bound for Veracruz, where he climbed painfully into the stagecoach that passed through Jalapa on its way to Mexico City. Eager though he was to see Magdalena, Ellis couldn't keep his mind from roaming back to Nacogdoches and the things he felt he'd left unfinished there. When the coach stopped at Jalapa, he asked the driver to let him off at Las Banderillas.

"We usually stop there for water when coming from Mexico City," the driver told him. "The lady who owns it always invites the passengers into her house and gives them *dulces* to eat. Then she asks every foreigner if he's seen her husband the colonel, and describes everything about him. You fit the description, only the man she describes is young."

"I'm the one," Ellis confessed, feeling ashamed. "I've been gone way too long."

When he alit from the stage and walked stiffly toward the vine-covered big house, he saw Magdalena at the door, surprised that the Mexico City coach had stopped. As he hobbled toward her, Ellis saw that she was stouter than before but still attractive. When she recognized him, she gave a happy cry and hurried into his outstretched arms.

"You're home to stay at last," she told him firmly. "I'll never let you leave again without me. I've been much too lonely all those years without you."

Ellis had little to do, for servants waited on him and Magdalena lovingly watched over him as if he were the child she'd never had. Whenever the coach stopped, he asked the passengers for any newspapers they could spare, and read each one several times. He tried hard to forget about Nacogdoches, but he badly missed his ranch and his friends there.

One day in late March 1844, the coach to Mexico City unexpectedly stopped, and Ellis felt gooseflesh on his arms when he saw Dr. Jesse Bean, looking more dignified than ever, alight. He knew at once that Jesse hadn't made the long journey to bring him good news; fears rising, he tried to imagine what calamity might have occurred. He winced from the pain in his hand when Jesse shook it.

"I hate to be the bearer of bad tidings," he said solemnly.

"I knew you wouldn't come all this way just to say howdy," Ellis replied. "What is it?"

"For one thing, Louiza Jane died about six months after you left, preceded by both children. Poor Lacey was naturally devastated."

"Louiza Jane! My God?" Ellis exclaimed. "She was so young. It should have been me instead."

"That's not all of it, I'm sorry to say. Here's a letter from William Roark that explains it in detail. Your nephew Sam wasn't up to your trust in him by any means. The long and the short of it is that he went through almost everything you owned before I could stop him." Groaning, Ellis cursed himself for not dividing his property before he left, as Jesse had advised.

Magdalena insisted that Jesse stay as long as he could, and they took him on buggy rides to Jalapa and on visits to other *haciendas*. Ellis sat in a daze much of the time, thinking only of Louiza Jane, but when Magdalena wanted to explain something to Jesse, he mechanically interpreted for her.

"I can't stay much longer," Jesse protested after several weeks had passed, "or I'll never be able to leave this delightful country. The talk of annexing Texas has revived in Washington, and who knows? This time it may be serious, and it could lead to war. I can't afford to get caught here in that event. I'll deliver any letters you care to write, and I'll assure your friends you're living in comfort and ease."

"Wish I could go with you," Ellis told him wistfully. "I aim to come when my rheumatism is better." He held up his gnarled hands and painfully flexed his crooked fingers. Jesse stared at him blankly, his expressionless face discreetly masking his doubts.

With great difficulty, Ellis scrawled a note to "Mr. William Roark my old friend Esq—Received your letter by Dr. Bean and see that Sam Bean is a Rascal. But one knows not who to trust. He is a Rogue and a Liar, but let him go. My fingers is stiff and I can't write good, but I am getting well fast. Dr. Bean can tell you all. Remember me to your lady. When the weather becomes cool you will see me. Remaining your old friend, Peter E. Bean." Because writing was so painful, Ellis sent messages to his sons by Jesse.

He followed the news as best he could, but it was impossible to get a clear picture of what went on in Mexico City or Washington, or in Texas, for that matter. It seemed certain that the government would retaliate if the U.S. annexed Texas, and late in 1845, he read that the U.S. had admitted Texas as a state. His friend Almonte, who was Mexican minister to Washington, had demanded his passport and departed in protest, thereby severing diplomatic relations between the U.S. and Mexico.

It was frustrating for Ellis to be so far away when exciting events were taking place in Texas. He'd often talked of visiting his friends in Nacogdoches. Why not now? he asked himself.

"I need to go to Texas and take care of some business and see my friends," he told Magdalena. "It looks like trouble is coming, and I should get there before it starts," he added, but without conviction.

Magdalena gazed at him fondly, and he knew she saw through him. "Of course, my dear," she replied, gently stroking his cheek. "But I can't let you travel alone. You keep on getting better; when you're well, and after the crops are in, we can both go. Our last journey together ended rather badly, remember? This one will be better." He'd almost forgotten the day his horse gave out when a troop of Spanish dragoons pursued them. If she hadn't made him take her horse. . . . He shivered at the thought of a lance blade thrust between his ribs.

Most days Ellis sat on a stone bench among the roses, inhaling the scented air, reveling in the sunshine, drinking the hot chocolate the servants brought him, and muttering endlessly to himself. From the papers he knew that Mexico was angrily preparing for war, but he couldn't tell if it was serious preparation or mere political bluster.

In May 1846, Ellis read that American troops had invaded Mexico by crossing the Nueces, which had been the border between Texas and the Mexican state of Tamaulipas. He recalled that Santa Anna had agreed on the Rio Grande as the boundary between Mexico and Texas, but the government had naturally disavowed all of the concessions he'd made to save his life. Later Ellis read that Mexican dragoons had captured American soldiers near the Rio Grande; the U.S. declaration of war soon followed. He saw that the two armies had fought at Palo Alto and Resaca de la Palma, but the papers were vague as to the outcome. They asserted, however, that Mexican troops were massing at Matamoros, which he took to mean that they had withdrawn or been forced back across the Rio Grande.

At sixty-three, Ellis suddenly realized that his life was rapidly slipping away; the years in the dungeons at San Luis Postosí and Acapulco were now taking their toll, and he felt feeble. I'm fixing to die, he thought, and far from my native land. He forgot about the war—it no longer mattered as he became obsessed with getting to Texas before he died. Down deep he'd never been reconciled to living out his last days at Jalapa, and now he felt the desperation of a trapped animal. It isn't fittin' for me to die so far from where I belong, among my children and friends, he thought.

That afternoon his face felt hot, and he stretched out on the bench half asleep. His clouded mind rambled aimlessly back over the years, and he saw Morelos engulfed in the smoke of battle. He saw William Roark and other friends, who smiled and shook hands with him. Then Louiza Jane appeared, wearing her favorite dress, and his pulse quickened. She beckoned to him, and he saw that her expression was sad. "Papa," she pleaded, "please come home. I want to be with you."

"I'll come!" he said aloud, and sat up, feeling a wave of energy sweep over his wasted body. He looked around for Louiza Jane, wondering where she'd gone. I must go to her now, he thought, while I still can. He walked firmly into the big house.

"Tomorrow I'm goin' to Texas to see Louiza Jane," he told the startled Magdalena. "She wants me with her, and I'm feeling pretty good."

Magdalena stared in amazement at his flushed face and feverishly bright eyes. Then she quickly lowered her gaze to conceal the terror that gripped her like icy fingers around her throat, for she knew Louiza Jane was dead. She anxiously hovered over him, fighting back her tears, until he fell into bed. Despite her desperate prayers and loving attention, that night, as she feared, Ellis closed his tired eyes for the last time.